A SIMPLE STORY

S. Y. AGNON

A Simple Story

Translated and with an Afterword by Hillel Halkin

SCHOCKEN BOOKS · NEW YORK

First published by Schocken Books 1985
10 9 8 7 6 5 4 3 2 1   85 86 87 88

Library of Congress Cataloging in Publication Data
Agnon, Shmuel Yosef, 1888–1970.
   A simple story.
Translation of: Sipur pashuṭ.   I. Title.
PJ5053.A4S52413   1985   892.4′35   85–2481

Design by Janet Halverson
Manufactured in the United States of America
ISBN 0–8052–3999–5

A SIMPLE STORY

1

THE WIDOW MIRL LAY ILL for many years. The doctors consumed her savings with their cures and failed to cure her. God in heaven saw how she suffered and took her from this world.

As she lay dying Mirl said to her daughter:

"I know I'll never rise from this bed. If you're angry with me for not leaving you anything, don't be. God in heaven knows I never spent a cent on myself. When I die, go to our cousin Boruch Meir. I'm sure he'll have pity and take you in."

Soon after, Mirl turned her head to the wall and gave back her soul to its Master.

Blume was left without a father or a mother. The neighbors came to console her, saw that the cupboard was bare, and said:

"There's a cousin named Boruch Meir Hurvitz who's a wealthy storekeeper in Szybusz. He certainly won't turn her away."

Blume nodded. "That's just what my mother said," she said.

As soon as the seven days of mourning were over, Blume's neighbors got together, hired a horse and wagon, gave her some provisions for the trip, and sent her off to Szybusz. "This cousin of yours is a very rich man," they told her. "Everyone in Szybusz knows him. Just ask for him and you'll be shown where he lives right away."

Blume boarded the wagon and left for Szybusz. When she reached her cousin's house she sat down on a chair in the entrance hall with her belongings beside her.

On coming upstairs from the store that evening, Tsirl Hurvitz saw a new face. She took it by the chin between her fingers and asked:

"Who are you, my dear? And what are you doing here?"

Blume stood up. "I'm Hayyim Nacht's daughter," she said. "Now that my mother is dead and I have no parents, I've come to you because you're my family."

Tsirl pursed her lips and said nothing.

Blume looked down at the floor and reached for her bags as though they were all she had to take hold of in the world.

Tsirl sighed. "It was very sad for us to hear about your mother, may she rest in peace. I never met her, but I've been told that she did not have an easy life. Not everyone is fortunate. Your father too was taken before his time. What a pity that was, because there was no better Jew than he. I've been told that he spent his whole life studying, and I suppose that he passed some of his knowledge on to you. I myself don't have much book learning. But I do hope that you were also taught a few things that a woman ought to know."

In a different tone of voice she went on:

"Well, you're not going back to where you came from tonight. Tomorrow we'll have a talk and see if we can think of something."

Then she showed Blume to a room.

Blume lay down to rest in her cousin's home. She was so tired that she fell asleep right away. In the middle of the night she awoke with a start. Where was she? The bed she was in was not her own, nor was the room. She began to fear that she would have to spend the whole night awake in this place. Never before had she been so afraid of not sleeping.

When she awoke again it was daylight. She tried to recall what had made her sleep so troubled and remembered dreaming that she was sitting on a wagon in a street back home. It embarrassed her to be where everyone could see her, and so she climbed down; just then, though, the horses bolted and galloped off, leaving her waiting with her arms out for the coachman to come and stop them before someone was tram-

4

pled. But he did not. She felt sure that some terrible accident would take place and hid her face in her hands so as not to see it.

No one was up yet in the house. Blume lay in bed, considering her situation. Carriage wheels rumbled through the street beneath her window. There was a railroad line connecting Szybusz with Stanislaw and a train that stopped in Szybusz twice a day, where it was met by the coachmen who brought passengers to and from the station. If one was not planning to take the morning train there was no need to rise early, but Blume had woken before the first carriage passed. She was used to it, for her bedridden mother had left all the housework to her; and yet though she was up early as usual, there was nothing usual about the day itself. Strange sounds came from the street and strange walls stared down at her. The ceiling was much higher than her parents', which made the room seem to float in air. Blume had lived all her life in a one-story house; now, lying in bed on the second story of the Hurvitz house, she felt precariously perched.

She could not go on lying there because it was already day, yet neither could she get up for fear of waking the rest of the household. For a while she lingered in bed thinking of her mother, who, while sick all her life and barely able to eke out a living, had never asked her cousins for anything. If ever one of the neighbors said to her, "You have such rich relations, why don't you let them know that you exist?" she would reply with a smile, "Do you know what the best thing about rich relations is? That you don't have to support them." Every year around Rosh Hashana they had received a New Year's greeting from the Hurvitzes. Blume remembered these cards well: they were made of stiff, heavy paper blazoned with gold letters. Every year they were placed on little straw ladders that her mother made in bed and fastened to the wall. There they stood until the gold letters peeled, the paper turned yellow, and they were finally thrown away. Now Blume's mother lay in the grave and her daughter in their cousins' bed.

Suddenly the bed felt too narrow. Blume jumped out of it,

5

washed, dressed, and went downstairs to prepare breakfast, using the same dishes that Tsirl had used the night before.

She heated a saucepan of milk and made coffee, set out cups, saucers, spoons, and knives, sliced bread, and cut a slab of butter from the churn. Then she opened her bags, took out some little cakes, and put them on a serving dish. When Mrs. Hurvitz came down to make breakfast, she found it waiting for her.

Soon Boruch Meir appeared, rubbing his hands. He said good morning to Blume, lifted the tails of his jacket, and sat down at the table, where he poured himself some coffee and regarded his cousin and the cakes she had brought with approval. He was followed into the dining room by his son Hirshl, who declared:

"Those cakes look awfully good!"

He took one of them, ate it, and said, "These deserve a special blessing."

"Who baked them?" asked Tsirl, breaking off a little piece and tasting it. "Did you?"

"No," Blume said, looking at her. She too tasted a piece. "But I can bake just as good."

"Thanks be to God," said Tsirl, her tone of voice changing, "that we aren't cake eaters and pastry nibblers here. Plain ordinary bread is good enough for us."

Blume looked down at the table. The munching of cake did not stop.

"Mama dear," said Hirshl, leaning toward his mother, "I have something to say to you."

Tsirl looked at her son. "Then say it," she said.

"It's a secret," said Hirshl with a smile.

Tsirl bent an ear toward him.

Hirshl put his mouth to it as though intending to whisper and said in a loud voice, "You must admit, Mother, that these cakes are delicious."

Tsirl frowned. "All right," she said.

Blume cleared the dishes from the table and went to the kitchen. Tsirl followed her and showed her where the dairy

6

sink, the wash basins, and the dishrags were while Blume took in the dairy counter with the corner of one eye and the meat counter with the corner of the other.

Tsirl watched her. "Can you cook a cut of meat?" she asked.

"Yes," Blume said.

"By the time you wash the dishes," Tsirl said, "the meat delivery will come. Here's rice, here's noodles, here's kasha, and here's everything else."

Blume nodded as if asking to be left alone. Tsirl watched her move about the kitchen, stepped out, came back in, stepped out once more, and did not come back again until half past one in the afternoon, when she returned to find the table set and dinner ready to eat.

It was a day in May, the first of the Hebrew month of Iyyar, when servants and household help renewed their annual contracts. Not long before Blume's arrival the Hurvitzes' maid had given notice and a new maid had yet to be found. When the employment agent came to Tsirl with a replacement, Tsirl said to her:

"Just where, please tell me, am I supposed to put her? A cousin of ours is staying with us and sleeping in the maid's bed."

So Blume went to work in her cousins' home. God in heaven gave her strength, and her small hands did every kind of task: the cooking and the baking and the washing and the mending. There was not a corner of the house in which her presence was not felt. Work came naturally to her; she had not been raised by a sick mother for nothing, and the same habits that had served her well then did so now too. It did not take Tsirl long to discover that Blume had indeed been taught all the things that a woman ought to know. Nor, since she was family, was there any need to pay her a wage. "After all," said Tsirl to her husband, "she is one of us, isn't she? He who rewards us will reward her too."

It might have seemed that Blume was being taken advantage

of; yet anyone considering the matter closely would have concluded that Tsirl was right. After all, was it conceivable that, when Blume's time came to marry, Tsirl would beg a dowry for her from some local charity? She would surely recompense her then for each year of work, and, if the match was a good one, even double the sum that was due her. Besides, what sort of wage could Blume expect to receive? She had never worked as a housemaid before and was learning the trade from Tsirl, which made her case the same as a shopgirl's who worked her first year without pay, or as an apprentice's who served his master for three years before earning even a penny.

So Blume lived with her cousins, cut off from the rest of the world. The girls from poor families who worked for the Hurvitzes' neighbors did not seek her company—nor, needless to say, did she seek theirs. The employment agents whom the housemaids tried to cultivate were not so shameless as to approach her—and, needless to say again, she did not approach them. Of necessity she was confined to the Hurvitz household, which was not one with many diversions. Its members were busy all day in their store, from which they returned only to gulp down a meal or to sleep, while if they went for a walk on the Sabbath or a holiday, or were invited to dine with friends, they always left Blume behind. A house needed watching, and who was there to watch it if not she? Thus, she was left to her own devices, with neither the amusements of a housemaid nor the entertainments of a better-off girl her own age to help pass the time.

Blume's stay with her cousins was a long one. Tsirl neither pampered nor picked on her. Indeed, Tsirl knew how to get along with people. She ran a shipshape shop, knew the customs of each customer, and never looked down at anyone, not even at the poorest of buyers. "Today he bought for a penny," she would say, "but tomorrow he can win a lottery and buy for a pound." The tiniest tot who came to make the smallest purchase was treated by her with affection, fondled by the chin, and given an extra little something. "Now that he's small," Tsirl said, "so are his needs. But when he's big they'll be great. If I'm nice to him now, he'll keep coming back then. Lots of rich men in this town used to come to my father once a year as boys to buy a carob pod on Tu b'Shvat. Now they buy whole bagfuls of almonds and raisins every day."

The Hurvitzes' store was not the only one in Szybusz. A whole row of shops ran along the big market, one squeezed tightly against the other, quite apart from those in the little market and along various other streets. Each had its slack and busy seasons, its good and bad days, except for the Hurvitzes', which was crowded with shoppers all the time. A man might have found himself hard-pressed to explain why he preferred it; yet even for ordinary smelling salts of the kind prescribed by the doctors and sold in every pharmacy, it was the place one went to, for Tsirl's cheery manner in itself was good for whatever ailed one.

And just as she was considerate toward everyone, so she was with Blume. If, for instance, she came across an old dress that did not fit her, or a shoe that had seen better days, she was sure to give it to her cousin. As long as it was usable, Blume could use it, and only when it wasn't was it discarded. "I myself save everything," Tsirl liked to say. "Not like our Blume, who throws out whatever she doesn't care for." Though a person might have thought that Tsirl was finding fault, anyone knowing her would have realized that she was simply stating a fact. And her husband was no less thoughtful; in fact, the slightest service performed for him by Blume always met with profuse thanks on his part. Not only did he never forget to say goodbye or hello to her when he left town on business or came back, he even thought of her when he was away, such as the time he brought her a small trinket from Karlsbad along with the gifts for his son and wife. "Most men," remarked Tsirl, "haven't the faintest notion of what a woman likes to get. But not my Boruch Meir. He knew exactly what Blume needed, and that's what he brought her. Or maybe he just felt it in his blood, because she is a blood relation."

Even Hirshl was friendly toward Blume and never forgot

9

that the two of them came from the same stock. If his shirt collar was creased while being ironed, he did not complain about it, nor did he ever ask her to polish his shoes. Hirshl did not have his mother's knack of making even his criticisms sound like compliments, nor did his eyes twinkle good-humoredly like his father's. He was young and still had to learn that a twinkle or a kind word could be turned to one's advantage. And yet, though he was only sixteen years old, he was old enough to know that life was no idyll. There were those who claimed that the whole problem with the world was its being divided into the rich and the poor. Indeed, that was a problem. Certainly, though, it was not the main one. The main problem was that everything was so painful.

Hirshl himself could not explain this pain. From the moment he first saw the light of day he never lacked for food or clothing, nor for the attention of good people who lavished him with kindness and lovingly fulfilled his every wish. Perhaps he had eyes to see that the same people who were so good to him were not always as good to others, which grieved him. And perhaps he was still only a boy with a somewhat impractical turn of mind.

2

HIRSHL WAS HIS PARENTS' only child, born to them when they were no longer young. Not until they had despaired of having a son were they finally granted one, whom they called Shimon Hirsh after his maternal grandfather. The first of these two names, however, vanished in the cradle, while the second gained an affectionate diminutive.

As soon as Hirshl was weaned, Tsirl went back to working full-time in the store. She was not expecting more children. Not that she sought to prevent them. Yet neither was she anxious to have them, especially since one never knew in advance who was lucky to be born and who was not. And though Hirshl was her only child, she was careful not to show him too much love in order not to spoil him. Boruch Meir, on the other hand, more than made up for this by loving his son to excess.

Boruch Meir was a man smiled upon by fortune. All his undertakings prospered, and whatever came his way increased in his possession. He never bothered to ask whether he deserved such success; nor, so it seemed, did success. In a dim way he felt sure that anyone who worked as hard as he did would get his just deserts in the end. He himself had started out in the store as a shopboy and was now its wealthy proprietor and the husband of its first owner's daughter.

Indeed, fortune's smile could be seen in Boruch Meir's face, glistening in his beard and sparkling in his eyes that were jolly even when he was alone. Life treated him well, his inner life too, for if conscience generally kept him from temptation, self-regard saw to it that, if tempted, he did not reproach himself overly much. On Sabbaths, holidays, and days of the New Moon he regularly attended synagogue, though had anyone told him, A man like you ought to pray in public more often, Boruch Meir would have gone daily, for he was willing to take advice and did not make a point of relying too much on himself. He was not especially generous; yet when asked to give to charity he did, sometimes more, sometimes less, and sometimes handsome sums to the beggars whom Tsirl simply scolded and told to go do something useful and stop bothering honest folk. "The world," Boruch Meir would say to her, "is not going to change if a single do-nothing does something, and I am not going to lose my shirt if I give him a penny." And just as he got on well with the world, preferring to let it have its way so that he might concentrate on his business, so he was on good terms with his own employees, whom he never was bossy with, though he did forbid them to nibble at the merchandise, since this made it unappetizing to the customers.

From the day Boruch Meir went to work in Shimon Hirsh Klinger's store he felt a special bond with his patron. At first sight the old man, who used to bathe in the river until nearly wintertime and insisted on attending to all his own needs, won Boruch Meir's heart. Indeed, Boruch Meir could not say which amazed him more, the fact that the whole world did not seem worthy to Tsirl's father of being looked at, or the fact that Shimon Hirsh knew all about it without having to look at it at all. The moment he stepped into his store, without even lifting his eyes, he knew exactly what and how much had been sold, even of bulk items like almonds, raisins, and the like. The town gossip had it that the old man went over his stock every night, weighing all the merchandise and checking each box and crate. Boruch Meir, however, did not believe a word of this. And since he could think of no rational ways to account for Shimon Hirsh's omniscience, he was left with irrational ones, which only increased his amazement. Shimon Hirsh Klinger, for his part, was sparing of explanations. "A store," he once said, "is not a synagogue, where everyone sits around and gabs." In fact, apart from an occasional "hmmmm," his employees never heard a word from him, a long "hmmmm" being a sign that he was pleased with them and a short one that he was not. Yet there were no slackers among them. Whoever landed a job in Shimon Hirsh Klinger's store soon taught himself to do its owner's bidding.

Boruch Meir had worked six and a half years for Shimon Hirsh Klinger and been spoken to by him no more than were his fellow employees when one night the two men happened to lodge in the same roadside inn. Boruch Meir was returning from his native town in high spirits, both because of an army exemption he had gotten and because of an attractive cousin of his whom he was about to take for a wife. In the room in the inn was a guest who was doing sums in an account book so loudly that no one was able to sleep. At last, feeling that Boruch Meir was looking at him, the man asked, "Am I disturbing you?" "Not at all," answered Boruch Meir gently, going over to the table as he spoke and blowing out the lamp. Shimon Hirsh Klinger was staying in the same room. "I liked that," he said to Boruch Meir. "I always thought you were an innocent lamb, but now I see that you have character." Whereupon he began to chat with him like a friend. Before they had gone their separate ways, Shimon Hirsh Klinger had given Boruch Meir his daughter's hand in marriage.

At first, even when he was already married, Boruch Meir felt uncertain whether his new wife saw in him anything more than her lawful husband; all day long he courted her as though they had just met and some part of her was not yet fully his. Often he would sit looking at her and wonder, What is it about her that she still is withholding from me? Not that she seemed to be concealing anything, but whatever she revealed was a mystery to him too. Every movement of her body, every dress that she wore, made her seem like a different person. Day by day he felt his love for her grow, yet the more he loved her, the more baffled by her he became. And this baffled her and made her ask, What does he want from me that he hasn't yet gotten?

Only with the birth of their son did Boruch Meir feel at last that all had been given him and that the most deeply treasured of Tsirl's desires was now in his hands. Did he not hold the boy in his arms, press him to his heart, and play with him even in her absence? Henceforward he loved her more than ever because of her son, just as he loved the boy because of his mother. And though Boruch Meir had never shirked work in his life, he now worked twice as hard. Not a day went by without some innovation in the store or some new item for sale there. He even began selling tanning and smelling salts, as well as house paints and sign paints, for Szybusz was changing with the times. Once, if a man had been sick, he was bled, whereas now he took baths full of salts; once, he whitewashed his house, now he painted it; once, the sign above his shop had hung there for a lifetime, while now shops went bankrupt as fast as they were opened and new signs were needed right away, sometimes with the name of the owner's first wife and sometimes with the name of his second. But whoever wanted to buy cheaply still bought from Boruch Meir, it being a known fact that his prices were the lowest in town. Even other shopkeepers had begun to order from him, because Boruch Meir obtained all his merchandise at the source and bought and sold at a discount.

3

Hirshl was seventeen years old when he went to work in his parents' store. He was neither as sharp-witted as his mother nor as quick on his feet as his father, but he did have the virtue of doing whatever he was told. As long as he had attended the old study house in the Little Synagogue his parents had hoped he would become a rabbi, yet in the end he had disappointed them by losing interest in such a career. Indeed, the study of Torah had lost its old prestige, so that many young Jewish boys nowadays were putting their religious books aside and turning to more useful occupations. The brightest of them enrolled in the universities, where they might acquire a well-paid profession, while those of more ordinary talents went into business or trade. There was also a third class of youngsters who neither studied religion nor did anything useful but who, supported by their parents, spent their days in such unworldly pursuits as Zionism or socialism. Neither the Zionists nor the socialists, however, were thought very highly of, the former because they were laughed at and the latter because they were feared.

Of course, there were adults in Szybusz who were pro-Zionist themselves, attended every Zionist function, and held receptions, complete with coffee and cake, for visiting Zionist speakers, whom they then took to see the local sights, such as the Great Synagogue with its sun, moon, and twelve signs of the zodiac painted on its ceiling and its copper lantern, etched in whose glass panels was the blessing for the New Moon, or the old study house with its illuminated Hebrew Bible that had a marginal gloss in Latin written by a cardinal and its copy of the original Venice edition of the *Sefer M'lekhet Makhshevet*, which bore on its frontispiece an unusual engraving of the author, Rabbi Moses Hefetz, his hair unrabbinically long and his chin unrabbinically beardless. Even on ordinary days you might find such people in the Society for Zion clubhouse, reading a newspaper or, if the need arose, preaching to the unconverted. Yet their ranks, it must be said, were restricted to those Jews who were already comfortable enough off to have put away a nest egg and to have no worries about making ends meet.

Hirshl himself was certainly bright enough to attend high school and university and even earn his doctor's degree. His mother's apprehensions, however, ruled out such a course, for Tsirl had had a brother who, instead of turning out normal, had been driven mad by his academic studies. Nothing done by his parents to cure him had helped in the least; when they tore up his books he had simply found others, and when they finally threw him out of the house he took to the woods and lived there on berries and plants like a beast until his vital powers failed him and he died. No sooner did Tsirl realize, therefore, that her son had tired of the Talmud than she hastened to put him to work in the store before he could develop any other interests. And though it started with no more than an odd day here or there, eventually Hirshl began to work full-time for his parents. There's nothing like a business, thought Tsirl, for keeping a man healthy, wealthy, and safely out of harm's way. Not that she respected religion and its scholars any less than the average woman did; still, like any occupation whose practical value was doubtful, it seemed to her less than ideal. Of course, there were rabbis who earned handsome livings too, but how many of them could you point to? Not even one per town, whereas the goods of a merchant were always in demand. And since Hirshl had given up his religious studies anyhow, what better future for him than the store?

The fact of the matter was that, even when Tsirl had wanted her son to be a rabbi, this had stemmed less from her piety than from her desire to atone for the sin of her grandfather's grandfather, who had once accused the rabbi of the town he lived in of an excess of religious enthusiasm. One time, that is, when this rabbi had done something that seemed quite deranged, Tsirl's great-great-grandfather had remarked to a fellow townsman, "I'm afraid that our rabbi is going out of his mind," to which the rabbi had retorted, "If anyone is going to go out of his mind, it's that man and his descendants." And indeed, though Tsirl's ancestor had spoken in an entirely disinterested manner, the rabbi's vengeful curse came true nonetheless, since not even the most principled dispute is ever above personal animus. From that day on there was not a generation in Tsirl's family without its madman—which was why, when Hirshl was born, his parents had sought to consecrate him to sacred studies as a penance for this ancient transgression. Not all men's plans, however, are approved by Providence, especially when their motives are not selfless. And since Tsirl saw that Hirshl would never be what she desired of him, she decided that he might as well be what she could make of him.

Hirshl's first day in the store came at a time when his father, who was away taking the baths at Karlsbad, had left Tsirl alone with two shopgirls. "Come, give us a hand until your father gets back," Tsirl had said to him, and Hirshl had folded down the corner of the page of the Talmud he was studying as though intending to return to it soon—nor did it ever cross his mind that he would not. Yet the smell of the ginger, the cinnamon, the raisins, the wine, the brandy, and all the other good things there proved more enticing than the Talmud, just as the customers he waited on appealed to him more than did his fellow bench-sitters in the study house. For who, after all, still frequented the study house in those days? Young men who were bored to tears with their studies, the very opposite

16

of the shopkeepers and their customers, most of whom seemed to know and do so much. By the time Boruch Meir returned from Karlsbad, Hirshl had become a shopkeeper himself. Instead of debating the Law in the study house he now haggled over prices in the store. Before long he never entered the Little Synagogue at all except to attend prayers on the Sabbath, holidays, and days of the New Moon.

Like other boys from well-to-do homes who had studied to be rabbis and stopped, Hirshl joined the Society for Zion. The society owned a large room to which its members came to read newspapers and journals, or else to play chess on a board that stood on a table in a corner. Not all the newspapers and journals dealt with Zionism, nor was everyone who read them a Zionist. There were some who came to the clubhouse simply to read, just as there were others who came to socialize, for one way or another it was never a dull place. Sometimes, of a winter evening, as darkness descended on the world and one was filled with vague yearnings, a few of the club members might begin to sing such sad songs of longing for Zion that all hearts welled together. At such times the youngsters gathered there would appear to be as winningly transfigured as once they had been by the study of Torah.

Among those who came to the clubhouse for non-Zionist reasons was Hirshl. It was difficult to say why, when most of the sons of the better-off families in town were Zionists, Hirshl was not. Perhaps there was something about the movement and its followers that he disliked. Perhaps he had simply not thought the Jewish problem through to the end. Or perhaps he had and had concluded that Zionism was not the solution for it.

In any case, Hirshl's parents had nothing against his joining the Society for Zion. As long as it did not interfere with his work and he did his fair share in the store, what objection could there be to his dropping in on the clubhouse at night to look at a newspaper? He might as well know what was going on in the world. Certainly it wouldn't make him any less eligible a bachelor. Suppose, God forbid, that he had been attracted to the socialists instead? A generation that could no longer control its own children had better keep its complaints to itself. More than one well-bred boy or girl of Hirshl's age had already fallen in with wild-eyed radicals, leaving their parents with nothing to do but groan and beat their breasts.

And so once or twice a week Hirshl dropped in on the Zionist clubhouse, where, between lighting a cigarette and chatting with his friends, he read the latest news, the political dispatches, and the literary and art pages. On Thursday nights, when the librarian unlocked the bookcase and lent out books, Hirshl would borrow three, one for serious and two for light reading. And on wintry Friday nights, when the Sabbath meal was over and his parents were asleep and three candles still burned on the dinner table, one for Boruch Meir and one for Tsirl and one for Hirshl himself, he would sit reading until he fell asleep too. Still another candle burned in Blume's room, where she too was sitting up with one of Hirshl's books. Blume liked books: they opened up worlds for her and reminded her of the distant days when she had sat with her father, might his soul rest in peace, reading aloud with him.

Hayyim Nacht, Blume's father, had married Mirl, who was supposed to have married her cousin Boruch Meir, who, blinded by Shimon Hirsh Klinger's fortune, had jilted her and married Tsirl instead. Shimon Hirsh Klinger, Tsirl's father and Boruch Meir's employer, was a wealthy storekeeper; yet after Tsirl's brother went mad and died it was hard to find a good match for her, even though she was the only child of rich parents. A man who had lost his mind and died without it was not an easy stigma for a family to overcome. Of all life's misfortunes, madness may have been the only one to which the afflicted person was himself insensible; to his family and relations, however, the blow was doubly cruel, for not only were other troubles gotten over and forgotten while this one was passed down from one generation to the next, but, while other

18

chronic patients could be put in special wards run by chronic idlers, nobody wanted to care for a madman: on the contrary, people either fled at the sight of him or else tormented him and turned him into a bogeyman to scare their children. And so when Tsirl's father saw that she was not getting any younger and that the matchmakers were not beating a path to his door, he decided to marry her off to Boruch Meir, who had a good head for business and was a hard worker with an impeccable record in the store. Moreover, being called Hurvitz carried a weight of its own, so that, even though Boruch Meir himself was not a direct descendant of the renowned sixteenth-century rabbinical authority Yeshaya Leib Hurvitz, the name still entitled him to respect.

Even after Boruch Meir's marriage to Tsirl, Mirl's parents stayed in touch with him; indeed, they seemed to esteem him all the more for having married into wealth. He too kept up his ties with them and sent them a New Year's greeting each year. And when Mirl married Hayyim Nacht, he sent them a yearly card too: as with father and mother, so with husband and daughter.

Hayyim Nacht was not well-off like Boruch Meir Hurvitz, nor was he regarded especially highly by others; for though he was a well-read and cultured man with a gift for languages, his education, like that of all the Nacht family, far outstripped his attainments. And though Mirl had married him with her father's consent, the old man never stopped reminding her vindictively that, having failed to win the heart of a successful businessman, she had had to settle for a spendthrift of a scholar who frittered away her whole dowry without earning a penny for himself.

Mirl, however, refused to criticize her husband. No matter how great a failure he was, she thought just as much of him. She was grateful to life for having delivered her from the hands of an overly strict father and given her a home of her own, and even when, as hard luck had it, she and her husband were left without a cent, she felt no less fond of him. Do I, she would ask, have to make him suffer at home just because he's no great shakes in the marketplace? And as she pitied him, she loved him even more with a love that sought no earthly reward. Whatever he did seemed right to her. If only everyone else were as honest as her Hayyim, he too would have done well; the trouble was that men were either successful or honest in this world, and that the first group grew rich off the second while the second gullibly let them. Was it Hayyim's fault that he had faith in people who fleeced him and made off with his capital? And since losing one's money meant losing one's credit along with it, Hayyim Nacht had lost all chances of ever recouping his losses. From sitting in a large shop he went to sitting in a small one; from a spacious apartment overlooking the big market he moved to cramped quarters where the sun never shone. For a while he still tried his hand at this or that small-time venture, trusting his luck to improve, but in the end he gave up and tried no more. He was not meant, he saw, for worldly advancement, and so he secluded himself with his books, which he studied in the hope of qualifying as an instructor of religion to Jewish students in the Austrian state schools. Yet here too he succeeded only partly, for while he passed his examinations he was never given a job, since wherever one was available it was bagged at once by some illiterate who had managed to bribe the school supervisors. Hayyim Nacht was not a man to get around anyone, not by flattery and certainly not by bribery, even if this meant leaving himself and his family in the cold.

Finally, when he saw that no school would hire him, Blume's father went and opened his own school—that is, he found a few pupils and tutored them in his home for a fee. Before long, however, not one of them was left, for the times were not what they once were: the desire for pure knowledge had vanished, and all that fathers now wanted for was their sons to get ahead in life, which meant that, if they were to receive any schooling at all, it should be something useful like bookkeeping rather than the fables, literature, and philosophy that Hayyim Nacht was cramming their heads with. True, there was not another tutor in town who could pen as fine a letter as he, but what good did his fine style do him if it was impossible to understand a word of his flowery phrases?

By then Blume was old enough to see and understand what was happening. She saw her mother stitching patch on patch to cover their poverty and her father sitting by the window with an unread book in his hand, his blue eyes filled with tears and his silken-soft beard clenched between his teeth. Sometimes he would take Blume's hand and say, "I know, my darling, that a man like me, a husband and a father who can't provide for his own wife and daughter, should be sent to Siberia." And how he cried when he read her the story of the thief who was brought before the caliph. "Why did you steal?" asked the caliph. "Because," answered the thief, "my wife and children had nothing to eat." "I acquit the man of thievery," declared the caliph. "Now take him and hang him for having let his family go hungry."

When the time came for Blume to be given some education, her father took to sitting her beside him and reading together with her. "I know," said Hayyim Nacht, "that I won't be leaving you any riches, but at least I'll have taught you how to read a book. No matter how black your life may be, you can always find a better one in books."

Blume was a quick learner. Almost before she knew all the letters of the alphabet she was reading fairy tales and legends. Yet it astounded her father, who shed so many tears when he read that they all but rotted the pages, how little feeling she showed. None of the passages over which he was used to weeping or heaving a sigh, no one's sufferings or sorrows, seemed to move her in the least. A tragic tale that made him break down in sobs left her totally dry-eyed.

"But Papa," she might say when he tried explaining the full poignancy of some character's predicament, "it's his own fault. If he hadn't done what he did, it would never have happened to him."

"Blume, my Blume," replied Hayyim Nacht. "How can any daughter of mine talk like that? A man does what he has to do. There isn't a thing we do or don't do that isn't already our destiny at birth."

"I'd better go help Mama now," Blume would interrupt him.

"Go, then," said her father. "Let your heart be your guide. You help your mother while I sit and hide my face from shame because the two of you must slave away while I do nothing. I tremble to think of Judgment Day. I tremble to think of the reckoning there will be. What will I say when I have to stand trial then?"

And, never doubting that he would, Hayyim Nacht sank back in his chair, buried his face in his hands, and burst into tears. One day he sank back and never sat up again. Sorrow and humiliation had killed him prematurely, leaving his wife and daughter destitute.

Blume remained alone with her mother. Little by little they sold off her father's books. Next came his clothes, desk, and bed, and finally they moved out of their small apartment into one that was even smaller. Mirl's father had died too by now, leaving them barely enough money to get by on. And then, whether because of her frailty, her grief, the damp quarters they lived in, or all of these things together, Mirl took sick. For years she lay in bed while the doctors and their cures consumed all her savings without curing her. God in heaven saw how she suffered and took her from this world.

Seeing that Blume was an orphan, her neighbors sent her off to her cousins in Szybusz, in whose home she found room and board, partly because she was their relative and partly because she was their maid. If it were not such a human trait to complain, Blume would not have had cause to, for God in heaven had given her enough strength, charm, and brains to console the unhappiest person.

4

BLUME SAT ALONE in her room, reading a book. A candle burned on the table, which was spread with a white cloth. The day before, Hirshl had borrowed three books from the library; two he had kept for himself and the third he had lent her. God in heaven had given her the wits to sit and read, and rest for the body is rest for the soul. Her father and her mother were long dead. They did not die all at once but rather bit by bit. In fact, their whole life had been one long waiting for death. Blume had cried enough while they lived, and now, from under her lashes, only the traces of that sorrow could be seen.

She sat in her cousins' home, her open book opening worlds. She was used to sitting at home, which was something she had learned to do while caring for her sick mother. She was used to reading, too, books having been a part of her life from the time she was little. Hayyim Nacht was a greater prophet than he knew when he had said to her, "At least I'll have taught you how to read. No matter how black your life is, you can always find a better one in books."

Blume owned nothing in the world. All she could call her own were her own two hands that she let out to others. But her mind was free and could rove where it pleased. The Sabbath candle made a pleasant sight in the room of this chaste young girl relaxing by its light from her week's labors. Who of you could doubt her good fortune? God in heaven had lavished her with graces, and no one thought the less of her because of them. Never was she scolded for anything. Boruch Meir was a kindly soul whose eyes twinkled fondly at her when he watched her at her work. Indeed, Boruch Meir got along well with everyone, let alone with those who were born to serve him. Now and then it crossed his mind that a daughter of Mirl's deserved better in life; yet if she was fated to be a servant, at least the Lord had found her a master like himself who, out of respect for her feelings, refrained from acting like one.

Tsirl was pleased with Blume too. She had never had an easy time with help. After her wedding she had been given her mother's maid, who managed everything by herself and left Tsirl without a worry in the house. But this old woman, whom Tsirl gladly would have kept till the end of her days, was soon called away by a letter from a distant town. Forty years after having been abandoned by the husband of her youth, she was informed by the man that he was on his deathbed and wished to see her one last time—and so, bundling up what possessions she had managed to accumulate during her long years of service, she set out. No one knew whether she found her husband alive there or how much longer she remained so herself. Tsirl's mother was not one for writing letters, and when Boruch Meir himself finally sent an inquiry to the rabbi of the town, the latter wrote back that he had never heard of such a woman. From then on Tsirl knew no peace. Not a servant was good enough for her. One was wasteful, a second was quarrelsome, a third was not a good cook. And since Tsirl herself was no expert on housework, she only made things worse with her advice. The servants took note of this and did as they pleased. "If you don't like it, ma'am," they snapped back if she complained, "you're welcome to do it yourself."

There was yet another problem with help these days, which was that at night they had a life of their own. The times were gone when you could find good domestics whose only thought was for their masters and who were ready to work around the clock for them. A new nation of housemaids had arisen in Szybusz that could not have cared less for its employers. No longer were songs and music heard in each house as its servants went about their work; a sense of hostility reigned there instead, as though it had fallen to enemy troops.

24

Who was to blame for this? None other than a local citizen named Dr. Knabenhut, who had brought to town the new gospel that all men were equal and that no man was better than another, which he preached at public gatherings that put a lot of half-baked notions into a lot of heads. Try calling a servant a nasty name nowadays and off she went to Knabenhut, who took you right to court for defamation of character. No longer was a housemaid part of the household. She found her pleasures elsewhere and put her earnings in the bank. Some were not even ashamed to call themselves socialists, or to behave toward the lady of the house as though she should serve them. Had Tsirl not been busy all day long in the store, she would have hired some Ukrainian peasant girl, but as it was, having no time to look after things at home or to make sure that the kitchen was kept kosher, she had to rely on uppity Jews.

Since the day of Blume's arrival, however, all this had changed for the better. There was nothing that Blume would not do. She performed all that she was asked to and a good deal more besides. Food was cooked, jams were made, laundry was washed, clothes were mended, socks were darned, and every corner of the house was made to sparkle without the least fuss or commotion. If a good housewife is no better than her help, Tsirl could once more consider herself the best of housewives. As good as were the days in which she had had her mother's old servant, the days in which she had Blume were even better. Whatever Blume did was done with a flair. Seven pairs of hands working seven days could not do what she did in one.

Blume was a credit to herself, a credit to the house, and not least of all a credit to Tsirl, who had reached the age when what concerns a woman most is what she has to eat and drink. Nor was Tsirl like some of her friends, who nibbled all day on almonds and raisins and, if they chanced to come across a pickled herring, ravaged it down to the tail. No, what Tsirl liked best was a proper meal: a good roast, stew, or cut of rare beef; gizzards, kishke, and spleen; stuffed goose neck; oven-baked egg farfel served in a gravy that made it melt in one's mouth; a chicken with a filling of groats. Even before it was dinnertime she would sit herself down at the table, her body overflowing her chair, and review in her mind each single dish that was about to be served to her; while when the food came, she leaned over it and filled her plate as lovingly as if it were a prize hen being fattened up to be sold.

The trouble was that not all of Tsirl's meals were what they should have been. A dish might be well cooked but not the way she liked it; or the way she had liked it yesterday but not how she wanted it today; or how she wanted it today but followed by the wrong dessert. As long as her mother's old servant was in the house everything had always been right: sweet horseradish for potted meat and hot horseradish for a roast; the roast today and the pot meat tomorrow; sweet stewed plums with the first and sour stewed plums with the second. One would have thought that any cook could have done as much—or at least, any cook who cared about whom she was cooking for. No matter what pains Tsirl took to teach her help what she liked, no meal was ever put on the table without something being the matter. Nature itself had gone awry, so that you had no idea anymore whether it was summer, winter, spring, or fall. Once upon a time a body eating cherry blintzes had known it was summer and one eating kasha cakes had known it was not, whereas now it was kasha and gravy, or else gravy and kasha, all year long, in hot weather and cold, on Sabbaths no less than on weekdays.

Since the day of Blume's arrival, however, nature had resumed its proper course as if the months of the year were inscribed right over the stove. Each season had its own dishes and each dish its own taste. The Lord only knew where Blume had learned it all.

5

HIRSHL WAS STILL a growing boy when Blume entered his life. In age she was almost his twin.

Blume had blossomed like a lily of the valley that is protected against all harm. No matter how often you looked at her, you could never look enough. Though she was thin when she first came to Szybusz, her limbs had now filled out, yet her every movement was still full of grace. Her work had made her agile, and she was as quick on her feet as a bird in flight. By the time your eyes came to rest on her there was nothing there but her shadow.

Hirshl had eyes for her alone. He saw her even when she was elsewhere. A skillful Artist had sketched her portrait in his mind, and her beauty was always on display there.

In the store he stood staring into space. Whole days passed with his lips slightly parted and his tongue firmly tucked in his mouth, as if he had been given a candy to suck on and wished to retain the taste of it. His heart quickened when he heard Blume's footsteps as she went about her work. Prudence alone kept him from seeking out the room she was in, reaching out his arms, and embracing the wondrous mystery of her that caused him such sweet distress.

Hirshl was no little innocent. He may not have known the taste of sin yet, but the thought of sin can be worse than sin itself. Nor does lewdness ever lack for company. Even in little Szybusz, the most dissolute of whose sons had scant opportunity for sowing their wild oats, there were young men who had lost not only their virtue but with it all sense of shame, so that they actually boasted of their deeds. Such loose talk stained

Hirshl's pure spirit. Sometimes, when he was alone, he imagined all kinds of women who existed only for men's pleasures. And such imaginings, once yielded to, made him want the pleasures themselves. It was hard to think about such things and hard not to. Shame, anger, and frustration came and went in him at will. If he tried not looking at women, he felt thwarted; if he looked, he felt ashamed; and one way or another, he felt agitated all the time.

Hirshl would have liked greatly to sit beside a woman who, her loose hair falling over him, gave him her hand to hold while brushing his ear with her soft voice. Once would be enough: he would be satisfied forever after. In perfect stillness he let his imagination conjure up the faces of the women singers and performers who came to town with their minstrel troops two or three times a year and sang songs put to bawdy lyrics. The men's collars gleamed; their shirts were always well starched; their eyes shone with a strange glitter that gave them a rheumy look; and they smelled of all kinds of things, such as tobacco, eau de cologne, and the dust of many roads. There was no telling whether the fancily dressed women talking and laughing in loud voices were their girlfriends or their wives. At night they set up a stage on which they sang, danced, and told jokes. Hirshl always went to see these performances, as did many of his young acquaintances—and while he never failed to pray that he had not been spied by them there, they were certain to be in the audience, praying the same thing about him. After the show, the fast set in Szybusz took the performers out to eat, drink, and carouse. Though Hirshl envied them, he was too embarrassed to join them. The minstrels' songs had made him shake with sin—how could he eat with them now?

Of course, times and attitudes had changed, and the same minstrels who once were held in low repute were suddenly being treated with respect. Students strolled with them in public, referred to them as artists, drank with them in the taverns, lectured on them and their folk songs, and gave their women bouquets of flowers while plying them with boxes of chocolates. Yet whether or not the minstrels had changed, Hirshl clearly had not. The good breeding he had received at home was not easily overcome. It was simple to wrap a box of chocolates but difficult to present it to a woman one did not know. And so, his heart as full as his hands were empty, he continued to watch from a distance while his friends went off to enjoy themselves.

Hirshl knew that his dilemma was not easily solved. The religious studies of his childhood still influenced him. If he eyed some peasant girl, they made him look away; if he imagined a rendezvous with her, they reminded him of stories of the sages, such as the tale of Rabbi Matya ben Harash, who never so much as looked at a woman until the Devil grew jealous and disguised himself as the most beautiful enchantress who had ever lived. Of course, Rabbi Matya turned his back on her the minute he saw her; yet seeing her again and again until he realized she could not be gotten rid of, he took a nail, heated it in a fire, and put out both his eyes.

Needless to say, a young shopkeeper in Szybusz was not a Talmudic sage of yore. Here, however, prudence again came to the rescue by pointing out the disgrace that was sure to follow even a single sin. Far better to die a thousand deaths than to be disgraced even once.

It almost seemed that with one hand God was making Blume more beautiful each day while with the other He was opening Hirshl's eyes wider every minute. Hirshl thought of a thousand different excuses to be with her. And yet his legs trembled when he was, nor could he say a word to her without stammering; indeed, he had not the slightest idea of what he was saying, and neither for that matter did she. But as the heart knows more than does the mouth, so can the ear hear what the tongue never speaks.

One day Hirshl entered Blume's room. Before he could say anything, the ground quaked beneath him; he felt as if a cavern had opened at his feet, revealing a hidden treasure that was his for the taking. All at once, though, his arms failed him, and, paralyzed, he froze. Blume too seemed dazed. Suddenly there was a great divide between them.

They were both bewildered. The smile on Blume's lips vanished. Hastily she reached up to arrange a loose wisp of hair, then shook his hand to signal him to go. Yet he did not go, nor did he release her hand. Their faces crimsoned as if they had been caught doing something wrong. She wrenched her hand free and left the room.

How long did Hirshl remain there by himself? Not very. Still, it was long enough to think of what many hours might not ordinarily have sufficed for.

What was it that Hirshl thought? That although they had not actually done anything, something had happened all the same. I must not let it happen again, he told himself. And yet no sooner had he done so than it seemed that nothing had happened after all.

Perhaps it had not. Perhaps that was the very reason for his turmoil. He had not hugged her or stroked her hair, though he easily could have; nor, when she finally wrested her hand back, had he sought to detain her. Though were he to think of her for a thousand years he would still find the wonderful light of her eyes and the bright shimmer of her hair lovelier each moment, Hirshl had the presence of mind to realize that he should not have clutched at her hand. Indeed, had she not left the room when she did, he would have had to leave it himself.

It was actually a relief for Hirshl to discover that he was still in control of himself and not a slave to his passion. He felt like a man awakening from a drugged sleep; while the effects of the drug were still wearing off his whole body felt numb, yet once they were gone he was perfectly normal again.

And so Hirshl went back to keeping shop. Not that he was all that keen on it. Just as when studying religion he had never really cared about being a rabbi, so now, working in the store, he did not really care about making money. If his father had wanted the rabbinate for him and his mother the life of commerce, he himself had no great expectations of either. And if after parting from Blume that day he threw himself into the

30

business, this was only because he saw that unless he kept occupied he would be at the mercy of his caprices.

It did Tsirl good to see all this. Hirshl had never been so involved with the store before. Although it was she who had introduced him to it, she had never dared hope that he would amount to much of a merchant. It had been enough for her to know that working there would keep him out of mischief. Now, however, she saw that he had the makings of a true businessman.

"I tell you, Boruch Meir," she remarked to her husband, "we may make something of the boy yet."

"Yes, indeed," nodded Boruch Meir. He himself had never worried about how his son would turn out. He was no teller of fortunes. The good Lord, who looked after all His creatures, would take care of Hirshl, too. Who could know what the future held in store for him? And even if one could, what could be done about it? Of course, if that was Tsirl's opinion, there was no point disagreeing. Yet Tsirl, he mused, wished to change Hirshl without realizing that there was no changing anyone. In the end he would do what he wanted, even if it was behind her back. Boruch Meir could see that his son was not cut out to be a practical man of affairs—which was all the more reason, he thought, to polish him carefully so that no fatal flaw in his character developed. Though Hirshl would have made a better rabbi than a storekeeper, since a storekeeper was what he now was, he might as well be taught to be a good one. He may be the only one of his kind, thought Boruch Meir, but then how many of a kind are like me? In a town full of merchants you can always find room for one odd one.

Tsirl's mood in the store was expansive. Not that there had been any cause to complain before, but at last Hirshl was shaping up and showing real business skills. Though it had taken him a few years to find his own feet, he was now solidly on them. Even the two shopboys had noticed the difference and were beginning to take him more seriously.

Getzel Stein, for instance, the son of the town's deposed chicken slaughterer, who had considered himself the store's mainstay before Hirshl came to work in it, and even afterwards had shown him scant respect, now whistled a different tune and consulted him constantly as a good employee should. Or take Getzel's assistant, Feyvel, who was both older and more educated than Getzel himself, with whom he was continually at loggerheads: though at first he had treated Hirshl no differently from Getzel, he now obeyed his every word and even addressed him as "sir."

Hirshl hardly noticed any of this. And by the time he did, he had already taken it for granted. Perhaps this should have struck him as strange, but it did not. He had other things on his mind, and not all that is strange to a shopboy is also strange to his employer.

Hirshl was not disposed to puzzle over things that others found puzzling. He did wonder, however, about things that they did not, such as the woman customer who entered the store one day and made some purchase from him. You might have thought it a simple matter to sell something to a woman, but not if you were Hirshl. Why, he remarked to himself when she was gone, I just weighed and sold her that item without even thinking how attractive she was! Why didn't I? Because I kept my mind off her, just as I've kept it off Blume. What you don't think of can't attract you; if she is not in my thoughts, she does not exist for me. Then, thinking of how Blume was not in his thoughts, he thought of Blume herself.

Blume was feeling irritable and low. When most people feel that way they can usually make themselves scarce, but when the person is a housemaid there is no place to hide, since a housemaid must be seen around the house. Like it or not, her feelings are there to see too.

Hirshl was the son of Blume's masters, and Blume was a servant in his home. Whatever her job demanded she performed irreproachably, for though a veteran in the Hurvitz house, she did not know what idleness meant. Yet if her two hands were the household's in exchange for her room, board, and clothes, her face and her heart were her own. Like it or not, they belonged to her alone. Perhaps indeed they did not belong to her either but to One even greater than her masters. In any case, Blume could not force herself to look happy when she was not. She came and went in silence when she served Hirshl his meals and kept her eyes on the table. God in heaven knew she had tact.

Hirshl sat eating his meal. Though a white cloth half covered the table, he saw neither the half of the table that was covered nor the half that was not. He had eyes only for Blume, who had just curtly left the dining room.

I see you're keeping accounts, thought Hirshl. If you mean to give me the silent treatment, believe me, two can play at that game: I can be as silent as you. And yet the fact was that it was Hirshl, the son and grandson of storekeepers who were used to weighing and measuring all things, who was keeping accounts. Nor should he have thought that he could play at Blume's game, because at the first opportunity the words tumbled out by themselves. Blume's eyes looked so anguished that he simply had to say something, and so he followed her back to her room.

"What's wrong, Blume?" he asked.

Blume sat down without answering.

The chair she sat down in was the only one in her room, which was not intended for guests. Hirshl was left standing limply, his mouth quivering as if wanting to say more. God in heaven knew what that could be.

Hirshl stood for a while longer in the middle of the room. Its walls bore down on him. How near he was to her and how far she was from him. And yet not so far as all that. He need simply reach out his arms and she would be closer than ever before.

In the end he obeyed his heart's counsel, extended a hand, and conciliatingly sought to take hers. Before he could do so, however, she was gone from the room.

He himself remained there. In her absence he felt her presence even more. The whole room was filled with her scent, which was like a freshly fallen apple's. He looked about, saw he was alone, and lay his head on her bed.

A thousand years might well have passed, for the world had ceased to exist for him. He lay without moving, suffused by a honeyed sweetness. Never had his body felt so fully alive. God in heaven knew how long it lasted. Then a woman's hand touched his head and stroked his hair. Who of you has not already guessed that it was Blume's? He came to his senses, rose, and left the room.

Hirshl grew taciturn. If alone in the store, he stared vacantly at nothing in particular. Though the store was stocked with merchandise that belonged to his parents and would one day be his, their only heir, this made him neither glad nor proud. He had other, more troubling thoughts on his mind. Sometimes he laid a hand on the scales, which rang against the counter without his noticing.

He did not speak to Blume, either. He was embarrassed to be with her. Even though he longed for her, he hid from her. Several days went by without their meeting. Yet the ray of golden light that shone from beneath her lashes when she looked at him was before him all the time.

Blume went about her work in the Hurvitz home, cooking, baking, washing, and mending. She did everything in the household except for such drudgery as scrubbing the floors, which could not be expected of a cousin. In a word, she was one of the family. And yet though many a young girl would gladly have traded places with her, she seemed to have no idea how lucky she was. Never once did she smile, while her mouth hung slightly open as if it had either given up talking in the middle of a sentence or else were about to scream.

God in heaven saw Blume's unhappiness and prompted Hirshl to approach her. God had made Hirshl an honest young man, nor was there any guile in Blume. No longer did their paths cross in self-imposed silence. Hirshl had much to say, and Blume was a willing listener. Though his conversation was trivial, it pleased her nonetheless. Let the nightingale sing what he wishes, his mate never tires of hearing it. And while Hirshl still began each tête-à-tête with a sigh, all this meant was, Though God in heaven will surely have mercy and never come between us, we had better be careful in the meantime not to upset my father and mother.

Hirshl and Blume were careful. Not that they had anything to hide. But being a good Jewish boy, the more honorable his conduct with a good Jewish girl was, the more Hirshl felt called upon to conceal it.

(This remark may seem to demand an explanation, perhaps even an illustration. The problem is, though, that any illustration will just lead us back to Hirshl and Blume.)

Tsirl began to take note. Had Hirshl not tried hiding his love, she would never have noticed it. But He who put the love of his cousin in his heart had not put the wits of his mother in his head.

6

THOUGH TSIRL SAW what was happening with her son, she said nothing. The same good sense that made her think, Why, the boy would have to be mad to fall in love with a penniless orphan, made her keep silent too. Let him have his flirtation with Blume, she thought. Once he grows up, he'll marry someone suitable.

Tsirl pretended that she saw and heard nothing. She neither discussed the matter with Hirshl nor sought to keep Blume away from him. On the contrary, she felt grateful to Blume for keeping Hirshl away from other girls, for even in Szybusz, she knew, youthful morals were not what they once were. As long as Hirshl had not found a mate for life, he was best off being friendly with Blume, who at least kept him out of worse hands.

One day, however, when it was announced that the draft board would soon be coming to Szybusz, Tsirl remarked that if a good match came her way she would not even put it off until after the army physical. Yona Toyber happened to be in the store. As he departed, Tsirl said, "By the way, Gedalia Ziemlich has a daughter named Mina. Don't you think that bears looking into, Mr. Toyber?"

Yona Toyber took out some paper and tobacco and rolled himself a cigarette. He broke it in two, stuck one half into the inner pocket of his coat and the other into a little holder, popped his head back into the store, lit his cigarette, popped his head back out again, and left.

Tsirl rubbed her hands together as her husband liked to do when he had reason to be pleased with himself.

Yona Toyber was a matchmaker. Though on the face of it he had never made a match in his life, no one in Szybusz married anyone in Szybusz without his help. True, if someone happened to mention in his presence that he had a marriageable son and was thinking of so-and-so's daughter, Toyber would not even deign to reply, as if such things were beneath him. The next day, however, he would be sure to run into the young man in question, nor would the two of them have parted before there was such camaraderie between them that the young man's heart was putty in Yona's hands. Not that Yona ever laid down the law to anyone; it was enough for him to mumble a word or two, and the rest simply happened by itself. No matter whom a youngster thought he loved, Yona could make him think otherwise, and whomever his parents thought he should love Yona could make him love too, so that in the end, as it were, he fell in love with her all by himself while Yona simply gave his approval. There were some quite educated people in Szybusz who snorted at the notion of an

36

arranged marriage without knowing that they themselves were a match made by Yona.

Yona Toyber had been one of Szybusz's bright young lights who had trained to be rabbis in the old study house. On his way to Lemberg to receive his rabbinical degree, however, he had stopped at an inn where he saw a man reading a little geography book. Yona took one look at it and was amazed. How many cities and countries there were in the world whose names he did not even know! Since by the time he finished reading it himself he had run out of money, he returned home to Syzbusz without his degree and without even having seen Lemberg.

Although his newly acquired knowledge did not undermine his faith, it did bring out an unexpressed side of him. In the middle of one night he awoke, took a pen, inkpot, and paper, and stayed up writing until dawn. That same day a visitor was in Szybusz and Yona showed him what he had written. The man read it and sent it to Yosef Kohen Tsedek in Lemberg, who printed it in his Hebrew review *The Eagle*.

This article of Toyber's was something of an enigma. If it was meant to be about geography, why all the homespun philosophy? And if it was meant to be about philosophy, why all the facts about geography? Yet back in the days when Yona Toyber was young and Yosef Kohen Tsedek edited *The Eagle*, a man's philosophy turned up in the strangest places. Had Yona lived among the fanatical Hasidim, they would no doubt have burned his piece in a bonfire, as they did with anything not penned for the greater glory of God. In the old study house of Szybusz, however, where there was a tradition of high-minded inquiry going back to the days when pious Jews with an interest in worldly knowledge still had more piety than worldliness—that is, to those Bible critics and grammarians of the last century who, when they prayed, made sure to pronounce every letter of the ancient Hebrew correctly and not like most Jews who swallow all their words until the angels themselves cannot make head or tail of them—nothing wrong was seen in Yona Toyber's article. On the contrary, it was spread out on the desks of the study house and parsed there verse by verse. Then, the conclu-

37

sion having been reached that its grammar could not be faulted, Yona's praises were publicly sung.

Though Yona Toyber never published anything else, nothing else was needed to assure his lasting fame. *The Eagle*'s wings drooped and folded, but Yona's reputation persisted. Noted scholars had lived in Szybusz before him; their works had made a name both for themselves and for the town; yet none were as renowned as he was. And he was especially looked up to by the youth of the town, which was a place where young bachelors were not thought fit company for their elders, so that any married man paying attention to a youngster could win his heart at once, let alone Yona Toyber, who actually enjoyed strolling with the younger generation in the marketplace and talking to them as one talks to a friend.

After his own marriage Yona Toyber had been supported for a while by his father-in-law; yet once this arrangement came to an end he was left in sore straits. His first dowry had been lost by his brothers-in-law, who had borrowed it to do business in his name, while a second given him to make up for it was frittered away by himself. True, if not for that geography book, he could easily have found some rabbinical post and lived comfortably at the public expense. Yet what had been his undoing proved his salvation as well. It so happened that a certain wealthy man in Szybusz who wanted to marry his daughter to someone from another town had, impressed by Toyber's book learning, asked him to write some letters of inquiry about the prospective groom, for which he paid him a matchmaker's fee. Having been paid it, Yona was considered a matchmaker, and being considered a matchmaker, he managed to make a few matches. Which was why Tsirl, having noticed what was going on between Hirshl and Blume, had said to him, "If I could find a good match for my Hirshl, I'd marry him off right away." And she even dropped a hint about Gedalia Ziemlich's daughter, who bore, so she thought, looking into.

Hirshl was going on nineteen. Though neither as strong as Samson nor as brave as David, he was certainly good enough to

38

serve the Kaiser. Younger and frailer boys than himself were already wearing uniforms and eating army messes. But Hirshl had no need to fear, for He who sent induction officers to Szybusz sent them the vice of avarice as well, so that whoever slipped them a sufficient consideration received a medical exemption. Once Dr. Knabenhut the elder, whose son Dr. Knabenhut the socialist still lived with him, had been the chief examiner; now that he was old his place had been taken by others, but they too had their price. Why then, if she was not worried about the draft board, did Tsirl say she wished to find a match for Hirshl before it came to Szybusz? Simply because the expression was a common one, events often being dated by whether they took place before or after the draft board arrived.

Gedalia Ziemlich came to Szybusz once a week. His village, Malikrowik, was not far from Szybusz, which was the market town for its wheat, the district capital for its taxes, and the shopping center for its provisions. As Gedalia's whole family consisted of only three people—himself, his wife Bertha, and their daughter Mina—he did not have much shopping to do; yet his business in Szybusz was considerable nonetheless, for though the town's district superintendents were not as easily bought off as their underlings, they had to be buttered up all the same. Bribing a department head differed from bribing a clerk: a junior official never objected to having his palm greased, whereas a senior one, as venal as he might be, could suddenly come down with an attack of nerves and throw one into prison for one's pains. And so the practice was that, in the days before Christmas, the wives of such men would set a room aside to which one might bring a modest largesse. Gedalia Ziemlich was in the habit of giving baskets of fancy foodstuffs, which was how he and the Hurvitzes came to be friends, for if he was a generous customer, they saved him the trouble of wrapping and sending his own gifts. In the course of time the two men grew close and Boruch Meir's store became Gedalia Ziemlich's regular stopover in Szybusz. And not just his store, either; for, since not everything between them could be discussed in public, or on an empty stomach, they sometimes went upstairs to the Hurvitz home to have a cup of coffee. At one time this had been accompanied by a slice of fried bread; since Blume's arrival, however, the coffee was drunk with a piece of such cake as she had learned to bake from her mother. Now and then Gedalia Ziemlich stayed to dine with the Hurvitzes too. And since, apart from weddings and other festivities, invitations to dinner were not the custom in Szybusz, such meals were a special occasion.

The year that Tsirl spoke to Yona Toyber about finding a match for Hirshl, Mina Ziemlich had begun to visit Szybusz by herself and to stop at the Hurvitzes, too. Indeed, Gedalia and Boruch Meir being such good friends, how could a daughter of Gedalia's come to town without being invited to Boruch Meir's? She would arrive in a buggy drawn by two horses and loaded with bundles, some of which, such as her dresses, hats, and shoes, were for her, and some of which, such as butter, cheese, and fruit, were for the Hurvitzes. After Tsirl had greeted her in front of the store and inquired after her parents, Stach the coachman unpacked the things and Mina went inside. There was an empty room in the Hurvitz house whose windows were never opened in summer because of the sun and in winter because of the cold, and in which, amid an odor of mothballs, stood some pile furniture that was covered all year round with white slipcovers against the dust. There Mina repaired to dab herself with cologne before going to see her friend Sophia Gildenhorn.

7

IT WOULD BE POINTLESS to criticize Mina in order to praise Blume, for Mina too was a well-mannered and attractive young lady. Even though she had grown up in a village she had the graces of a city girl, having gone to a boarding school in Stanislaw where she learned to speak French, embroider, and play the piano, so that nothing about her so much as hinted that she was the daughter of country Jews. When she accompanied her parents to Szybusz, her elegance contrasting with their simplicity and her leisurely gait with their hurried one, one might have thought her the daughter of a Polish nobleman besieged by two Jewish peddlers. The transformation undergone by her was so complete that her own father and mother scarcely seemed to belong to her anymore. Not that she was ashamed of them—it just could not be said that she was particularly proud of them either. She had other concerns, foremost among them how much longer she would have to stay in Malikrowik before returning to Stanislaw.

Spending the summer in the village had been an ordeal for her. Like other well-to-do students who spent their summer vacations in the country, Mina had come back to Malikrowik, yet she was not happy there. Perhaps she should have exchanged her city clothes for country ones, or perhaps she was simply used to the bustle of the city, which was so different from the village, where there was nothing to look at but chickens, cows, and trees, and every breeze stank of cow manure and milk and blew away your hat and mussed your hair. Not a day went by without her wishing that her vacation would already be over. Meanwhile, she came to Szybusz as often as she could. It may not have been Stanislaw, but at least it was a large town.

Although Mina had overheard her parents discussing a match for her, she had not bothered to express her opinion on the matter. True, her life belonged to her and her alone, but though she had friends younger than herself who were already married and friends older than herself who still were not, she knew, without being sure which of them were better off, that she could not live in a boarding school forever and that sooner or later, or at the latest later than that, she would have to get married too. In that case, what did it matter if it was sooner?

She had nothing against young Hirshl Hurvitz, whom her parents wished her to marry. If she judged him by his clothes, he was a modern enough young fellow, and if she judged him by his manners, he had plenty of them. No doubt there were other things to be desired in the man a girl pledged her heart to, but Mina was too inexperienced to know what these might be. It only surprised her a bit that, though she had been in his house several times, he had never talked to her about anything but the most ordinary matters. What kind of modern young man let his parents do all his wooing?

Yet if one could not exactly say that Hirshl Hurvitz was the young man of Mina's dreams, neither could one say that he was not. Something about him attracted her. She herself did not know that it was the power of the inarticulate love that she felt for him whose heart was already pledged to another.

The days went by unobjectionably, each profitable in its own way. The only thing objectionable was Dr. Knabenhut, who had persuaded all the shop clerks to quit work at eight P.M. and to stop behaving like serfs.

Getzel Stein and his assistant, to be sure, were not enlisted in Knabenhut's legions, but the pressure of the socialists was too much for them and, reluctant to break ranks, they now walked off the job at eight o'clock sharp and went home. One's God-given compassion alone kept one from laughing in their faces, for what good did this do them? A more dismal place than their homes would be hard to find.

Indeed, when God is on one's side all clouds have their silver linings. Despite her raving at Knabenhut for inciting her help to quit early, Tsirl was glad of it in the end, since once the two clerks were gone and Hirshl had left for the Society for Zion clubhouse, she and her husband had a chance to be alone at last. Just to be safe, they rolled down the shutter halfway. Customers wishing to buy learned to come earlier, while those wishing simply to chat turned around and went elsewhere. Even at the hour of nine o'clock there were thresholds in Szybusz that could be crossed without having to crawl on all fours.

And yet if the shutter was halfway down, the cash register

was fully open. Boruch Meir and Tsirl sat in front of it counting the day's take, arranging the bills in wads and the copper and silver in stacks.

Could there be a greater pleasure in life than sitting at night in one's store with one's profits laid out before one? Schilling rose above schilling on the counter, and all was right with the world. Out in the street the young couples went by and sometimes even dropped to their knees. If one's hearing was good one could make out their heartbeats in their footsteps. Ah, how many more long nights of courting like these did they still have ahead of them, nor was the outcome certain even then! Meanwhile, one sat with one's wife in one's store amid a fragrance of cinnamon, figs, and raisins. A last parting trace of the warmth of the sun lingered on in these fruits, which retained it even dried and packed in crates.

Silently Tsirl and Boruch Meir sat listening. What could they be straining to hear? A line of a song sung in faraway climes by the planters of such southern vines and trees? The last echo of a kiss that a shepherd gave his love beneath them?

There were people in Szybusz who swore that the apogee of true love was a certain rich lady in town who had run off with her butler and refused to return to her imploring husband even though her new lover beat her. There were others who told you to look for it in the person of the unrepentant Mottshi Shaynbart, who had lost his leg chasing after a woman and now had a wooden one in its place. Still others insisted that only the man driven out of his senses by passion could claim to be love's acolyte. In each of these cases, the passion for love misled them about love itself.

Tsirl and Boruch Meir, in any event, had no time for such diversions. Boruch Meir never pretended to be Tsirl's lover, and Tsirl never drove Boruch Meir out of his senses. He simply was as happy with her as she was with him. Their days passed in the making of money, and if now and then they chose to rest from it, they generally did so in silence.

Yet sometimes their silence was broken. When one has been hard at work, a bit of conversation can be welcome.

43

"You know," said Tsirl, putting down the coins she held, "no matter how far ahead you try to look, you never can look very far. If you're wondering what's on my mind, it's Gedalia Ziemlich's daughter. I do believe that she's suited for Hirshl, don't you?"

Boruch Meir was not in the habit of contradicting his wife. Sometimes he would simply repeat what she had said and sometimes he would add a few words of confirmation. A tiny something in Tsirl's voice, which Boruch Meir was every bit as fond of as he had been during their first year of marriage, still reminded him of that year. Yet now that she had raised so momentous a question regarding his son's life, Boruch Meir hesitated, played with his gold watch chain, shut his eyes, and took time out to mull the matter over. Unlike his father-in-law, who had been able to think unassisted, Boruch Meir needed to concentrate on his watch chain.

Tsirl looked at him. This too was a sign of the times. Her father could read a man's thoughts blindfolded, but Tsirl liked to see whom she was talking to. Besides, it was a good opportunity to study her husband without his being aware of it.

At last Boruch Meir opened his eyes, let go of the watch chain, and said, "We'd better see what Toyber thinks about it."

"I wouldn't dream of depriving Toyber of a livelihood," said Tsirl, "but I wanted to hear what you thought first."

"Ziemlich," said Boruch Meir, "has money. That's undeniable."

"And Mina?" asked Tsirl.

"Mina," said Boruch Meir, "is a lovely girl. That's undeniable too. It's just . . ."

"Just what?" asked Tsirl.

"Just that in matters like these," said Boruch Meir, "you don't really need me. I believe you're a better judge of them than I am."

"We're in perfect agreement, Boruch Meir," said Tsirl.

"So what now?" asked Boruch Meir.

44

"Now," said Tsirl, "the time has come to talk to Toyber.'

"That's just what I said," said Boruch Meir.

"So you did, Boruch Meir," said Tsirl. "I only wanted to know what you thought about it first."

"We're in perfect agreement, Tsirl," said Boruch Meir.

"A person should always seek advice," said Tsirl. "No one should make important decisions all by himself. One person will tell you this, another will tell you that, and little by little things sort themselves out. But just so you don't think I've been up to anything behind your back, I had better tell you that I've already spoken to Toyber."

"And what did he say?" asked Boruch Meir.

"As if you didn't know Toyber."

"I'd still like to know what he said."

"He didn't say anything. He left the store."

Boruch Meir rubbed his hands contentedly and said, "Toyber just stood there and said nothing?"

"And left the store."

"Where did he go?"

"I personally," said Tsirl, "did not follow him. But I heard that he was in Malikrowik."

"And what did he do there—say some more nothing?" asked Boruch Meir.

"That," said Tsirl, "is something we can ask him when he comes for his matchmaker's fee."

"Oh, we most certainly shall," said Boruch Meir, rubbing his hands together.

Blume saw what she saw and came to her own conclusions about Mina's visits. Although she had heard nothing definite, something told her what was happening.

She was surprised at herself for not feeling angry or bitter. But just as it was pointless to berate herself when her fate was still in her hands, so it was senseless to feel aggrieved when she saw clearly what must be done. And the first thing to do was to change her situation before Mina's family arrived for the betrothal and she was made to wait on them. One way or another, she would have to look for another job.

One day, when Hirshl went down to the cellar to tap the wine barrel, his mother followed him. She's snooping on me to see if I'm having a rendezvous with Blume, he told himself. It infuriated him to be suspected of such a thing. He felt ashamed of his mother's meanness for even thinking it and pretended not to notice her. I'm afraid I'll just have to disappoint her, he thought angrily.

Tsirl shut the cellar door behind her. "Hirshl," she said, "I want to talk to you." She groped her way toward him. "Why don't you say something?"

"I believe it's you who want to say something," said Hirshl. "I'm waiting to hear what it is."

"That's very well put," said Tsirl, not sounding as if she thought it was at all. She pursed her lips, then changed her tone of voice, let out a preliminary sigh, and said, "You know Ziemlich. I don't think I have to tell you the sort of man he is."

Although it came as a great relief that his mother was not spying on him but had simply come down to talk business, Hirshl failed to see why she was having so much difficulty doing it.

"Ziemlich," Tsirl went on, "is a wealthy man, and he has an educated daughter. What do you think of her, Hirshl? If you ask me, she's what's called nowadays a modern girl. And as for the dowry she'll get, we should only make that much from the store in a year. But why even mention the dowry when one day everything that her father owns will be hers? A bachelor can be free to follow his heart, but what would the world come to if he didn't put his romances aside when the time came to get married? A fine place it would be if everyone followed their hearts! I wouldn't envy it. Far be it from me to say a word against Blume. There aren't many Blumes around. But you can't just ignore the fact that she hasn't a cent to her name. We were good enough to take her in and provide for all her needs, and I'm sure she knows her proper place and would never

46

want to come between you and good fortune. You were born into a good family, Hirshl, and you're meant for better things than Blume."

Hirshl did not answer. Nor had his mother expected him to. She was merely seeking to put him in the proper frame of mind.

Hirshl's arms felt numb. It was all he could do to hold on to the pitcher of wine. Although he hadn't drunk a drop of it, his head was reeling as if a whole cask of grapes was fermenting there.

All that day he looked for Blume. He had a thousand things to tell her. Even though he had not talked back to his mother, he felt quite heroic. But Blume had disappeared. Her footsteps were nowhere to be heard. And when he finally came across her, her bottom lip was in her mouth and something had happened to her. How he had fought for her, and here she was looking right through him! His heart sank. How had he wronged her? God in heaven knew that he had not.

If Hirshl was seeing less than he wanted to of Blume, he was seeing more than he wanted to of his mother, whom he tried avoiding just as Blume was avoiding him. As dearly as he loved Blume, not only was she giving him no encouragement, she was actually spurning him.

In a vague way Hirshl began to feel that, if he did not stand steadfast forever, this would only be because Blume had abandoned him. He could never have a change of heart unless she changed toward him. Not that he had ceased to care for her. He still felt the same about her. Yet now he felt a grievance too.

Tsirl made good use of her time and moved quickly. She did not raise the subject with Hirshl again or pester him in any way. And since he didn't raise it with her, she misconstrued his silence to mean that he had seen the error of his ways and wished to make amends.

47

8

IF ONE WAS LOOKING for Blume, she was to be found only in Hirshl's thoughts, for she was gone from the house. Blume had another job. She had packed and left without warning, ending her stay with the Hurvitzes.

Blume moved into her new home, arranged her things there, and hung her father's photograph above her bed. The picture had faded, giving the blond beard that ringed his face an ethereal, otherworldly look. She had never been close to her father as a child. The pity she had felt for her mother had made her angry with him for reading and sighing over his books all day long. Yet his death had made him dear to her, so that anything reminding her of him filled her with emotion. Now that only his photograph was left, it made her think how good a man he must have been.

Blume folded her arms and looked at her new bed, her second since leaving her mother's. She felt as if she were being orphaned all over again. Would she, she wondered, have to remain a housemaid all her life? Did leaving Tsirl's home mean leaving her hopes behind too? She remembered the day of her arrival there. Not that there had been much cause for hope then either—yet it had been a far better day than the painful one of her departure.

Just because Hirshl is tied to his mother's apron strings, thought Blume, is no reason for my world to come to an end: he may be her slave, but I have my freedom. And yet who could say whether this freedom should have meant taking herself elsewhere or trying to free Hirshl too?

There was a tap on the door. Her new employer, Tirza Mazal, entered the room and inquired, "Is there anything I can do for you?" She glanced at the photograph on the wall. "Is that your father?"

"Yes," said Blume. "It's my father."

Mrs. Mazal gave her a curious look but said nothing.

"I look like my mother," said Blume, reddening as if caught in a lie.

Silently they regarded the photograph. The face of the man in it was sad and gentle, yet peaceful too, as if any complaints he had against life were not meant to be taken too seriously.

Blume stared at the floor, and Mrs. Mazal slipped out of the room. The little she had said made Blume see her father in a new light.

One day Hirshl heard sounds coming from the room with the pile furniture. He went to have a look and found Mina Ziemlich sitting and embroidering a handkerchief. "Excuse me," he stammered. "I should have knocked first."

"If anyone is an intruder in this house, it's me and not you," said Mina, putting down her embroidery.

Hirshl felt as if he were seeing her for the first time. That is, he had seen her before, but he had paid no attention to what he saw. Now that he was standing in front of her, he felt at a loss. He knew he should say something, but he had no idea what. Why, he kept thinking, she knew just what to answer me and here I am gaping at her like a fool. She must think I have no manners. She lives in a city, and studies in a boarding school, and knows French, and goes to the theater and to concerts, while I've never been out of Szybusz, except for one time I took the train to Piczyric, which is an even smaller place than Szybusz is.

How sad it is to think the less of oneself just because someone else has seen a bit more of the world. If only one knew how grand that made the other feel!

The days came and went. Hirshl quickly forgot the momentary discomfort of his encounter with Mina. She was not, after all, the center of his life, nor need his mind dwell on her. If it must dwell on someone, that was Blume.

The more Hirshl thought about Blume, the less he could say what made her special. Was it simply her being gone?

He could not have been more wrong about this. It would have made no difference where Blume was. She had always been special for him. He had been drawn to her from the day he ceased being a boy. He felt about her as one might feel about a twin who has suddenly been abducted.

Hirshl was an unrealistic young man. Though he thought about Blume constantly, it never occurred to him that she might be working somewhere else. For all he ever considered the matter, she could have been living on starbeams. He imagined everything possible having happened to her without it crossing his mind for a moment that she needed a roof over her head.

Even when he finally learned where she was, he did not stop indulging his fantasies. The case of Mrs. Mazal, who had fallen in love with her mother's former tutor and married him, cast a romantic glow over Blume's new home. Hirshl imagined a conversation between the two women in which, Tirza Mazal having told Blume about her love affair with Akavia Mazal and Blume having told Tirza about Hirshl, Blume would realize that a woman had to take the first step. In fact, he was sure that she would take it. When at first she did not he felt surprised; then he began to hold it against her. If she did not do something soon, it would be too late.

Such self-indulgence was not for Blume. If the Angel of Dreams himself had whispered his sweet promises to her, she simply would have laughed at them. She bustled about from morning to night, busying herself with a thousand different things to keep her mind off herself. In vain the Mazals chided her for working herself to the bone. She was in seven different places at one and the same time. There was no chore in the household that she did not perform. She even took such good care of Tirza's little baby that Tirza was heard to complain that she no longer knew if the child was hers or Blume's.

Hirshl waited on customers in the store, which was crowded with housewives and domestics, selling them sugar and kerosene.

He went about his job as usual, standing in front of the scales and weighing, wrapping, and handing out merchandise. The goods were of good quality, the scales were balanced, and neither the customers nor the Kaiser had any cause for complaint. And just as Tsirl kept boosting Mina, so Hirshl too deserves a good word. There was profit in everything he did.

Between customers Hirshl stood by the scales staring off into space and wondering why he put up with so much in silence. Perhaps it was because he felt sure that nothing would come of it anyway.

In fact, however, much had happened since the day Tsirl spoke to her son in the cellar, and even more was about to. It puzzled Hirshl why he was not angrier with Mina for coming between him and Blume. Dimly he felt that not she but Blume was to blame, since if Blume had been nicer to him, there would have been no question of Mina.

Hirshl's mind kept changing. If one day it surprised him that he was not angrier with Mina, the next day his anger at Blume did not surprise him at all. He thought, It's all because she walked out on me and left me with my father and my mother and everyone else who wants to run my life.

Why, Hirshl asked himself, do I put up with it? Because nothing will come of it anyway. Yet something already had come of his mother's activity. Hirshl's and Mina's parents had met and agreed on a dowry. It only remained to convene the young couple beneath the wedding canopy.

His mother did not argue when Hirshl was moody with her but simply sighed along with him and said, "No one chooses his own fate. Better to marry a woman who respects you than to run after one who doesn't care." Tsirl was clever enough to know that she lived in an age when no parent could force a son to do anything, much less to marry against his will. Had she

51

behaved like most mothers, she simply would have antagonized Hirshl. Yet as she continued to be her loving self, he was hers to do with as she pleased.

Indeed, just being near his mother made Hirshl dewy-eyed these days. As distant as he had felt from her, there was now no one in the world who seemed closer to him. Once, when he had been a small boy, a friend had jilted him; seeing how hurt he was Tsirl took him in her arms, where her kisses and caresses soon put the friend out of his mind. And although Hirshl was now a young man, the same thing had happened again.

It was the middle of the winter. The houses were waist-high in snow, and a column of smoke rose from every roof—a lower and fainter one from the far roofs and a higher and thicker one from the near ones. The river was frozen as flat as the sky, and a cross of ice stood upon it. The Christmas holidays were at hand, and every store was crammed with goods and customers. Horse-drawn sleighs jingled down the streets, the clear, cold chime of their bells resounding all over. The rich estate owners came to town wrapped in their bearskins and wolf-skins. Szybusz was bright and bustling, and the shopkeepers had their hands full, for there were no better shopping days than those before Christmas, when the Poles and Ukrainians bought each other gifts. There was not a shop in town that did not do a booming business.

Gedalia Ziemlich arrived one day at the Hurvitzes'. Tsirl was sitting in the shop, warming her hands over a brazier of hot coals. She smiled at Gedalia when he entered and nodded toward a stack of boxes that was redolent of wood and groceries. Boruch Meir came out of his office, handed Gedalia a sheet of paper, and said something to him in low tones. Gedalia Ziemlich took the page and read from it aloud while wiping the icicles from his mustache. His kind, weary eyes lit up with the pleasure it gave him to think of what so many officials and their wives would soon be eating and drinking at his expense.

Hirshl stood to one side with a sneer on his lips, his fingers drumming on the counter. Senses of right and wrong differ. It irked him to think that men appointed to enforce the law should take bribes; worse yet, that even though the Christian bribe takers considered the Jewish bribe givers their inferiors, the bribe givers were as pleased with themselves as if they were giving to a deserving charity. And yet it was neither socialism nor a sense of Jewish honor that made Hirshl think this way. It was simply his dislike for the Jew from Malikrowik.

Tsirl saw her son's expression and sought to change the subject. Pushing aside the brazier of coals, she asked Ziemlich, "And how is Miss Mina?" Even though the dowry had already been settled, she still referred to Mina as "miss."

"We expect her home any day now," said Gedalia Ziemlich, putting down the sheet of paper.

"She'll be most welcome here," said Boruch Meir, rubbing his hands.

"Will she be returning to Stanislaw as soon as the vacation is over?" Tsirl asked.

"She won't be returning at all," said Gedalia.

"Why not?" Tsirl asked.

Gedalia Ziemlich let out a heartfelt sigh. "Because the headmistress of her boarding school has gone and married a Pole."

"A Pole!" exclaimed Boruch Meir and Tsirl in alarm. "Imagine, she married a goy!"

Gedalia Ziemlich nodded and sighed again. Boruch Meir ran his left hand through his beard, distraughtly flipping its hairs upward as if throwing them away. Tsirl warmed her fingers in front of her mouth, lowered her eyes, and said nothing. Boruch Meir smoothed his beard down with his right hand, gripped his watch chain, and said:

"I hate to think of a young lady like Mina having to spend her whole vacation in the village."

"Why not think of how happy her parents will be to have her," said Tsirl.

"Well now," stammered Boruch Meir, "if you look at it that way, I'm happy too."

"I do hope, though," said Tsirl, "that Mr. Ziemlich will not hide his daughter at home, so that we can get to see her also."

"I do believe she'll be more in Szybusz than in Malikrowik," said Gedalia. "She's already invited to stay here with Sophia. That Sophia is absolutely turning her against Malikrowik."

"Ah," said Boruch Meir in the tone of a man whom friendship has made an expert on another man's business. "You must mean Miss Gildenhorn, Eisy Heller's daughter."

Gedalia Ziemlich nodded. "She doesn't let Mina alone. The minute Mina arrives from Stanislaw Sophia runs off with her to Szybusz. She tells her that the cows in Malikrowik will give milk just as well without her."

"The Gildenhorns have a big house," said Tsirl. "There are always gay times there. It might not be a bad idea for Mina to stay with them."

"That's what I think," said Gedalia. "But her mother is against it. When a child's been away for so long, a mother wants her by her side when she's home."

"Well," Tsirl said, "we'll be glad to see Miss Mina when she comes. Tell me, Hirshl, will the Zionists be having their Hanukkah party this year?"

Tsirl cared for neither the Zionists nor their parties, but she thought it would make Hirshl glad to know that she took an interest in the same things he did.

Sophia Gildenhorn was two years older than Mina, though she looked two years younger. She was married to a commercial traveler named Yitzchok Gildenhorn, a carefree young man who made a good living selling life insurance to gullible provincials. His house, which was a quiet place when he was away, teemed with activity when he was home, especially during the Christmas holidays, when the shops were closed and there was much partying and the fast set in Szybusz gathered at the Gildenhorns' to stay up all night eating, drinking, playing cards, and telling jokes. Sometimes the revelers invented comic names for various inhabitants of the town, or even composed satirical sketches about them that were posted in the marketplace, where others felt free to change or add to them as they pleased. More than one marriage had been called off because of these lampoons, which cast whole families into disrepute. Indeed, the decline and fall of Szybusz's old patricians had begun on the day that Gildenhorn moved into town. Anything went in Szybusz these days, and every rogue felt free to raise his head; nor could anyone do anything about it, since half the local residents were afraid of Gildenhorn and the other half were on his side. Anyone promising good times and free drinks is certain to have lots of friends. And anyone dropping in on Gildenhorn was certain to find the unlikeliest people in his house.

9

ON THE FIRST NIGHT of Hanukkah the Gildenhorns invited the Hurvitzes to a pirogen party that they were giving with the proceeds from a winning lottery ticket bought by Sophia.

When it was time to set out, Tsirl said to Hirshl, "Your father and I aren't ready yet. Why don't you go now, and we'll come later. You know who's going to be there, it's not something you would want to miss. Judging by the amount of liquor they bought in the store today, there's going to be lots of fun. Perhaps you had better put on a fresh shirt for the occasion."

When Hirshl arrived at the party, Yitzchok Gildenhorn was already at the card table with his friends. Hirshl was perfectly presentable, yet unaccustomed to society as he was he kept touching himself to make sure that his tie was still in place and that his socks had not fallen down. He stood there uncertainly, running a hand over his clothes as though he had lice.

A large crowd of people was at the Gildenhorns'. Among

them was the likable Leibush Tshortkover, as light of head as he was heavy of beard, sitting at the card table with his mentor and host; Gimpel Kurtz, who taught religion at the Baron de Hirsch School; the joke-loving amputee Mottshi Shaynbart, nattily dressed and gay-looking, his wooden crutch smelling of fresh paint; Gildenhorn's father-in-law Eisy Heller; and many others besides, not all of whom Hirshl knew. As soon as they had greeted him, they went right back to their cards.

Hirshl was left sitting by himself until he was discovered by Sophia, who told him how happy she was that he had come and asked when his parents would arrive. Before he could answer her, though, she was gone, for she had left the pirogen on the stove and had to keep an eye on them. Left alone again, Hirshl sat looking at Yitzchok Gildenhorn, who always made him feel of no account. Gildenhorn was the sort of man who put you in your place whether you wanted to be there or not. It was not that he was so clever—in fact, there were far cleverer people than he; it was because, unlike most Szybuszians, who ate so much starch that they grew sideways rather than up, he was exceedingly tall. The good Lord was parsimonious: if one would rather be round, He gave the height to others.

Thinking about the card players made Hirshl wonder about their names. You would imagine that someone named Tshortkover, for example, would come from a family of Tshortkov Hasidim, whereas Leibush was in fact a Bobov Hasid. A man's name could even be his opposite. True, plump Gimpel Kurtz, whose last name meant "short," was just that, but Mottshi Shaynbart, whose name meant "fine beard," had no hair on his chin at all, while Leibush Tshortkover, who was named after the wrong city, should have been called Shaynbart instead. The fact was that names and people rarely went together. Take Balaban, for instance, who was chain-smoking next to Eisy Heller. What in the world did a name like that mean?

Watching Balaban smoke made Hirshl want to smoke too.

56

He took out a cigarette and searched his pants in vain for a match. Though Hirshl did not particularly relish smoking, a young man his age was expected to smoke whether he relished it or not. Indeed, the reason he never went anywhere with matches was that the nuisance of having to borrow them kept him from smoking more.

Hirshl went over to ask Balaban for a light. Balaban, who was absorbed in his cards, took the cigarette from his mouth and tossed it to Hirshl like a coin to a bothersome beggar. Hirshl blushed and took an angry puff of smoke, which only made him even angrier. As soon as the cigarette was finished he lit another. The more he smoked the stupider he felt, and the stupider he felt the more he smoked. The befuddling odor and taste of the tobacco mingling with the heavy smell of grease coming from the kitchen made him gasp for air. He was afraid that he would disgrace himself by throwing up or fainting. The cards jumped so quickly from hand to hand that, strangely enough, the hands themselves had disappeared. Then the cards vanished too and there was nothing but little red and black faces dancing mockingly in front of him.

Hirshl rose bewilderedly to his feet. He knew that such small people did not exist anywhere. He must have been looking at the pictures on the cards. He glanced about the room. The cardplayers were still puffing away at the table, and their smoke was making him dizzy. He was about to step outside when he remembered a story he had once heard about a man who left a party without informing his host and was accused the next day of stealing an object of value. Though he knew he would be accused of no such thing, Hirshl removed his hands from his pockets as if to protest his innocence.

Just then the door opened and in stepped Mina. Hirshl collected himself and gladly went over to shake her hand and help her out of her coat and gloves.

A moment later they were talking like old friends.

Hirshl kept up a steady stream of conversation and took care that it did not flag, for he was afraid that Mina would abandon him for the card table and leave him alone once more. He talked to her about everything under the sun. Never in his life had he said so much at one time. Before he had finished with one topic he had already gone on to the next.

Mina had never heard such things discussed in her life. She stood rooted to one spot, hanging on every word, her large, heavy earrings at rest in her little ears, which, Hirshl noticed, were flushed. He looked over his shoulder, and, seeing that no one engrossed in the card game was paying him any attention, pulled up two chairs to sit down on. Then he resumed talking while Mina went on listening in silence. And though her silence made no great impression on him, the fact that she was listening did.

Apart from four or five teachers in her boarding school, some of them bachelors and some of them married men who carried on like bachelors, Mina did not know many young men. Unlike other girls in the school, she had never been the favorite of any of her teachers, much less gone walking with one in the park or been kissed by him, and she was for the male staff simply one more student whose tuition helped pay their salaries. Even her tutorials were kept to a minimum, so that now, sitting with Hirshl, she felt doubly amazed: at him for not tiring of her company, and at herself for being so interesting. At first she wondered whether any of the men her girlfriends were always running after could be as charming as Hirshl. Then she stopped making comparisons and simply concentrated on him.

Hirshl sensed her thoughts and strove not to disappoint her. Whatever he could think of, he said. He spoke in a well-modulated voice, nor did he stammer, as when talking to Blume. In this he was aided by Mina's eyes, which did not regard him suspiciously like Blume's.

Hirshl sat and talked. He did not seek to impress Mina as he would have had she been Blume. The two of them were different, and so was talking to them; yet having talked to no one at all for the last several days, he would gladly have talked now to either.

All at once Hirshl felt that they were being stared at. He turned red, forgot what he was saying, and broke off in the middle of a sentence.

Gildenhorn, who was holding a hand of cards, chose that exact moment to laugh and exclaim, "Just look at the two lovebirds cooing to each other!"

Hirshl was embarrassed. In fact, he was mortified. Not only had he been publicly insulted, Mina had been too. The slight to their honor, which he saw no way of defending, enraged him. He felt too shamefaced to look up. And yet when he returned the stares in the end, each one of them was friendly. Indeed, he had never seen so many pairs of eyes looking alike, each more doting than the next. Before he could absorb what was happening, Gimpel Kurtz stepped up to him, took his hand, and murmured some lines of poetry about a young man in a beauteous garden who was urged to pluck its fruits. His wink left no room for doubt that the young man was Hirshl, the garden Mina, etcetera, etcetera.

What must Mina think of him, Hirshl wondered, for having disgraced her so? He could not bring himself to look at her. He was so immobilized that it seemed as though nothing short of a fire or a war could ever get him to move again.

Yet Providence had other plans. Indeed, when Hirshl was still a twinkle in his mother's eye an angel in heaven had proclaimed, "Hirshl the son of Boruch Meir to Mina the daughter of Gedalia." And so, when Hirshl finally stood up, he was holding Mina's hand. It clung to his. Her eyes were bright with the light that had been waiting to shine forth from the day of that angelic proclamation.

What made Hirshl take Mina's hand? He had only wanted to say to her, Please do not think I am to blame. Before he could say it, however, Yitzchok Gildenhorn came over, clapped him on the shoulder, and said, "That's the brave fellow! Now you're a man among men."

Aghast, Hirshl withdrew his hand from Mina's. Gildenhorn seized it and declared, "*Ich gratuliere.*"

Saying *ich gratuliere,* to be sure, was not quite the same as saying mazel tov to a groom. It was more like something one might say to the winner of a card game. Yet as the same angel who had announced Hirshl's betrothal in heaven now chose to speak on earth in Gildenhorn's voice, not a single guest doubted that Hirshl had been congratulated on his engagement.

Sophia ran over to Mina, hugged her as hard as she could, and kissed her loudly on the mouth. Then she smiled at her and said, "I've never been so thrilled in my life. You absolutely must tell me how Mr. Hurvitz proposed to you. And him playing the innocent, you'd never have guessed that he was after you! Doesn't still water run deep!"

She grabbed Hirshl's hand as she spoke and pumped it until she was red. Everyone gaily crowded around the couple to shake hands and wish them good luck.

Leibush Tshortkover rose, took the money from the card table, and sent someone out with it to buy champagne. Then he took the bowl the money had been in and smashed it against a wall.

Mottshi Shaynbart rapped his crutch on the floor and shouted, "Mazel tov, mazel tov!"

"You had better go tell the parents of the bride and groom," said Eisy Heller to Gimpel Kurtz. Before Gimpel could go for them, however, they arrived on their own. A sixth sense must have told them what was happening.

Gedalia Ziemlich laid a hand on the breast pocket where his money was kept, as if meaning to present the dowry then and there. Boruch Meir rubbed his hands with pleasure and kept repeating, "Friends, friends," as though to make clear that he held everyone responsible. Tsirl held out her hand to Gedalia. He took it with his left hand, since his right hand was still on his left pocket.

"Why don't you hold your heart with your left hand," said Bertha. "It's nearer to it."

Ziemlich noticed his faux pas and switched hands. "Where—" he started to ask.

"—is the groom?" interrupted his wife.

Gedalia nodded like an invalid who managed to be understood. "And Mina?" he asked. Although he had just been informed of her engagement, he still found it hard to believe.

10

THE PROCEEDS of Sophia's lottery ticket stood ready to eat on the table. Although her winnings had been small, one would never have guessed it from the amount of food and drink served.

After the appetizer Yitzchok Gildenhorn got to his feet, raised his glass, toasted his guests and the two families newly joined in wedlock, and proposed drinking as well to the health of his wife, whose pirogen with their hidden filling of meat were the perfect symbol of Hirshl's love, which too had been hidden until now. He was followed by Kurtz, who gave a speech that started with Schiller, ended with Heine, and avowed that all poets were agreed that the highest theme of poetry was young love. "And so," Kurtz concluded, "I invite you to rise and drink with me to the charming young couple that is making great poetry here tonight."

Leibush Tshortkover poured himself another drink and said to Kurtz, "In case you're wondering why I'm staying seated, it's because it says in the Bible, 'Stand not in the way of the great.' "

Mottshi Shaynbart rapped his crutch on the floor and exclaimed, "Ai, just listen to the old peg laugh."

Hirshl sat wondering what he was doing there. He felt dazed and dejected. Several times he tried thinking things through and gave up. His mind kept jumping until it settled on a story he once was told as a child about a man who, finding himself at a wedding, suddenly noticed that the bride and groom were

made of straw, that the guests were all trolls, and that everything in the house was an enchantment. Just as he was about
to flee for dear life he saw that the wedding ring was real gold
and decided to take it. No sooner had he done so than the
bride stuck out a finger and he slipped the golden ring onto it.
The trolls roared with laughter and so did he. His new wife
seized him by his jacket tails and never let go of him again.

Tsirl caught her son's eye and ran a hand over her forehead.
Hirshl, however, did not take the hint to smooth the frown
from his brow. Though he was being stubborn, Tsirl simply
curled her lip in a smile as if to say, If that's how he wants it,
let it be.

When the guests could stuff themselves no more they began
to sing folderol to the tune of old Passover songs. It seemed
odd to Mina that anyone could laugh so hard at words that had
no meaning. Gedalia Ziemlich was troubled at first that the
Passover service should be spoofed by young men so unregen-
erate that they did not even cover their heads when they ate;
yet seeing his new in-law enjoying himself, he felt reassured:
Boruch Meir was a God-fearing Jew and never would laugh at
anything improper.

Boruch Meir put an arm around Hirshl and beamed at him.
The fact that Hirshl was sitting next to Mina, that he and Tsirl
were sitting next to the Ziemlichs, and that the table was piled
with good food that was heartily being devoured made him
feel indebted to his son, for he had been worried all along that
the dowry negotiations would prove a waste of time.

As for Tsirl, she kept her eyes on Boruch Meir. Other
wives might not have spent their son's engagement party
looking at their husbands, but Boruch Meir was no ordinary
husband. At the age of forty-seven he was still young in body
and mind.

Tsirl was every bit as spry. Her forty-eight years did not
show on her. Her face looked washed with virgin rainwater
and her eyes bathed with fresh egg whites. Indeed, how can
we have mentioned Tsirl so often without having mentioned
her eyes? Although she had only two of them, their power was

great—and never so much as now that she kept them fixed on Boruch Meir while never taking them off Mina, for whom she felt a special affection for having agreed to become her daughter-in-law, thus saving Hirshl from the clutches of Blume.

All along, thought Hirshl, I was sure that the matchmakers could never lay hands on me, and here I am with my head in their noose. How will I ever talk to or look at Blume again? If only he could slip away home now, bury his face in his hands, and quietly sit listening to her footsteps as she made the bed in the next room. Of course, she was no longer there, yet thinking of her made it seem as if she were.

The party grew gayer and gayer. Boruch Meir sent to his shop for some almond and raisin cordials. The drinkers kept drinking, and the non-drinkers kept eating. Few of the guests could remember anymore why they had been invited in the first place.

Gimpel Kurtz stared at his glass. "You know," he said to Sophia, "I wouldn't mind if it were bigger."

"But you only have to fill it again," said Sophia. "Why should you want it to be bigger?"

Kurtz nodded as if his faith in human reason had been restored and replied, "*That* is the question, Sophia."

"The point is, Sophia," said Leibush Tshortkover, "that if his glass were bigger it could double as a bathtub."

"I already have a bathtub," said Kurtz. "What I need is a birch rod for after my bath."

Mottshi Shaynbart rapped his crutch on the floor and said, "Watch out for your beard, Leibush."

"Let him bathe his own beard," said Leibush, clutching his chin.

"He doesn't want to bathe your beard," said Mottshi. "He wants to make a birch rod out of it."

"The Devil rot your crutch, Mottshi," said Leibush, "if Gimpel's mustache isn't birch rod enough for ten men his size."

"Leave my crutch out of this," said Mottshi. "The Devil

63

has greater things in mind for it. He's going to stoke the fires of hell with it for saints like you."

"Drink up, gentlemen. Down the hatch!" called Gildenhorn, tapping the wine pitcher in front of him.

"Here's to you, Gimpy!" cried Leibush, raising his glass.

"And to you, Leibush!" answered Kurtz. "May it be granted that—"

"That . . ." declared Leibush, ". . . that we drink the wine of paradise without spilling a single drop."

"Amen in the name of all Jews!" said Eisy Heller.

"Amen and amen," repeated Mottshi Shaynbart.

"Here's to you, Reb Gedalia!" said Kurtz. "May it be granted that—"

"That . . ." said Leibush, ". . . that . . ."

"That God have mercy on us sinners," said Mottshi.

"And on our dear Hirshl," said Gildenhorn.

"Hirshl, pour yourself a drink," said Leibush. "Or are you afraid of ending up like the fellow in the story who got pie-eyed at his father-in-law's house?"

"At his own father-in-law's?" said Eisy Heller. "My, my! What did he do then?"

"Puked his guts out," said Balaban.

"In the old man's bedpan," said Leibush.

"Hear, hear!" cried Gildenhorn.

"And when his wife saw it in the morning," said Leibush, "she said to her husband, 'Why, you old rascal, you, I've a good mind to go tell your son-in-law.' "

"You see, Hirshl," said Kurtz, "you have nothing to be afraid of. Pour yourself a drink and take your medicine."

There is nothing to be done, thought Hirshl. I'll just have to sit it out to the end. Maybe my mother's brother wasn't crazy after all when he ran away to the woods. Maybe he knew what he was doing.

Balaban looked Hirshl over and said, "I can read your thoughts, Mr. Hurvitz. I know every one of them as if they were written on the palm of my hand."

Hirshl turned crimson.

64

"And I know, Mr. Hurvitz," continued Balaban, "that this day on which you have plighted your true love is the happiest of your life. I felt the same way when I was engaged to my late wife. So does everyone. But I tell you, today is nothing compared to how you'll feel on your wedding day. Just look at him turning red, he's the picture of innocence! Well, I'm all for innocence. It becomes a young man the way . . . the way . . . what a pity I can't find a good comparison. But why look for comparisons when we already have one ready-made? Yes, innocence becomes a young man as a bridal gown becomes a bride! And so I say it's the wedding day that matters, not the engagement or anything else. Believe me, gentlemen, all our toasts tonight are just a rehearsal for then. Here's to the day when Mr. Hurvitz and Miss Ziemlich stand together beneath the wedding canopy!"

Balaban looked lovingly at Hirshl. Who would have thought that this gallant mind reader was the same man who had tossed him a cigarette as though he were a beggar! But such is human nature: when things go our way even our minds interest others, while when they do not no one will give us the time of day.

"To your health, groom, to your health!" Numerous hands reached out to shake Hirshl's and to congratulate him. One by one he had to clasp each of them and say thank you. Glasses clinked and the room kept getting hotter. Tsirl, flushed from the meal, smiled at Bertha, and Bertha smiled back at her.

Boruch Meir refilled his glass and said, "And now let's drink to the bride."

"Fair is fair," said Kurtz.

"May my drinking hand wither," said Mottshi Shaynbart, "if I didn't think of suggesting that long ago."

"Then why didn't you?" asked Eisy Heller.

"Because his glass wasn't empty," said Leibush. "A toast calls for a new drink, and he never finished his old one."

The guests quickly emptied their glasses and drank to the health of the bride.

Sophia felt in a dither. After the first rush of it, her excitement had cooled. Yet the more she asked herself why, the less she was able to say. "And now let's drink to the groom," she declared, raising her glass. Although her voice trembled, she gripped the glass bravely, downed it in one gulp, banged it on the table, and turned it bottoms-up.

"O woman of valor!" sang out Leibush Tshortkover.

"And now let's drink to the groom's father," said Bertha Ziemlich, raising her glass.

"And now to the bride's mother," said Boruch Meir.

"And now to the bride's father," said Gildenhorn.

"And now to Jews everywhere," said Leibush.

"And now to the whole world," said Eisy.

"And now to whoever made the world," said Leibush.

"To God's health! Ai, ai, ai. L'hayyim, l'hayyim, l'hayyim!"

It was an hour after midnight when Hirshl walked home with his parents. He had to halt once or twice on the way. His legs felt as heavy as stones. He himself had not drunk a drop, but the smell of all the liquor and food had left him feeling groggy and shaky.

"The snow is melting," said Tsirl.

Hirshl looked up at the cloudy sky.

Tsirl yawned. "Thank God we're home," she said. "I'm sleepy."

"Raising children has its trying moments," said Boruch Meir with a smile.

"Why don't you take out your key and open the door," said Tsirl.

Boruch Meir stuck his key in the door. "What's this?" he said. "It doesn't open."

"What do you mean it doesn't open?" said Tsirl.

He peered into the keyhole. "There's a key on the other side."

"Who on earth could have put a key there?" Tsirl asked.

"I imagine," said Boruch Meir, "that the girl must have locked up without realizing that we weren't home."

"What girl?" asked Tsirl.

66

"The new maid."

Tsirl knocked on the door and shouted angrily, "Open up there!"

"Who is it?" asked the maid, coming downstairs.

Tsirl knocked even louder and yelled, "Will you stop giving speeches and open up!"

"Is that the missus?" asked the girl, groping her way to the door. "I'll open in a jiffy."

"It's the missus and the mister and the young master," said Boruch Meir, "and they'd like to be let into their house. Will you kindly open the door?"

"Just a minute while I put a dress on," said the maid.

Tsirl pounded on the door in a rage. "Just listen to her! A dress she wants to put on! You might think this were a formal visit."

"How did Leibush Tshortkover put it?" asked Boruch Meir. "May your crutch rot in hell, Mottshi, if that door doesn't open at once."

"I have to sleep," Tsirl moaned, "and the man stands here making jokes."

"Look, it's opened," said Boruch Meir, rubbing his hands.

The little night lamp flickered feebly inside. Tsirl inspected the house before undressing. Boruch Meir wound his watch and placed it beside him. Taking a deep breath, Hirshl stretched out in bed. Tsirl sleepily put out the lamp and got into bed too. After a while she turned toward her husband's bed and asked:

"Are you asleep?"

"No," said Boruch Meir. "I'm not."

"Neither am I," said Tsirl.

"I know," said Boruch Meir.

"How?" Tsirl asked.

"Because," said Boruch Meir, "you wouldn't be talking if you were."

"It amazes me how people can drink," said Tsirl. "What are you laughing at?"

"At a joke I just thought of," said Boruch Meir.

"Who thinks of jokes in the middle of the night?"

"It's about a man who does nothing but drink. Once his wife decides to see how he spends his time. She goes to the tavern and finds him sitting there with his friends. They buy her a drink, and then another. Pretty soon she's so potted she falls off her chair and rolls right under the table. 'So, my darling,' says her husband, 'now you can see for yourself that I haven't had an easy life.' "

"You may be in fine fettle, Boruch Meir," said Tsirl, "but I feel that my nerves are all shot. I'm too sleepy to even fall asleep."

"I promise you," said Boruch Meir, "that you'll sleep very well. Good night, Tsirl."

"Who's that snoring?" asked Tsirl. "It's keeping me up."

Boruch Meir strained to hear. "I don't hear a thing."

"It sounds like a stuck pig."

"I imagine," said Boruch Meir, "that the maid is in a deep sleep."

"A minute ago," Tsirl said, "she wanted to try on all her dresses, and now she's in a deep sleep. I wish I were. Blume never snored like that. Just look at me, I'm yawning my head off and still it stays wide awake. It must be two o'clock by now. Oy, am I tired. I must sleep."

11

HIRSHL SLEPT WELL that night. His mood on awakening in the morning was mixed. Though it was not an especially bad one, there was nothing terribly good about it either. What's done is done, he thought, recalling what had happened. I'll just have to forget about Blume and start thinking about Mina.

Resignedly he reviewed the events leading up to his engage-

68

ment to a girl who meant nothing to him: the party at the Gildenhorns', the crowd of guests, Balaban's cigarette, his relief when Mina arrived and there was someone to talk to at last. It would never have happened, thought Hirshl, had Blume let our love bloom. As though in a vision he saw the curve of her face that was full without being round and the wordless look of her blue, blue eyes that were neither happy nor sad. He would have given anything to be allowed once more to smell the fragrance of her that had suffused his whole being that day in her room.

Hirshl was a responsible young man and knew that there was no turning back. He had to put Blume out of his mind and make room there for Mina, his fiancée. Yet was she truly? Once, as a boy, having asked someone how marriage was proposed, Hirshl was told that one went down on one's knees and kissed one's true love's hand. He had been a child at the time and should have known better by now; yet the description had stuck with him, so that, it having been otherwise with Mina, their betrothal did not seem quite real to him.

Whereas until now Hirshl had tried thinking of everyone but Mina, now he could think of no one else. As detached as he felt from her, there was no escaping her existence. And yet—though he did not, God forbid, wish her any harm—to escape it was what he most wanted. He prayed for something to save him, such as his family losing its fortune overnight, which would force Ziemlich to call off the wedding and himself to go to work as a shopboy in another town. One night, without knowing how Mirl's dead parents, Blume's grandparents, had sat reading Boruch Meir's letters to them before Boruch Meir became engaged to Tsirl, Hirshl dreamed that he had written them. If worse comes to worse, he thought, I can always run away to America. Though he knew that an only child like himself could do nothing of the sort, imagining it kept him from despair.

Indeed, there were sons of Szybusz who really had gone to America—workmen looking to better themselves, for instance, or bankrupt merchants fleeing the law. Boruch Meir's own shopboy, Getzel Stein, had two brothers there. Some of these emigrants sent home letters and magazines, while a few even returned to visit with wondrous tales about steamships, weeks of navigating icebergs bigger than cities, and huge propellers that shredded sea monsters capable of swallowing whole boatloads in one bite. Strutting around Szybusz with gold chains on their vests and gold teeth in their mouths, their speech larded with English words, they poked fun at their former fellow townsmen for wallowing in poverty when they too could be living it up in the New World, where everyone got to be president, which was a kind of king for four years. Just how one managed to live it up there, however, was a subject they were a bit vague about. Perhaps they had yet to reflect on their own experience, or perhaps they would just as soon not have had to. Meanwhile they made the rounds of the town and ate dinner at house after house, where they put away the kasha cakes that Szybusz was famed for and no end of other good things while telling their hosts about the mountains of gold that anyone owning a pickax could chip away as much of as he wanted. The problem was that these mountains were far from New York, which was where most Americans lived, and that it took several months to reach them. In New York itself, though, there were long green bills called dollars, each one of which was worth two and a half Austrian gulden. It fired imaginations in Szybusz to hear of such things, and some people even pinched and scraped in order to buy a ticket to America too.

Yet the food of Szybusz was oddly habit-forming, so that ultimately few of these visitors ever went back to America themselves. This had nothing to do with the sea monsters, which were in any case beheaded by the propellers, nor with the fear of icebergs, which was more than offset by the lure of the solid gold mountains; it was simply a matter of being too full of good food ever to want to go to sea again. Those who still had a few dollars left exchanged them with the locals, who liked to save foreign currency for wedding presents, while those who did not sold their gold chains and opened some business in town, where they proceeded to wallow in poverty like everyone else. If a gold tooth broke and he could not afford a new one, it being a well-known fact that the curse of Columbus rested on the renegade who had abandoned America's shores, its owner swore roundly at the day of his homecoming and quickly got over it, admitting with the next breath he drew, "On the other hand, I must say that the air in America is nothing compared to that here."

And if something as insubstantial as air could keep a man from leaving Szybusz, a weightier substance like a blanket or a pillow had an even more powerful effect. No matter how often Hirshl thought of running away, each time he laid his head on his pillow and pulled his blanket up over him he knew that he would never go anywhere.

12

THAT SATURDAY NIGHT, after the Sabbath was over, Gedalia Ziemlich's carriage arrived to fetch the Hurvitzes to dinner in Malikrowik.

Although Boruch Meir and Tsirl had received the invitation on Friday, they managed to look as surprised when the carriage drew up as if they knew nothing about it.

Hirshl had been sitting with an unbound book, its pages freshly cut and arranged before him on the table, that he was in the middle of reading. He put it down, took out some cigarette paper, rolled himself a cigarette, lit it, and eyed the leather thong of the whip in the hand of the Ziemlichs' coachman.

Boruch Meir produced a bottle of brandy and poured Stach a glass. Stach put down his whip and swallowed it.

"How about another?" Boruch Meir asked.

Stach studied the empty glass. "Well, perhaps just one more wee one to your health, sir."

Tsirl surveyed her son's clothes, smoothed out her own, and said, "It's a lucky thing that I'm still in my Sabbath outfit and needn't keep you waiting while I change."

Boruch Meir put on his weekday hat and said, "Hirshl and I are still in our Sabbath clothes too." Then, like a man who has kept his share of a bargain, he folded his arms and waited.

Tsirl inspected the table, locked the pantry, put away the key, and asked, "Are you ready?"

"Ready as can be," said Boruch Meir.

Stach went out, came back with three fur wraps, helped the Hurvitzes into them, seated them in the carriage, and spread bearskins over their knees.

Tsirl glanced at the house. "You there!" she shouted at the open door. "Lock up and don't forget to take the key out. Did you hear me?"

The maid gave a nod. Then, uncertain whether it had been seen, she stepped outside and said, "Don't you worry, ma'am. I won't leave that key in for a second."

Tsirl stretched her legs out comfortably in the carriage and turned up her fur collar. "We're off," she said.

"So we are," said Boruch Meir, tucking his hands into his wrap.

"Are you covered, Hirshl?" asked Tsirl. "Turn up your collar."

Hirshl bundled up in Ziemlich's wrap until it tickled his neck, grunted as if something hurt him, reached into his pocket, took out a handkerchief, and placed it over his mouth.

Tsirl looked at her husband and whispered, "I do believe that our driver is rather high in spirits."

Boruch Meir regarded the whip in Stach's hand. "I daresay he's waving that palm branch of his as though he were saying hosannas."

Tsirl approved of Boruch Meir's witty rejoinder every bit as much as Boruch Meir approved of Tsirl's deft double entendre.

Stach let out a whistle and the carriage started out with a lurch.

The road was easily traveled. The snow on the ground made the night pleasantly frosty, and the horses trotted gently. After an hour or so they made out what looked like a necklace of lights and heard the barking of dogs.

Stach twirled his whip until the thong was wrapped around the handle, pulled on the reins, and cried, "Whoaaa!"

The horses took a few more halting steps and the carriage stood still.

"What are we stopping for?" Tsirl asked Boruch Meir.

"We're stopping," said Boruch Meir, "because we've come to a place called Malikrowik."

"Already?" asked Tsirl in amazement.

"Already," Boruch Meir said proudly, as if he had accomplished something rare.

"It's so short a trip?" asked Tsirl, a note of gladness creeping into her surprise.

"Try walking it sometime," said Boruch Meir, "and you'll see how short it is."

"You're very sporting with my feet," Tsirl said. "Hirshl, we're here."

Hirshl picked up his handkerchief, which had fallen on the bearskin, and put it back in his pocket.

Gedalia Ziemlich's house stood amid trees and shrubbery, surrounded by barns and stables that were half covered with snow and half projecting like loose beams of lumber. As soon as the carriage swung into the courtyard the dogs began to bark in harmony, the tenors for the returning Stach and the altos for his passengers.

Stach clambered down from his seat, crouched low, drew back a foot, and booted one of the dogs in the belly, sending it flying into the snow. Then he kicked it again head over heels into the other dogs. The cur shook the snow off and stared back imperturbably as if to say, Well now, that wasn't half bad for a knucklehead like you. "Knucklehead" was the dogs' pet name for Stach because of the iron studs like knuckle-dusters that he wore on the soles of his boots.

73

Boruch Meir jumped out of the carriage and gave his hand to Tsirl, who gave her hand to Hirshl and helped him to the ground. Hirshl rubbed his eyes with a wet glove and looked at the brightly lit house. Out here in the country, he thought, there's not a care in the world. Yet as soon as he remembered the reason he was there, the house lost all its splendor and he his envy of it.

Gedalia and Bertha came gaily out to greet their guests and sought to relieve them of their wraps. Boruch Meir, however, pulled his more tightly around him and growled, "Look out for the bears," which made the servant girls giggle, while Tsirl struck a statuesque pose in her fur. When Mina came to the doorway Boruch Meir shook her hand and said merrily, "The bears have brought you a little deer from the forest." He was referring to Hirshl, whose name meant "little deer" in Yiddish.

The house was all lit up. A fire burned in the fireplace. An agreeable odor of sappy wood and roast meat pervaded the rooms. Both the guests and their hosts were wearing their best. All faces shone. Even the servants were jolly.

The Hurvitzes split up upon arriving, Boruch Meir and Tsirl going off with Gedalia and Bertha and leaving Hirshl and Mina in a room by themselves. Mina was wearing a long black satin dress that was wide in the whalebone-stayed skirt and—apart from the rounded bust—narrow from the waist to the the collar, which was trimmed with two fingers of lace. The chandelier on the ceiling made her face glow and brought out the color in her cheeks. Her uncertainly shaded hair was braided in a circle at the neck. She seemed different from the way she had looked that summer or even from the night of their engagement. Suddenly Hirshl no longer knew what to think of her. An unfamiliar feeling of respect combined with another, less easily definable emotion gave her new stature in his eyes.

They talked little, however, for Hirshl could hardly put a sentence together. Indeed, anyone seeing him who had been at

74

the Gildenhorns' party might well have wondered if he was observing the same person, for now words failed him completely. Yet though she could not help noticing this, Mina did not find it peculiar. After all, she thought, what do I expect him to do, recite Schiller and Lessing for me? (This was because it was the custom in those days for a boy and girl getting together to recite poems to each other, such as Schiller's "The Bell" or "The Lad at the Fountain," taking turns saying each line by heart. It might take them a long while, but then this was precisely the point—and although it was easy to joke about such things, the jokers themselves had behaved no differently when young.)

How odd, Hirshl thought: just a few days ago she rescued me at a party, and now I need to be rescued from her. He had not felt so uncomfortably self-conscious since the day he walked into the unused room in the hope of finding Blume and discovered Mina instead. All I need do, he thought, is say something beastly and I'll be rid of her for good. Being too much of a gentleman for this, however, he rather broke out in a torrent of uncontrolled speech. Things that he did not even know he knew came tumbling out of him. Mina looked at him wide-eyed, her large earrings glittering.

Although she had studied in Stanislaw, Mina had not even known when the city was founded, much less that it was sacked by the Tatars in 1692, let alone that such great scholars had lived in it that it had supplanted Tisminic as the center of Jewish learning in Galicia, not to mention the fact that a well-known Hebrew poet who did translations on commission from the Kaiser still resided there. And though none of this could be said to matter very much to a young lady like her, she listened raptly to it all and even sighed "Oh!" over each new disclosure, spurring Hirshl on to ever greater efforts.

It is possible to know something without knowing all of it; or to hear something and wish to hear more; or to learn something but not fully understand it: imagine then one's gratitude when someone comes along and fills in all the missing pieces.

Suppose, for example, that you had once heard a story about a party of Jewish refugees from Rumania who appeared one day before you were born in Stanislaw, where the bailiff of the community refused to take them in for fear of their becoming a burden, so that they were forced to squat in squalor with their wives and children before the city gates until their cries for help reached the heavens; suppose, moreover, that you were only a child at the time and did not have the presence of mind to ask how the story ended; indeed, suppose you so regretted not asking that you went and forgot the whole thing—or that, on the contrary, you never managed to forget it at all; and suppose that you were now suddenly told everything you had ever wished to know about it: even though it had happened long ago and nothing could be done anymore to help the poor Jews who had died or wandered on, or to demand restitution from the hard-hearted bailiff; was not hearing about it from Hirshl every bit as good as reading it in a history book? And even if such an incident, which was a far from unusual one in Jewish history, was of no particular interest to Mina, who may have wondered about it no more than she did about any of the world's other problems, the very fact of Hirshl's telling it made it seem so fascinating that she regarded him with astonishment. How curious, she marveled, thinking of the hard-hearted bailiff: I've been in that man's house to visit his granddaughters and never found him cruel at all. In fact, he once even gave me a friendly pat on the back. And even if his cheeks are blue and he always looks unshaven, what sort of proof of cruelty is that?

Hirshl was still talking when Tsirl stepped into the room with a gay smile. Hirshl fell silent, feeling annoyed. Just then Mina did not seem to him someone his parents wished him to marry but simply a young lady with whom he was having a good time that his mother had come to put an end to. He took her hand and squeezed it as if it were his only support in the world.

A minute later a servant girl appeared and summoned them to dinner.

13

"WHAT, YOU TOO ARE HERE?" Yona Toyber asked Hirshl in amazement.

"So it would seem," replied Hirshl.

Boruch Meir rubbed his hands with pleasure. Such a comeback had not even occurred to the condemned man in the joke who was asked the same question by the hangman. Boruch Meir was in too good a mood to notice that the comparison was not auspicious.

Toyber shut his eyes as if he were having a pleasant dream.

The guests washed their hands and sat down to eat.

The table was set with braided breads and three kinds of brandy, one ordinary, one flavored with fennel, and one with a fruit infusion for the ladies. The appetizer was a dish of mushrooms marinated in vinegar and bay leaves. They drank to each other's health and broke bread.

Tsirl and Boruch Meir were not used to eating mushrooms in wintertime and consumed so many of them that their hostess grew worried that they would be too full for the rest of the meal that she feared having labored on in vain, the main course of which was a roast in gravy and a bird called *grechky hiener*, that is to say, Greek chicken. Although this guinea hen, to call it by its proper name, which the Jews of the region were wary of eating because of its strange size and shape, laid eggs with one round and one pointy end as prescribed by law and had not only been declared indubitably kosher by the leading rabbis of Galicia, who had found in it all three signs of gallinaceous legitimacy, namely, a spur, a crop, and a membranous gizzard, but was in addition sanctioned by the weight of tradition, observed to mate with ordinary roosters and produce chickenlike offspring, and reported by reliable eye-witnesses to be eaten with relish by the Jews of the Holy Land itself, it still was not on sale in Szybusz, the only place to obtain it being from the barnyards of the rich, which was the reason that Bertha so wanted the Hurvitzes to have room for it.

"Just look at me," said Tsirl. "In the summer when the forests are bursting with mushrooms you can't even get me to look at one, and now I can't stop eating them."

"Enjoy them," said Bertha. "Enjoy them, mother of the groom, eat as much as you want. I have more jars put away."

"I have a cousin," said Boruch Meir, "who is so afraid of being poisoned that he won't eat a mushroom on the day that it's cooked. He always first waits a day to make sure no one else in his family has been killed by it."

"Do you think that's the reason I don't eat mushrooms in summer?" Tsirl asked.

"I think," said Boruch Meir, "that that's the reason they taste so much better in winter."

As they were talking, a serving girl appeared with a china dish shaped like a goose. Bertha rose, removed the lid, and ladeled out gravy from it. The china bird stood flat and back-less, its beak angrily open as if the food had been snatched from its mouth. Hot, fatty vapors clouded the overhead lamp before Bertha could replace the lid.

Hirshl was dining out for the second time that week. The first time, at the Gildenhorns', he had not given the matter much thought. Now, though, it struck him as odd that one should travel all the way to someone's house just in order to eat.

Gedalia Ziemlich looked approvingly at his guests enjoying the food. Although he enjoyed it too, he could not help anx-iously wondering with each bite whether there would be any leftovers for tomorrow.

"You city folk," said Bertha, "are used to finer fare, but as long as you've made the trip out here, I hope you've found the fixings good." Not that she thought she had anything to be

78

ashamed of, but she did appreciate the Hurvitzes' having come to Malikrowik.

Tsirl helped herself to seconds. The carriage ride and the happy occasion had given her an appetite. Even the ordinary dishes on the table tasted better than they did at home, and she asked for the recipe of each of them. Bertha found herself liking her more and more.

Yona Toyber sat unobtrusively behind some serving dishes and ate a great deal. As long as his wife had been in good health she had fed him well, yet since the day she took sick he had hardly touched his food for fear of depriving his children, so that now that he was dining without them at the Ziemlichs' he made the most of the opportunity. Throughout the meal he kept his eyes half shut as though meditating on something of a highly private nature.

The dinner was a leisurely one. The company took its time eating and kept asking for more. At long last the last fork was laid on its plate and the last face was wiped clean.

Boruch Meir stroked his beard with a backward twist and reflected that after so much food and drink a bit of conversation was in order. And so, noticing that Hirshl had hardly eaten, he remarked, "From the looks of your plate one might think this were a fast day," and then, turning to Mina, "What a nice place you have here, miss."

Bertha stared at him in surprise. "I should think," she said, "that you might call your daughter-in-law by her first name."

Yona Toyber opened his eyes to look at Mina, who said nothing. Boruch Meir glanced at him and rubbed his hands as if anticipating an after-dinner speech. Yona pretended not to notice, or perhaps he really did not, yet in the end he cleared his throat and said:

"Let me tell you all something. And not just anything but something worth hearing. Once I happened to spend a day in the dinkiest little town I ever saw. Apart from a flock of geese in the marketplace there wasn't a sign of life. It was a burning hot summer day and I was dying of thirst. I looked around, saw what seemed to be a grocery store, and went in to buy a lemon to make myself some lemonade. The storekeeper looked at me as if he had never heard of a lemon before. So I asked for a glass of beer and got the same look. You would have thought I was asking for the moon. Finally I asked for a glass of plain water. And here's the point: I won't tell you that I wasn't given the water, but neither will I tell you that it came in a glass, because that water was brought in a black, crumpled can that had specks of rust floating in it. While I was trying to decide whether to drink it or not I looked up to see who it came with. Why, if she isn't a princess, I thought, that's only because no princess would ever live in a dump like this."

If Yona Toyber had some parable in mind its message was none too clear, for the Ziemlichs' dining room bore no resemblance to a grocery store, and Mina, however well-bred and attractive, was certainly no princess; yet the mere telling of it made the mood more relaxed. There is nothing more awkward than a room of silent people at the end of a big meal.

Hirshl, who had hardly eaten, glanced about at the company, which looked exhausted from its labors. Though he did not enjoy being hungry, he was glad his stomach felt so light. Just a few days before, he had come across a pamphlet attacking the consumption of meat, fish, wine, and other extravagances, and now that he saw so many full people still cramming their stomachs with food he wondered whether his late uncle might not have been a misunderstood vegetarian who took to the woods to lead a healthier life; perhaps indeed the pamphlet was right about overeating and the craving for luxuries being the root of all evil. If my mother did not have her heart set on Ziemlich's money, thought Hirshl, I would not have to be sitting here right now with all this cooked dead flesh in front of me. He looked up to see if anything was left of these abominations, whose smell was making his mouth water, and caught sight of Mina. She too seemed ill at ease. Perhaps she was thinking the same things. He wished he could ask if she was.

It simply is not true, thought Hirshl, that hunger dulls the mind. On the contrary, the emptier one's stomach, the clearer one's thoughts. Being hungry has made me realize that it's time I made something of myself. Only how can I make anything of myself when I'm still so dependent on my parents? He looked again at Mina and wondered if she could read his mind.

Mina wished she were somewhere else. Her corset was pressing on her. The poor child's done herself up too tight, thought Bertha, noticing her distress. Thank God, thought Tsirl, giving her a fond look, that when I was a child such tortures were not yet invented.

The serving girl reappeared with a large cornmeal pudding in the shape of a derby hat, stuffed with plums and walnuts and sprinkled with sugar coins. Though everyone except Hirshl was bursting at the seams, the aroma proved irresistible. Even Hirshl took a large slice and ate it with gusto.

"You must admit, Hirshl," said Tsirl, flashing him a smile, "that this pudding is delicious." Hirshl blushed. After priding himself on his self-restraint, here he was being a pig like the rest of them. Nor was that the worst of it. The worst of it was that his mother's words were the same as those he had spoken to her on the day of Blume's arrival in their house, when she had brought with her the most delicious home-baked cakes.

Following the grace after meals they retired to the drawing room, in which stood a table with cigarettes and sweets. This was an innovation brought back from Stanislaw by Mina, who had seen it at a dinner party there.

"Gedalia," said Bertha, turning to her husband, "why don't you tell us where these cigarettes come from?"

Gedalia looked puzzled. "What is there to tell?"

"Oh, come," said Bertha. "It makes a good story."

Tsirl looked coaxingly at Gedalia and said, "Come on, father of the bride, tell us where they come from."

"Our local count," said Gedalia, taking a deep breath as if he were under suspicion of smuggling, "has a rather free-spending younger brother who brings these cigarettes with him each time he comes to Malikrowik."

"But you left out the whole story, Gedalia!" exclaimed Bertha anxiously.

"He's still in the middle of it," said Tsirl, coming to his defense.

Gedalia wiped his brow and went on:

"The story is that these cigarettes are made exclusively for the count's brother by a factory in Paris according to a special formula. And since our count keeps his brother on a short leash because he's such a big spender, the brother uses cigarettes as money. If a servant helps him out of his coat, or a coachman takes him for a ride, that's what he tips them with. Well, yesterday the count's coachman stopped for a drink at our tavern. He paid the tavernkeeper with these cigarettes, and the tavernkeeper sold them to me."

"Aren't you curious to see what a count's brother smokes, Hirshl?" asked Boruch Meir, rubbing his hands. "Here, have a cigarette. Your mother and I will excuse your smoking in front of us."

Toyber took a cigarette from the box, inspected it carefully, and stuck it in his mouth. Then, still without lighting it, he put his hand on Hirshl's shoulder and steered him away from the company. Whether it was because he had nothing more to say to Mina, or because he was relieved to stretch his legs after sitting so long at the table, Hirshl was glad to be taken aside.

"A cultured young lady," said Toyber, his face as blank as a sleepwalker's.

One might have thought it was Culture itself that was being praised.

Toyber squinted as if searching for the right word, shook Hirshl's hand, and declared, "And now, Mr. Hurvitz, I must bid you good night. My constitution is not of the best, and I need sleep."

With which he lit his cigarette and left.

Hirshl remained standing by himself. His hand felt warm where Toyber's had gripped it, and the matchmaker's voice still tingled in his ears.

82

The grandfather clock began to chime. Boruch Meir stifled a yawn and said, "Ten o'clock."

"It's time we started back," Tsirl said, getting up.

"What's the rush?" asked Bertha.

"We have a store to open," said Tsirl with a smile.

"But you needn't open it until the morning," objected Gedalia, taking her literally. "Where's Yona?"

"Toyber has already gone to sleep," said Bertha. "If you had his habits, you'd live to be a hundred."

"I say he should live to be a hundred and twenty," said Boruch Meir, "and enjoy every minute of it."

Stach harnessed the horses. Boruch Meir, Tsirl, and Hirshl put on the Ziemlichs' fur wraps and climbed into the carriage. The dogs bayed, fell silent, and bayed once more. Stach cracked his whip and clucked to the horses, who set out.

They traveled in silence. The snow, which had been powdery on their way to Malikrowik but was now packed hard, glistened on either side of the road. The only sound was the clip-clop of the horses and the jingle of the bells around their necks.

Stach leaned forward, flicking the horses' haunches and singing to himself.

Boruch Meir chuckled.

"What's so funny?" Tsirl asked.

"I once had an old woman for a neighbor," said Boruch Meir, "who groaned whenever she saw a horse whipped. 'Leave it alone,' she'd say. 'Being a horse is hard enough as it is.' "

Hirshl sat huddled in his fur, trying to remember what he had been thinking about. Could it have been about the healthy life and making something of himself? Yes, I was thinking of making something of myself. How soft Toyber's hand is. A person with his habits really could live to be a hundred. But as long as I'm living with my parents, not even my habits are my own.

83

14

SZYBUSZ HAD NOTHING bad to say about the match between Hirshl and Mina. On the contrary, the whole town was as happy for the Hurvitzes as it always was. Indeed, Szybusz without Boruch Meir and Tsirl was no more imaginable than gefilte fish without pepper. Not that they weren't poked fun at now and then—but if anyone laughed at such jokes it was only to be polite. When God is with one, one's fellow townsmen are likely to be too. Boruch Meir had started out as a petty shop clerk and was now a wealthy merchant. His very movements, which were never hasty or impulsive, even his beard, which was neither too long nor too short, showed what kind of person he was. A man like Boruch Meir need fear going nowhere, not even to the baths in Karlsbad. He never quarreled with anyone and had no grudges held against him—apart, that is, from one time when, in the local elections, he had chosen to support Bloch against the wishes of the town's leading citizen, Sebastian Montag, who came out for Bick. Yet in this Boruch Meir was far from alone, nearly all of Szybusz having voted for Bloch, and the fact that Bick was elected anyway is another story that need not concern us here.

In any case, a great deal of water had flowed down the Stripa since then to wash Szybusz of its sins, and Boruch Meir and Sebastian Montag had made up, the best proof being that more than one delicacy served on Montag's table had its source in Boruch Meir's store. There was even a special page in Boruch Meir's account book that bore the heading "Gifts for R.Z.," that is, for Reb Zanvil, which was Montag's original name. Whenever R.Z. Sebastian Montag stepped into the store Tsirl greeted him with brandy and something to eat,

84

while home deliveries were made to him without his even having to ask. It was a good thing they were, too, since otherwise Mrs. Montag might well have starved to death, Sebastian being a terrible wastrel who squandered all his money on cards and "nebbichlach," which was his compassionate term of endearment for the young demimondes that he spent all his time with. Indeed, Sebastian Montag was the most generous of men and was always sure to be refinanced when insolvent, inasmuch as it would have been an insupportable scandal to send the town's richest Jew to the poorhouse—to say nothing of all his friends and relations, who could turn quite devilish if not treated with the milk of human kindness, let alone the more ordinary residents of Szybusz, who had to eat too. Not all of the town's eight thousand Jews were comfortably off. Some, who lived in large houses and breakfasted on white bread and cocoa, had no cause for complaint; yet there were others who could not even count on black bread and onions or on a roof over their heads. Boruch Meir never turned a poor man away without a penny, nor was he unmindful of the once but no longer rich. Though others might shout at a beggar to find a job, it was Boruch Meir's considered opinion that the world would be no different if he did; while of anyone who had gone bankrupt he would say, "Why, we should be grateful that he went out of business, because who knows whom else he might have dragged down with him if he hadn't?"

The Hurvitz house stood in a row of shops and houses in the center of town. It was no bigger than the buildings around it and was conspicuous only by virtue of an abandoned dovecote on the roof, Tsirl's father having raised pigeons as a hobby. The top half of the structure was a large home with many rooms, while the bottom was a long, narrow store which, though three or four customers could make it look crowded, never had less than five or six at a time. The counters were lined with scales heaped with merchandise, at the first of which, by the entrance, sat Tsirl. Tsirl did not touch the merchandise herself but was simply there to make conversation. Unlike her father, who thought that a store was not a synagogue in which to sit around and gab, or her husband, who was busy with his accounts, or Hirshl, who was always measuring and weighing, or the shopboys, who had no end of parcels to wrap, she had time to chat with each customer, which she did while signaling to one of the men to come sell him something he had never originally meant to buy. Certainly the store could not have done without Boruch Meir, who kept the books and made the entries and did all the ordering on time; it could not have done without Hirshl either, who handled the actual sales; it could not even have done without the shopboys, who packed and unpacked and waited on customers and delivered; yet least of all could it have done without Tsirl, who knew from talking with each customer just what he was worth. Perhaps in her father's time, when the world had been simpler and it was more obvious who was poor and who was rich, no great effort had to be expended on such things; nowadays, however, when the poor pretended to be rich in order to obtain credit and the rich pretended to be poor in order not to give it, one had to draw a man out. And when it came to knowing where he stood, there was no one like Tsirl for getting him to give himself away. He could be dressed like a lord; he could keep his hands in his pockets as though they were filled with gold coins; he could wipe crumbs of white bread from his mustache and moan about the stomachache he had from overeating; sooner or later the false moan would turn into a real one and the truth would come out that he had less clothes than creditors, that his pockets had nothing but holes in them, and that he would gladly give his right arm for an onion or a radish to munch on. Or the opposite might happen and someone would enter the shop in the most threadbare of suits, his shoes unpolished, his hat coming apart, his pockets hanging out of his pants; try getting him to part with a penny and he would groan as if he were being robbed of his last sou; yet let Tsirl listen to the sound of that groan and she could tell you at once that it was one of well-heeled bliss. How, if she were not such an artful conversationalist, would she ever have found out that Ziemlich was worth a good twenty thousand? Certainly not by the looks of him, nor by what he wore. A man's money, though, had its own voice that spoke when he did.

Ever since taking Gedalia Ziemlich's true measure, Tsirl had gone out of her way to befriend him and to invite him upstairs for coffee or even, if it was lunchtime, to dine. The stairs themselves were narrow and cracked, stained with oil and kerosene, and littered with sugar, grains of rice, broken matches, squashed raisins, and crushed coffee beans; the hallway was lined with cartons of candles, cans of paint and turpentine, and boxes of pepper and salt; yet Blume had managed to keep the Hurvitz home spotless, and, when a new maid replaced her, Tsirl saw to it that she did too, for Tsirl was not too old to learn.

As for Hirshl, he was an irreproachably affable youngster who never put on a rich man's airs. One would have thought that the son and grandson of well-to-do businessmen would not have argued with the common belief that making money was a sign of intelligence, yet this is just what Hirshl did. "What exactly is so intelligent," he liked to ask, "about selling something off a shelf?" Though no one in Szybusz was taken in by this, socialism did sound much better when expressed with the authority of wealth.

No less well liked in Szybusz than the Hurvitzes were the Ziemlichs. Gedalia Ziemlich had never hurt a fly and, however well buttered his bread, he aroused no one's envy, for he was not a man who paraded his good fortune. A generous giver to charity, he practiced it in strict privacy, discreetly letting others distribute it for him so as not to seem competitive about it. In fact, there were wealthy Jews in Szybusz whose reputation as philanthropists rested entirely on Ziemlich's magnanimity.

Although the story of Gedalia's success was seemingly an ordinary one of hard work and frugality, there was still something miraculous about it. His father, a dairyman, had never done well, since every self-respecting household had had its own cows in those days and did not need to buy milk, while his equally unsuccessful brothers and cousins had all left the vicinity of Szybusz for greener pastures, where some of them had died of hunger and others were never heard from again. One had even traveled all the way to Germany in search of his fortune, which he found in an unknown grave.

If Gedalia was not a happy man, then, this was not because he did not have enough but because he feared losing what he had and sinking back into poverty. He was keenly conscious of the fact that, while he lacked for nothing, lived in a grand house, and rode about in a carriage of his own, other no less worthy Jews lived in penury—which was why, though he meticulously performed all his religious and human duties, he never stopped worrying that life's kindness to him was only a ploy to make his ultimate downfall more dramatic. He dreaded the day of reckoning that would come. So great was this anxiety indeed that any stranger knocking on his door was immediately suspected of having come to turn him out. He still had clear memories of himself and his family going to bed without supper, rising without breakfast, and lunching on dry bread and onions. Not that the cows had given no milk, but the milk that they gave was never drunk by the Ziemlichs, for it was too precious to be wasted on themselves. Nevertheless, Gedalia had fond recollections of his days of making the milk rounds when, before the Almighty, so to speak, had even awoken in heaven, he and his father were up and about with their cans on their shoulders, although they never started work without first attending the early prayer at the synagogue in Szybusz.

Eventually Gedalia grew up and married Breyndl, the daughter of the keeper of the village tavern, which Gedalia managed with his father-in-law until the latter died and he became its sole proprietor. He would gladly have remained that, being unambitious and content with his lot, which seemed to him a token of divine beneficence, yet Providence helped him put his pennies together until they turned into schillings and gulden. Before long he became the count's estate manager, a position that only heightened his concern that his success might be some sort of test. Who, though, was testing him? He could hardly believe that God Almighty would take such an interest in him, especially as He must have His trusted agents on earth to manage His finances. It could only be then, thought Gedalia, that the count himself had made him his steward for the purpose of ignominiously dismissing him. When he had lived as a child in a wooden shack that leaked from both roof and floor, and the frost had drawn mocking pictures on the windowpanes, and his parents could not bring themselves to scold his brothers and sisters who were crying from hunger, Gedalia had sat reading tales of the saints who magically provided poor Jews with livelihoods, and had rejoiced in the knowledge that God looked after His own. Yet he had never expected such miracles for himself, so that when one befell him and the count leased him all his holdings, rather than look upon it as a case of heavenly intervention in his behalf, Gedalia had considered it a private joke on the part of the count, who was just waiting for the right moment to send him packing in disgrace.

Becoming the count's manager, therefore, had not gone to his head. His house was still open to rich and poor alike and he himself waited on each guest. Whenever he had a free moment he read Psalms to himself, while each Monday and Thursday he journeyed to Szybusz to hear the Torah read in the synagogue. Far from a jealous man by nature, his only envy was of those Jews who could double their merit by putting on two pairs of tefillin each morning, one according to the formula of Rashi and one according to that of Rabbenu Tam—and if he did not emulate them it was not for lack of time but because he feared that, since many pious and learned Jews made do with one pair, it would be vainglorious of him to insist on two. As it was, he took great care of his tefillin, inspected them constantly to see that they were in order, and made sure never to engage in unnecessary conversation while wearing them. It was his custom too to buy a new prayer shawl before each holiday and exchange it for the torn one of some poor but God-fearing scholar—and indeed, his tongueless tefillin and torn prayer shawls were apt symbols for the man himself, who never said a word to anyone about how torn he felt inside. If

89

his clothes befitted his station in life, this was not because he cared about them but only because he did not wish to embarrass the count. In fact, had it not been for his wife, his clothes would have looked like his prayer shawls.

As surprised as Gedalia Ziemlich was at God's goodness to him, he was no less amazed at his wife for taking so naturally to wealth that she screamed at the servants whenever they broke a dish or did anything that displeased her. Why, he thought, tomorrow God could easily switch us around so that Bertha and I would have to serve them; does she think they would fail to remember how mean she was to them? If he himself got through a week with nothing breaking he would wonder whether his good luck in this life was not meant to facilitate his being sent straight to hell in the next without any right of appeal.

When Mina was born, Gedalia's dread of the future lessened somewhat. He worried so much about her falling, or breaking an arm or a leg, or being bitten by one of the dogs, that there was no time left for worrying about himself or his good fortune. Besides, he imagined that even if God did not pity him for his own sake, He would at least do so for his daughter's. Now that Mina was engaged to Hirshl Hurvitz, however, his sense of unworthiness was obsessing him again. And the anxiety that accompanied his happiness for Mina was even worse than it used to be, since while once it had been only for himself, it was now for Boruch Meir too, whom he feared would be ruined along with him. Each day that passed without disaster seemed a miracle to him.

A man like Gedalia might appear likely to be hen-pecked, yet in fact he was not, for Bertha was a simple woman and did not put herself above him. Her own character had been fully formed before they came into money, and she was as self-sufficient as he was, the difference between them being only that she did not second-guess the Lord for having improved her station in life. Indeed, if she rolled up her sleeves each day and increased what He had given her, she did not do so out of cupidity but simply so as not to be idle. Did anyone really expect her to sit gossiping all day long with the neighbors? She had been a hard worker ever since childhood and did not intend to stop now; surely it was no fault of her own if her work, which once had brought in a small profit, now yielded a large one. God be praised that there was even enough to share with her and her husband's families. Gedalia gave little thought to his relations: he was glad to help when they turned up, but he seldom thought of them when they did not, and in general he never remembered where they lived and scarcely knew where the post office was. Had Bertha not taken it upon herself to send them money and gifts they would all have gone hungry, while Gedalia would have gone wild with grief and guilt the minute he found out.

The fact was that, though she might sometimes shout at the servants, Bertha too was not at all stuck-up and gave no one cause for offense. When she first decided to change her name from Breyndl the local wags had joked that becoming rich must be like becoming ill, a condition for which a change of name was known to be efficacious. Eventually, however, everyone grew used to calling her Bertha, or else "Mrs. Ziemlich" to her face and, behind her back, "the Lady of Malikrowik."

As for Mina, she was hardly known in Szybusz and, since she studied in Stanislaw, was seldom seen there. Sometimes one of her Szybusz friends ordered a copy made of a fashionable hat or coat of hers, but by the time the milliner or tailor had it ready Mina was already forgotten.

15

HIRSHL HAD NEVER been so popular as now that he was a model bridegroom. Once, in the good old days, the Jews of Szybusz had married with each other, and there were still families in town that, though maintaining no ties between them, could trace a relationship by marriage going back many generations. Subsequently, however, when it became the common practice to marry out of town, the greater the distance the bride or groom came from, the more distinguished the match was deemed to be. Such newlyweds walked the streets of Szybusz like counts and countesses. Whatever they did produced volumes of commentary and whatever they said was repeated over and over until, lapsing slowly into the routines of daily life, they became like any other Szybuszian.

Nor was there a family in Szybusz that did not have its favorite adventure stories of travels to faraway weddings, of robbers and swindlers encountered on the way, and of in-laws and matchmakers met upon arrival. Indeed, as times grew harder and a decent match rarer, one had to range farther and farther to look for it and be less and less picky about what one found. Thus, Hirshl's engagement combined the best of both worlds. You could say that he was marrying locally, and you could say that he was marrying out of town, for though Szybusz was not Malikrowik, Malikrowik was only two miles away.

When strawberry season arrived, the Ziemlichs began fetching the Hurvitzes in their carriage to come eat fresh berries with them. It would be the time of day when the cows were being driven back from the meadow by singing village girls; slowly the sun went down; the moon and stars came out; and, under Bertha's doting eye, Hirshl sat beneath a tree with his parents, his fiancée, and her father, before him a loaf of yeasty-smelling, appetizing black bread, bowls of butter and cheese, a pitcher of buttermilk, and lots of red berries swimming in sweet cream. Servants smelling of tar and wood waited to do his every bidding, bringing him new dishes, taking away old ones, and filling his empty glass. Thus pampered, Hirshl felt like a well-cared-for patient. Such attention indeed could make even a healthy man ill.

Hirshl and Mina did not talk much to each other. The evenings and nights of early summer were not conducive to conversation. They sat lost in thought, or perhaps in the absence of it. Sometimes Mina glanced up at the stars. Although once, before her engagement, she had known some of their names, she had forgotten them by now—or rather, it was not their names she had forgotten but which name belonged to which star. Had her nature teacher asked her about them, she would have been at a loss.

But Hirshl was not Mina's teacher and had no interest in astronomy. He sat lazily on a wooden bench with his feet barely grazing the ground, half listening to the snatches of voices that drifted from the village. Some peasant girls were singing a song about a mermaid who married a prince. What did the prince do when he realized that his bride was half fish? The village girls were far, far off, and their voices barely reached him.

It had been daylight when the Hurvitzes arrived in Malikrowik, and now Hirshl and Boruch Meir rose and went inside to say their evening prayers. Gedalia Ziemlich had already said his with the first stars, yet, always ready for more, he accompanied the two men into the house. Unlike Boruch Meir, who prayed quickly, Hirshl took his time. Perhaps he had things to pray about and perhaps he had thoughts that kept him from praying at all. He still had not finished when Stach the coachman appeared with his whip to take them back to Szybusz.

It was an hour after nightfall when they started home. Stach flicked the haunches of the horses and sang sad, sweet peasant songs. Although the world seemed his for the asking, Hirshl felt that he too was sad and that a man might have all the good food, pleasant surroundings, wealth, possessions, honor, and fame that could be wished for, everything but one thing, and still feel that happiness eluded him.

What was that thing? If his own father and mother did not know, it was unlikely that anyone did.

Yona Toyber may have been given his matchmaker's fee, but he still put an arm around Hirshl when they met and talked to him of interesting things—and while there is no knowing whether he ever told Tsirl about what happened on his first visit to Malikrowik, what he said to Hirshl is no secret. There were in Szybusz, besides those in the cemetery, many old graves that kept turning up whenever a new foundation was dug. Akavia Mazal had even written a lengthy book about them that was reviewed in the *Neue Freie Presse* of Vienna— and, though Toyber had not read it, he was no slouch on the subject himself, for when Hirshl mentioned it to him he replied, "Yes, they even found a couple of them underneath the old study house when it was renovated. You'll come on an old grave anywhere you stick a shovel in Szybusz." It was a moot question, he said, whether a descendant of the priestly caste, who was forbidden to enter a graveyard, should even be permitted to live in the town. If Mazal had written one book, Toyber could have written two, yet Hirshl still craved to hear more. Perhaps Mazal, who could have filled more books than Toyber, might have told Hirshl what he wished to know, but Mazal lived at the far end of town while Hirshl lived in its center, and the divine economy never brought them together as it brought him together with Toyber. Indeed, it was a pity that Mazal did not know Toyber, because Toyber was a mine of erudition. Hirshl wondered what Mazal would think of him.

Yet Toyber's and Mazal's paths never crossed. Had Blume Nacht's father been alive and rich and looking for a wealthy match for his daughter, Toyber would surely have sought Mazal out, since Blume lived in his house. As it was, though, Blume was simply a poor orphan who once had worked as a housemaid for the Hurvitzes and was now employed by the Mazals.

Toyber and Hirshl would walk the streets of Szybusz with their cigarettes in their mouths, Toyber's slenderly glowing and Hirshl's absentmindedly unlit. Although it amazed Hirshl how Yona Toyber could let his cigarette burn down until the flame practically touched his lips, each time he was about to warn him of the danger Toyber seized the burning stub with two fingers, flung it at his feet, and stood there regarding it as though it were an unfinished thought. Perhaps he was thinking that had he cadged it from Ziemlich rather than from Hirshl it would have borne the coat of arms of a count.

Though he was careful to speak no ill of Szybusz when talking to Mina, Toyber was more candid with Hirshl. Neither of the two men were Zionists; yet both agreed with the Zionists that an entire people could not subsist on buying and selling, and that Jews must be made to return to tilling the land. This was one reason that Toyber thought highly of Gedalia Ziemlich, who lived on a farm and did well there, while as for Mina—well, Mina was a cultured young lady.

Had anyone else linked Mina with Culture his listeners might have wondered which came first, but with Toyber there was no room for doubt that Culture gained most from the liaison. In a word, Zionistically speaking, it was all to the good that Mina's father ran a farm; culturally speaking, there was no denying that she was cultured; and if there were things in Hirshl's life that neither Zionism nor Culture had anything to do with, he should count his blessings nonetheless, since no one could ever have everything.

Hirshl was being outfitted for his wedding. Before he could sit down to breakfast, the tailors would arrive to measure him up, down, and across, in the collar, the shoulders, and the chest. Tsirl was clothing him not only for God and man, that is, for both the Sabbath and weekdays, but for halfway between them too, so that, for example, should Hirshl wish to go for a casual Saturday-afternoon stroll he would not be in the position of certain other stylish young men in Szybusz who, having only two kinds of outfits, could not possibly wear either, their Sabbath clothes being too formal to be casual and their weekday clothes too casual for the Sabbath, and so ended up sitting at home like mourners.

Mina too was busy assembling her trousseau. Though Bertha had wanted to order everything from Stanislaw, when Gedalia pointed out to her that no one from Stanislaw ever came to buy in Szybusz, and that if people like them did not support local merchants no one would, she agreed to make her purchases in town. If any item was a large one she made sure to consult Tsirl about it, not because she needed Tsirl's advice, but for Tsirl to see that money was no object with her. Indeed, neither of the Ziemlichs was sparing of expenses, Bertha because she wanted a grand wedding and Gedalia because he wished to propitiate his latest stroke of good fortune. Every day the couturiers arrived with new samples of velvets, satins, fine silks, and fancy tweeds, over which Bertha fussed while Gedalia watched and wondered how his baby daughter, whose bones were barely strong enough to bear the skin upon them, was going to wear such mountains of clothing.

As it was not the custom for a betrothed couple to spend time together, Mina no longer visited the Hurvitzes. Whenever she came to Szybusz she stayed with Sophia Gildenhorn, who was more than happy to have her because her husband was away on a long trip. The two of them spent the days shopping with Bertha, while at night Mina slept in Yitzchok Gildenhorn's bed.

It was peaceful at the Gildenhorns'. The pretty flowerpots in the windows gave off a fresh fragrance, so different from the liquor and tobacco smells of the men. The house and its contents were quietly resting from Gildenhorn and his crowd, as was Sophia herself, an old, girlish nightgown over her slim shoulders as she lay in her bed. A tired Mina lay next to her, for it had been a hectic day, full of dresses, sweaters, and coats to try on. The clock ticked loudly. In fact, since the day of Gildenhorn's departure it had been ticking more loudly all the time.

Sophia turned to look at Mina. "It's ten o'clock already," she said.

"Is it?"

"Didn't you count?" asked Sophia.

"No," said Mina.

"You must have been thinking."

"There isn't a thought in my head."

96

"You can't tell me that," said Sophia. "I know just what you were thinking about."

"You know what I was thinking about?"

"I know you were thinking about him."

"About whom?"

"Come closer and I'll whisper it to you."

"I'm as close as I can get."

"You were thinking about him."

"You already said that."

"It's the truth."

"I still don't know what you mean by that."

"If I have to spell it out for you, I will."

"Because I wasn't thinking about him at all."

"About whom?"

"About Heinrich Hurvitz."

"Then who were you thinking about?"

"Why don't you let me go to sleep?"

"Wait, there's something I want to show you."

"You can show it to me tomorrow."

"No. It has to be now."

Mina sat up without a word and stared at her friend, who was behaving very strangely.

Sophia had gotten out of bed and was changing into another nightgown, the likes of which Mina had never seen. It was, Sophia informed her, unable to restrain herself any longer, the gown that she wore whenever Gildenhorn was at home. Mina could hardly look at it. Whatever had possessed Sophia suddenly to start modeling nightgowns?

What had possessed Sophia was the irresistible desire to share certain facts of life with her friend, and when Mina turned angrily away from her she did not know which to feel more, amusement at her anger or amazement at her innocence. Though Mina was only two years younger than Sophia, Sophia had been married for that period of time and knew things that Mina did not. Indeed, sometimes she wished that she too did not know them, which was partly why she liked being with Mina. Yet Mina was turned the other way. It was already past eleven. The clock ticked more loudly than ever. Neither of the two friends heard it, however, because one was fast asleep and the other was deep in thought.

Sophia's thoughts were mostly of an intimate nature. She was still in her teens when she married Gildenhorn, who could pick her up in one arm and carry her about the house from room to room. How she had loved his stylish checked pants and swooned at the sound of his voice! Now, however, his voice had grown worn from selling too much life insurance, while no sooner was he home than the house filled up with his friends. Nor, though Sophia was a good wife and wanted to make him happy, did he himself always know how this might be done. From feeling that she lacked nothing in life she soon had gone to feeling that she lacked everything. After two years of marriage she still had no children.

It was not like Sophia to think only of herself. Sometimes, even when she was not in the mood, she put her problems aside to think of other people's. There were thoughts one did not even want, and others one had a craving for, like that she once felt in the Hurvitzes' store when she saw a woman buying shelled almonds and immediately went to tell Hirshl that she must have shelled almonds too.

The clock ticked away. It was the only thing in the house that never rested. It had just chimed eleven, and here it was already chiming twelve. In eight more hours it would be time to rise. Yet Sophia was still not sleepy. It was good to be alone with her thoughts, and she did not want them to end. Next to her Mina was sleeping soundly. Nothing ever troubled her. She had the mind of a schoolgirl.

Another hour went by. Sophia looked at her friend. She was still sleeping peacefully, as people sometimes do when, though their lives are about to undergo a great change, they as yet have no inkling of it.

Though Hirshl was a modern young man, the old ways were still observed with him. On the Sabbath before his wedding his well-wishers gathered at his home and escorted him to the synagogue. There Boruch Meir presided over the Torah blessings, and when the bridegroom's turn came Hirshl was showered with almonds and raisins from the women's gallery while the cantor and the leading male voices sang, "He Who blessed our fathers Abraham, Isaac, and Jacob." When the service was over the entire congregation was invited to the Hurvitzes' for a Sabbath dinner, after which Hirshl's friends remained with him until nightfall, serenaded with hymns and Psalms by the cantor and his choir. As soon as the Sabbath ended the charity warden came and received a large donation to distribute to the poor. Then all of Hirshl's former teachers arrived to congratulate him, and each one was presented with a gift.

"The wedding contract without discord has yet to be written," said the ancient rabbis. In the case of the Hurvitzes and the Ziemlichs this adage was refuted, yet the discord broke out somewhere else. In the Little Synagogue there was a seat of honor in the easternmost corner, facing Jerusalem, that was customarily reserved for bridegrooms. This seat was not synagogue property but belonged to a certain old man who was generally happy to yield it. When Hirshl was led up to it, however, the seat owner refused to budge and declared, "He doesn't look like a bridegroom to me." He was referring to Hirshl's lack of a shtreimel, the traditional round fur hat customarily worn on such occasions. Fortunately, a Jew standing by, who was as clever as he was learned, said to the old man, "Why, you yourself know that it is written that a bridegroom should be treated like a king. Does anyone tell a king what to wear?" To which the anxious sexton added, "If you'll be kind enough to forgive the shtreimel, I'm sure that Mr. Hurvitz will be happy to donate a new Ark to the synagogue." Boruch Meir nodded and the old man gave up his seat.

More serious was the disagreement between the two families over where the wedding should be held, for though the common practice was to have it in the bride's house, Tsirl insisted that it be in hers. In this she was supported by a number of prominent citizens, who argued that, since there were several weddings being held that day in town, they would have to miss all the others if the Hurvitzes' was held in Malikrowik, which would cause bad blood between families. The rabbi and the cantor seconded the point, for they could not possibly manage to officiate in one day both in Szybusz and in Malikrowik. "Besides which," put in the sexton of the Great Synagogue, "there's only one wedding canopy in all of Szybusz, and I can't have it sent out of town when brides and grooms need it here." When Bertha and Gedalia saw what they were up against, they agreed to hold the wedding in Szybusz.

16

ON THE NIGHT THAT Hirshl and Mina were married, several other couples in Szybusz were married as well. Yet the most special wedding was Hirshl and Mina's, for while the others too had singers, musicians, and guests from far places, only Mina and Hirshl's had a guest from abroad. And though Jews from Germany were not a total rarity in Szybusz, one seldom saw them at a wedding.

Money did not grow on trees anywhere, not even in Germany, but if proof was needed that anyone with wits and ambition enough could make it there too, it was provided in the person of this royally dressed son of Gedalia Ziemlich's cousin whose fortune was found in an unknown grave. A wholesale poultry and egg dealer with outlets in many cities who had often considered a business trip to Galicia, young Herr Ziemlich had finally come on one. On the day that he happened to be in Szybusz he heard that another Mr. Ziemlich was marrying off his daughter. Any Ziemlich, he thought, must be a relative of mine—and so, dressed in his best, off to the wedding he went.

The fact that Gedalia and Bertha were happy to meet their

rich cousin from Germany must not be taken to mean that they were ashamed of their poorer relations. On the contrary, any down-at-the-heel members of their families wishing to attend the wedding had their tickets sent to them by Bertha, who also bought them a new set of clothes and a wedding present in their name. After all, not all of the Hurvitzes' guests were rich either. Rothschild, in fact, was a good deal richer than any of them. What sizable wedding gifts Hirshl received came entirely from merchants and manufacturers who did business with the firm of Hurvitz, while as for Boruch Meir's family, you could add its presents to those of Tsirl's and tie both to the tail of a mouse without giving the cat an unfair advantage. The one exception was a long green bill called a dollar, which was worth a good many of the other gifts combined. True, its exchange rate was only five Austrian crowns, but it came with a poem attached.

While a coin remains the same coin no matter what Kaiser minted it, and a president's face on a dollar does not make it worth a cent more, a few lines of poetry have a value-enhancing effect. As Boruch Meir's brother Meshulam could not afford to come to his nephew's wedding, he took a sheet of paper, composed a poem on it, clipped it to the bottom of a dollar bill, and sent it off in his stead. Indeed, though Boruch Meir and Meshulam may have been brothers, the resemblance ended right there, for while Boruch Meir owned a large store Meshulam owned a small one, and while Boruch Meir was always busy with his customers Meshulam had time to spare, which he passed by writing verses for each holiday and special occasion.

The Jewish prayer book has no room for more prayers; the Jewish heart, however, is infinitely big, and when a Jew pours it out in Hebrew verse the very angels and seraphs break off their song to listen and bring it before the Mercy Seat, where the Holy One Blessed Be He adds it to His own private breviary and has mercy on His people when He reads it. In a word, if Meshulam Hurvitz did not own a store like his brother's, or measure and weigh as much goods, he was no less occupied weighing words, measuring meters, and being wrapped up in his verse. These poems did not appear in *Ha-Maggid*, *Otsar Ha-Sifrut*, or any other Hebrew publication. They were kept in a straw basket beneath Meshulam's bed, and when his wife went out shopping for a few pennies' worth of vegetables and found them there, she put them under the pillow and replaced them in the basket when she returned. The only poems of Meshulam's to have an audience were his New Year's greetings. An ordinary person might rather have received one of Boruch Meir's greeting cards, which had gold letters and gilt edging around them, but connoisseurs of literature preferred his brother Meshulam's, written though they were on plain paper and in ordinary ink.

What did Hirshl's Uncle Meshulam write on the note that he clipped to the bottom of the dollar? He wrote:

> *Many a mile came this dollar,*
> *E'en from a distant land.*
> *Share its good luck with each other,*
> *Underwritten by my hand.*
> *Long may you be happy together,*
> *And remember me, for I am,*
>   *Your Uncle Meshulam.*

Right timing is all. Though Meshulam Hurvitz had written reams of poetry and never acquired a reputation, he was made famous overnight by these few lines, which were explicated word by word, rhyme by rhyme, and even letter by letter. Why, for instance, did they begin with an "M"? One school of critics held that this was because "M" was the first letter of Mina. A second school argued that "M" was the first letter of Mazel Tov. A third school insisted that both of these opinions were wrong and that Hirshl's uncle had meant to write his own name, using the first letter of each line. Where then, asked the first and second schools scornfully, was the final "M" of Meshulam? It was, came the triumphant answer, in the last letter of the poem's last line.

But Hirshl did not remember his Uncle Meshulam, neither before his wedding nor after it. If anything, he thought of his mother's family, that is, of her brother who went mad and of her grandfather, who was said to have once put a chamber pot on his head and worn it instead of a skullcap.

Hirshl and Mina were married amid a great throng of guests, some in shtreimels and some in top hats, some more distinguished and some less so, some truer friends than others. The rooms of the house were filled to overflowing, and the tables were heaped high with wines and cakes. Even the room with the pile furniture was used for the occasion, its white slipcovers having been removed and its smell of mothballs admixed with that of food. The waiters ran back and forth, scanning those present as if in the hope of discovering a hidden tipper among them. The guests sat talking in groups, Gildenhorn on a couch with young Herr Ziemlich from Germany, with whom he was discussing affairs of note. Though the German wore a beaver and Gildenhorn an ordinary hat, the latter, being a good head taller, had to keep bending down; still, the German seemed no shorter than he, for there was something about being German that made even a little man look big.

"You know," said Gildenhorn's father-in-law Eisy Heller, who was Tsirl's age and had grown up next door to her, "I can still remember Hirshl's maternal grandfather, the one he was named after. A strange man that was. He never seemed to enjoy life much, but he never complained to anyone either, and in fact he had little use for people. I don't think he had a real friend in the world. All he cared about were the pigeons he kept on his roof. You should have seen with what love he took care of them. Once, while I was watching him climb a ladder to bring them food and water, one of them fell off the roof. I felt sorry for the old man having to climb all the way back down for it, and so I stood there waiting for him to ask me to bring it up to him. Well, he didn't, so finally I asked him if he'd like me to. He didn't even bother to answer. He just looked at me, climbed down the ladder, picked up the bird, smoothed out its feathers, and climbed back up with it."

"Are you sure that's really what happened?" asked Hayyim

Yehoshua Bleiberg. He was not in a particularly good mood that day and was for some reason irritated by Eisy's story.

"Of course I am," said Eisy Heller.

"Something tells me you dreamed it," said Hayyim Yehoshua.

"Why should I have dreamed it?"

"Something just tells me you did."

"Since when is what something tells you any reason for me to have weird dreams?"

"They couldn't be any weirder than the story you just told us."

"What's so weird about it?"

"If it wasn't weird," said Hayyim Yehoshua, "you wouldn't have bothered to tell it in the first place."

"But it's God's truth!"

"It's God's truth," said Hayyim Yehoshua, "that the groom doesn't look like a groom to me."

"And the bride?" asked Mottshi Shaynbart.

"The same goes for the bride."

"I never saw such a thing in my life," said Leibush Tshortkover. "An only daughter marrying an only son."

They were indeed two only children. Their parents had put all they had into them and given them the finest wedding that could be asked for. Had the whole town not known that it was taking place, it would have realized as much from the commotion; even a deaf man passing by might have guessed that a celebration was under way from the sight of Boruch Meir's closed store, its shutter rolled down as on Sabbaths and holidays and its two locks glinting in the sun. But there was no one passing by, for whoever was not attending one of the other weddings in town was already at Hirshl and Mina's. Even Boruch Meir's two shopboys, who could have been asked to mind the store, were invited by him and as cordially received as if they were his own in-laws. In fact, Boruch Meir had invited everyone he knew. Getzel Stein was there in his best, though he was not as gay as he might have been, for he had been hoping to see Blume, and Blume was not to be seen.

Though Blume knew that it was the day of Hirshl's wedding, she refused to feel downcast or upset. She spent the day in Akavia Mazal's house, playing with the baby as usual, or perhaps even more than usual. Not that she was indifferent to Hirshl. Blume loved Hirshl. But as Hirshl had married someone else, it did no good to think about him.

Hirshl stood wan and tired beneath the wedding canopy. His bride stood beside him. Mina was as pale as a tallow candle, and Hirshl was like her reflection in a mirror.

(What brought this image to mind? The candles that were lit beneath the wedding canopy in honor of the bride and groom.)

The white candles with their rims of red flame suggested bitterly crying eyes. Suddenly one went out in a draft. A candle that goes out beneath the wedding canopy is supposed to be a sign of bad luck, but neither Hirshl's nor Mina's parents noticed it—while as for Hirshl, his thoughts were elsewhere, though hardly anywhere in particular. His glance wandered from the rabbi to the flask of wine in his assistant's hand, and from there to the slowly dripping candles that were staining the blue ribbons tied around them. He remembered having once read or heard of a Hindu sect that, when a man and woman were divorced, put them in a room with two candles, one for each of them, where they waited to see what would happen. If the man's candle went out first he departed at once and never came back, leaving the house and its possessions to the woman, while if his wife's went out first she did the same.

Just then Hirshl's glance shifted and he saw that a candle had gone out. God in heaven knew whose it was. The bridesmaid holding it blushed and relit it from the candle of the bridesmaid next to her. Hirshl looked away and wondered whether the bridesmaids had tied the white candles with blue ribbons because they were Zionists, or whether the colors were a coincidence. I suppose that if they had tied them with red ribbons, he thought, I would wonder if they were socialists. If they didn't, then they must be Zionists. Still, I would have liked red better.

The rabbi concluded his blessings, and the best man led the bride and groom to a large room with many chairs squeezed together and many people seated on them. Mina hardly knew any of them and did not raise her head to look at them. The guests dipped into their soup bowls, the spooning of the soup and the smacking of their lips making a single greasy sound. How much soup could there be in one bowl, and how long could it take to get it down? And after the soup and its spoons would come the meat and its forks, and after the meat the dessert. All her life Mina had lived in a cozy little world from which soup slurpers and meat spearers were excluded. The wedding had already exhausted her. God in heaven knew she had to rest. Yet well-bred young lady that she was, she soon rose to circulate among the guests. The fiddles struck up, and everyone merrily finished the meal, after which the rabbi gave the wedding address while Mina sat by Hirshl's side wondering why such a great to-do was made about love. Not that she had anything against Hirshl. Far from it. But she had been content with her life before he came along too.

When the grace after meals had been said, it was everyone's turn to dance with the bride. First the rabbi took a handkerchief, held it by one end, gave the other end to Mina, and did a perfunctory jig. Then the handkerchief passed to Boruch Meir, then to Gedalia, then to the guests of honor, and then to all the other guests, each one circling with Mina as much as his strength and love of dance permitted, while Gildenhorn and Kurtz capered around them, leaping over and dodging under the white cloth, Gildenhorn, who was as tall as a ship's mast, practically scraping the ceiling, and Kurtz, who was as short as a dwarf, barely higher than the floor. Then all the men danced with the men and all the women with the women until the rabbi went home, when men and women danced together until dawn while the wedding jester made up comic verses, the musicians fiddled away, and Kurtz, Gildenhorn, Mottshi Shaynbart, Leibush Tshortkover, and assorted other guests and gate-crashers played practical jokes.

A pale, chill light trickled through the windows. One by one the candles went out and the guests rose and departed. At last Mina and Hirshl rose too. The cantor and his choir sang them a parting song, and the Gildenhorns walked them to their new home.

17

THEIR HOME HAD TWO ROOMS and a kitchen, in which the servant girl slept. In the larger room were two beds that stood side by side, a chest of drawers with a big wall mirror above it, a round table in the middle of the floor surrounded by six chairs, and two closets, one for Hirshl's clothes and one for Mina's. Apart from the chairs, which were fashioned from straw in the style called "Viennese," everything was made of walnut. The smaller room served no purpose and was set aside for the future when, God willing, there would be children. Indeed, the larger room was not strictly necessary either, for the couple could have lived with the Hurvitzes, as Tsirl had suggested one day while talking to the Ziemlichs. The house and table that had been good enough for Hirshl to grow up in and eat on, she said, were good enough for Mina too. Sophia Gildenhorn, however, who happened to be present and knew that Mina would never want to live with Hirshl's parents, had remarked, "Two's company, more's a crowd." Tsirl took the hint and rented a small apartment for Hirshl and Mina.

When the wedding week was over, Hirshl returned to the store. The charmed air of a newlywed still hung over him. He had trouble concentrating on his work and yawned without realizing it in front of the customers, who commented on it with a smile. All day he waited for evening to come, yet when it did he lingered in the store until Tsirl had to chase him out and remind him that Mina was waiting. "Here," she would tell him, handing him a bag of sweets, "give this to Mina." Whomever

Hirshl told Mina it was from, Tsirl, conventional wisdom notwithstanding, clearly begrudged her new daughter-in-law nothing.

Though often Mina seemed happy to see him when he came back from the store, sometimes Hirshl could feel her withdraw from him. He knew that women's hearts were fickle, yet he no more understood what made her glad one time than what made her sulky the next. At such moments he grew moody himself, in response to which she retreated into a mournful silence. If that's what she wants, he would think, let's see how long she can stand it. He would begin to put her to the test, or else get up and sit down again with a noisy scraping of his chair, but Mina's silence only grew more woeful until the whole room was filled with such anguish that, suddenly alarmed by it, Hirshl would start to talk in spite of himself. At first she would answer him grudgingly; then willingly; then in a tone of relief. By the time he rose from his chair again the two of them would have made up.

Sometimes he returned from work to find Sophia Gildenhorn, who always vanished the moment he appeared. Occasionally Mina's mother was there. Bertha lit up when she saw him and he too was friendly toward her, answering her questions, asking more of his own, and talking in lively tones. Not that she had much of interest to say, but her interest in Hirshl drew him out and made him loquacious with her.

Gedalia was seldom in Szybusz. Getting in the harvest, which was a big one that year, kept him busy all summer, so that it was all he could do to steal a few minutes here and there in which to visit his daughter, ask her and Hirshl how they were, sit with them a short while, say "Godspeed," and depart. On his way out he made sure to touch the mezuzah on the doorpost and to invoke the Lord's blessings on his daughter's home.

The days came and went. Though no two days in the world are ever alike, no day in Hirshl and Mina's lives was ever different from any other. Their mood might change a thousand times in the course of it, but its own course stayed the same, with Hirshl waiting on customers in the store and Mina knitting or embroidering at home. Sometimes she put on her going-out clothes and went to visit Sophia, stopping on her way to say hello to her husband. No longer did she arrive at the Hurvitzes' in a dancing carriage piled high with bags to unload. God in heaven had given her a home of her own, and she did not need theirs anymore. Her only baggage nowadays was her purse and her parasol, which were easily portable and no trouble at all.

Sophia was generally free during the day and was always glad to see Mina. If it seems odd that the two found so much to talk about, the Rabbis themselves once declared that, out of ten measures of talk that God gave the world, nine were given to women. Certainly Sophia's conversation appealed to Mina more than Hirshl's, since whenever Heinrich told her some news, say of some incident in the store, she was never quite sure why he had bothered, which was not at all the case with Sophia. Had Hirshl kept abreast of women's fashions, he and Mina would have shared a common interest, for Mina owned many elegant clothes and changed them many times a day; yet to Hirshl, unfortunately, all outfits looked alike and one dress was as good as another. Indeed, even had he been more sartorially minded it might not have mattered very much, Mina's weakness for fine clothes being less a matter of good taste than of having the money to buy them with and a tailor who knew how to make them.

Hirshl might also have talked to Mina about the books that he read, yet after two or three tries he gave up on this too, for though she had studied various subjects, she had lost all interest in her own education from the moment she left school. Indeed, Hirshl never knew whether to smile or to wince at how what he told her went in one ear and out the other. In the end he learned to keep both his books and his knowledge to himself. Sometimes, it was true, Mina asked him what he was reading, but no sooner did he begin to explain than she started to yawn. If not for the hot blood of youth that they shared, there would have been nothing between them. As it was, intellectual compatibility was not everything.

Hirshl's routine was unchanging. He spent his days in the store and his nights with his wife. His mother had raised him to be regular in his habits, and though he sometimes wished that he did not have to spend every evening alone with Mina, this was not a wish that came true. Even Bertha and Sophia had conspired of late to strand him with her, Bertha because she was busy in the village and Sophia because . . . but only God in heaven knew why Sophia behaved as she did. It almost seemed to Hirshl that she visited his home for the sole purpose of disappearing when he arrived, leaving him no choice but to sit up with Mina by himself.

Hirshl resented being cooped up with Mina all the time. Sometimes he wondered angrily how she could fail to see that it was bad for them—yet when she kept away from him, he felt annoyed by this too. And though Mina also thought it would be better to spend less time together, the power of regularity proved stronger than the power of thought. Were their closeness not only physical, she would not have minded it. Since it was, it made her unhappy too.

What, wondered Mina, did other people do? Had Sophia encouraged her at all, she would have gladly told her all her problems. But the same Sophia who had egged Mina on so before her marriage now seemed almost meekly unassertive.

A welcome change came from an unexpected quarter. The month of Elul arrived with its penitential prayers, and though, apart from their first and last night, Hirshl did not rise in the small hours of the morning to go to them, the mood of mild forbearance that descended on the town affected him and Mina too. They might not have put it that way, but it did make them realize that there were more important things in the world than the conversations of husbands and wives.

The summer and High Holy Days passed, as did the first four of the eight days of Sukkos, the Feast of Tabernacles.

The sun was banked by clouds that cast their changing colors earthward and formed strange apparitions in the skies. Birds called from the bare fields, and heavy yellow pears hung from their branches, offering up their sweetness to the world. In Malikrowik the peasant girls sat on their doorsteps, braiding heads of garlic and knotting corn and onions before hanging them in the sun to dry. Preparing to set out, the birds measured their shadows each day and took to the air in little, probing flights. Overhead the clouds drifted together, coupled, and went their separate ways again. If no rain fell from them, this was doubtless because the Feast of Tabernacles was not yet over and Jews had not yet begun to pray for precipitation in the Holy Land and elsewhere.

Gedalia Ziemlich had had a bountiful year. The harvest was a good one, and so were the prices it brought. Poultry and egg prices were up too. Indeed, when the Lord decides to be generous He does not take half measures. Hard though it was to believe, the same chickens that cackled in refuse on Gedalia's farm were now ceremoniously received at the railway station by a trainman wearing the peaked cap of the Kaiser, who sent them and their eggs off to Germany. Not even in the days of the Mishnah, when a whole tractate called *Betsa*, which is Hebrew for "egg," was composed, were eggs ever treated with such honors. And though they had always done well in Szybusz, they were never so profitable as now that Arnold Ziemlich, Gedalia's cousin from Germany, had a special agent there to buy and ship them.

Of course, there were those who accused Herr Ziemlich of driving up egg prices, but there were just as many others who praised him for providing a livelihood not only to the chicken growers but also to the carpenters who made the coops and crates, the peasant girls who sorted and wrapped the eggs in straw, and the clerks who filled out the shipping forms. Not that there were no chickens or eggs in Germany—yet you could not compare the taste of a German chicken or egg to one from Galicia. If prior to Herr Ziemlich's appearance the children of Szybusz had come running at the sight of a single German stamp, there was now not a child in town without his own collection. And even though the price of eggs may have gone up, people went right on eating them. Indeed, whereas there were old folk in Szybusz who still could remember when eggs were so scarce that a single one cost a whole kroner and housewives stopped glazing their Sabbath breads with egg yolk, one now ate as many eggs as one pleased even on ordinary weekdays.

Hirshl and Mina spent the holiday in Malikrowik and were gladly wined and dined there. Though they were given Mina's old room, which had not been used since the day of her wedding, its floor sparkled like a mirror and its walls gleamed as though freshly whitewashed, for while Gedalia had been building the holiday sukkah Bertha and the servant girls had been getting ready for their guests, sweeping, mopping, and cleaning out cobwebs. An unlived-in room was not easily made habitable again: although the mezuzah on its doorpost might keep out the evil spirits, there was nothing in the world that could keep out the dust with which Heaven signaled its displeasure that, while some Jews had nowhere to live, others allowed rooms to stand empty.

Once more Mina's bed stood freshly made and smelling of cologne. Next to it stood Hirshl's. Had it not been for the cologne, he could have smelled its new wood. It indeed was one of God's mysteries how Bendit the carpenter, who had never slept in a bed in his life and spent his nights curled up on the floor, could have made such a fine piece of furniture, out of which only three or four days' use stood to be gotten. And even then, as comfortable as it was, Hirshl did not sleep in it very much, since each morning of his stay in the village saw him up before the crack of dawn. Day and night might exist in all places but they were not the same everywhere, and Hirshl liked to see the houses, cottages, barns, stables, trees, and bushes of the village waking up beneath their blanket of white mist through which the moon and stars shone with a halo of mutable light and the first villagers stepped outside to care for the farm animals that lowed and bleated happily to see them. Yet it was not a world that he could remain in forever. Soon he turned around and headed back for the Ziemlichs'.

Mina usually slept till nine o'clock. "Are you up already, Heinrich?" she would ask in surprise when she awoke, opening her eyes and stretching her still-tired arms. Hirshl would answer with a nod so as not to disturb the peaceful silence of the morning before Mina's old nurse came along with a basin of hot bathwater, a cup of coffee that was more than half cream, and some pastries filled with raisins and cheese. "What day is it today?" Mina would ask, sipping the creamy head of her coffee while cutting herself a piece of pastry. Then her parents arrived to look in on her, Gedalia with fresh willow leaves in his beard, for he had been down to the river before dawn to gather willow shoots for the holiday lulav, and Bertha with a bowl of yellow pears.

"Did you sleep well?" Bertha asked.

Mina reached out for the clock on the table with a yawn. "If you're asking how many hours I slept, the answer is more than enough. But if you're asking how I feel, the nights here are too short for me."

"Then turn over and go back to sleep," advised Bertha. "We won't be having dinner for a while yet. Come," she said to Gedalia, pulling him after her out of the room, "let's let the child sleep."

The two of them left.

Hirshl went to the sukkah that Gedalia had built. It stood in a pleasant nook, garlanded with fruit and ears of grain. A breeze lifted the patterned sheets that formed its sides, revealing a world of woods and fields. A new day was starting, and men and women were already silently at work, it being still too early to be singing about mermaids or indeed about anything else.

Hirshl wrapped himself in his prayer shawl and began to recite the morning prayer, thanking God for watching over his soul while he slept and restoring it to him in the morning. He felt as rested and at home in his body as a man does in his own house when every room is tidy and clean. He said the *pesukei de'zimra*, the *shema*, the *shemoneh esreh*, the *hallel*, and the *musaf*, feeling at peace with the world. Gedalia was out making the rounds of the farm, Bertha was cooking in the kitchen, and

Mina was still in bed, her limbs spread lazily over the sheets and not in the least annoyed with her over their lack of exercise. Szybusz was just an hour's walk away. The shops there would be opening now and their owners comparing their lulavs and esrogs, each certain he had the best that money could buy. The sight of his father-in-law's sukkah gave Hirshl a festive feeling. There was nothing like it in the narrow, crooked streets of Szybusz, where each holiday booth looked like a pack on a hunchback's back. More than once on the Feast of Tabernacles Hirshl had preferred to skip a meal rather than eat it in such a sukkah. Perhaps Jews like Akavia Mazal who lived on the outskirts of town built nicer ones.

Hirshl had not thought of Akavia Mazal for a long time. Once he had mused often about this man, who had fallen in love with and married his ex-pupil's daughter Tirza, who sat talking with her friend Blume about her husband and young Hirshl Hurvitz. One day, however, Hirshl had sat down with himself and decided to put such thoughts out of his mind.

Meanwhile Gedalia came back from the fields, Bertha set the table in the sukkah, and Mina appeared in a morning dress. Though for her part she could have slept more, she had not wanted to keep the rest of them waiting for their dinner. "Good morning, Heinrich," she said with a bob of her head, standing so close to him that their noses nearly touched. Unlike Napoleon, however, Hirshl was no Frenchman; he did not like the smell of Mina's cologne and gave his nose the order to retreat. "Well then," said Mina, looking down at the set table, "I think I'll go and change before we eat."

She stepped out of the sukkah, whose own fragrance reasserted itself. Its garlands of fruit were beginning to bruise and spoil. A jack-o'-lantern hanging from a chain of strung walnuts swung back and forth in the breeze. Hirshl was not hungry. Mina's parents had been feeding him well. If he could have been allowed to sit all day in the sukkah without munching on more than a walnut, he gladly would have done so.

The two men sat without speaking, Hirshl because he was

feeling too peaceful to say anything, and Gedalia because a sukkah was no place for idle talk. His prayer book open before him, he sat praying that God would make the world His tabernacle as His people had made the sukkah theirs. The breeze rippled through the branches of the roof, which gave off a pleasant aroma.

Mina returned in an afternoon dress, sat down beside Hirshl, dipped a slice of bread in honey, and said the blessing over it. A servant girl entered with a platter of freshly cooked fish. Gedalia Ziemlich put down his prayer book and stared at the unexpected dish in surprise.

"I ordered fish for the last day of the holiday as usual," explained Bertha, "but it came today by mistake. At first I thought of pickling it and serving it as planned, but then I thought that pickled fish would be too sour for a holiday meal, so I decided to cook it today."

"Bless God for each day," mumbled Gedalia, tucking a napkin under his chin while dunking his bread in the aspic and chewing it slowly. Hirshl ate a great deal despite his lack of appetite, for the fresh air and his mother-in-law's cooking had given him one just in time. Indeed, his stomach seemed to have expanded since his arrival in Malikrowik, and his interest in vegetarianism and the simple life was a thing of the past. "Your own mother would be proud of such gravy," remarked Bertha as she watched him take a second helping. Hirshl ate in silence, his eyes on the angry beak of the china goose. Once he glanced up and saw Mina. What on earth, he wondered, was she doing there?

Mina looked thin and pale. She ate little, and the little that she ate did not stick to her bones. Did she think she had to diet all her life so her tailored clothes would go on fitting her? Not that Hirshl did not like having a wife who dressed well. Still, he would have liked even better having one who ate a bit. Though he himself had grown up in a wealthy home and had never gone without anything, much less without three meals a day, so that, unlike some people, he was not obsessed with food, he still could not help noticing that Mina ate less than she left on her plate. After all, she was his wife and her health was his business.

The servant girl cleared away the dishes and brought them plum tarts for dessert. Mina, thought Hirshl, had not even finished the bread and honey she had started with; who could possibly expect her to eat a plum tart? All that cologne, he felt sure, must be spoiling her appetite.

A fly landed on Mina's slice of bread and was trapped for a moment in the honey. Fighting free, it paused to rest on her plum tart. She shielded her face with one hand and pushed away the tart with the other.

The dogs began to bark. Someone was outside. Bertha went to quiet them and ushered several visitors from Szybusz into the sukkah, where she set food before them and urged them to bless it and eat. Clearly they were knowledgeable Jews, for though they had dined already, they did not refuse what she brought them but ate and drank again in order to recite the blessing over sitting in a sukkah. True, there were rabbis who held that the blessing could be said without partaking of food, the main thing being the sukkah itself, but it was best, the guests explained to Gedalia, to be on the safe side. Though it was by no means the first time Gedalia had heard this question debated, his respect for learning was such that he listened as avidly as though it were.

"The divine serenity of this place," said one of the guests when he was done eating, "is something I envy you. Why, if it weren't for the dogs one might think this heaven on earth!"

An agreeable tranquillity did envelop the sukkah. Hearing her home compared to heaven was music to Bertha's ears. Gedalia looked down and half stifled a sigh as he prayed that he might indeed be found worthy of Paradise and not of hell. He was once again beset by the fear that this life had been kind to him only so that he might be roasted all the more thoroughly in the next. Nevertheless, he was glad to have guests. It was known that the spirits of the Seven Patriarchs who came to visit the sukkah of each Jew liked seeing nothing better than hospitality.

The sun was going down. The eastward shadow thrown by the sukkah grew longer. The visitors said the grace after meals, rose to go, and exclaimed with an upward glance:

"What a fine holiday, what weather we've had! Just see how when Jews sit in their sukkahs, God sends them sunny days!"

They started back for Szybusz just as the peasants were coming in from the fields. A chorus of animal sounds, bird calls, and human song carried from the gardens of the houses. Storks circled high above, ready for their long journey, and the village girls stopped singing to look at them. The sky turned color after color, then faded and grew dark.

Gedalia stepped outside, looked up at the sky, and said, "Still no sign of rain. We haven't had a Sukkos like this, without a meal rained out in years. How charitable the Lord is to us."

He took his prayer book and went to say the evening prayer. Then supper was served and they all sat down to eat. Gedalia opened his book again and blessed the spirits of the Patriarchs in the whisper of a man charged with greeting honored guests and afraid of being too familiar.

While they were eating, several Jews from the village stopped by to pay their respects to the young couple. They had a bite to eat, sat with them for a while, and left.

Mina returned to her room and Hirshl went out for a stroll around the barnyard. Stach was attending to his horses, talking to himself. "What I was saying," he continued out loud to Hirshl when he saw him, "is that that God of yours must think a great deal of you folks to give you such fine days and nights for your holidays. I don't suppose by any chance you smoke, sir, do you?"

Hirshl took out a pack of cigarettes, gave one to Stach, took another for himself, and looked up at the sky.

Stach bent to rub a horse's belly and said, "I'd say that the moon's too far off to give us a light, wouldn't you?" He produced a strip of tinder, struck a flint, lit it, and then lit the two cigarettes.

A woman's footsteps echoed in the yard. Hirshl gave a start. "Who's that?" he asked.

Stach grinned. "Oh, just one of your fraid-to-be-alone-at-night-by-herself types. I reckon her legs will find her company enough."

The woman saw the young master talking to Stach and slipped away. Hirshl said good night and went to rejoin Mina.

18

THE FEAST OF TABERNACLES ended, and Hirshl and Mina went home. That same day Gedalia sent them enough firewood, potatoes, cabbages, broad beans, kidney beans, fresh and dried fruit, and smoked meat to last the winter. Tsirl was quite right when she said that, if for no other reason, Mina needed a house of her own just to put all her father's gifts in.

Through the parting of its white curtains, which were trimmed down the middle with red, Hirshl and Mina's snug apartment looked out on a triangular world. Mina, however, rarely stood by the window. Why bother looking out when everything was so cozy within? She and Hirshl were a couple. They may not have been all that happy, yet they were far from the opposite too, and they lived in comfort and lacked nothing.

One night Gedalia Ziemlich dropped by. Mina sat knitting a sweater by the lit lamp on the tablecloth. Gedalia looked at her and thought, Why, it's barely three months since I bought her a whole trousseau and she's already making herself more clothes. He hung his head guiltily and asked, "Do you need anything?"

Mina laid her knitting in her lap and considered out loud. "Do we need anything? We get cocoa, coffee, sugar, rice, kasha, oil, and kerosene from the store. We get butter, cheese, eggs, chicken, and chicken fat from you. What more could we need?"

Gedalia Ziemlich ran a hand back and forth across his beard. For the first time in months he did not have to rush through his visit. Little by little his beard fanned out until it resembled the Kaiser Franz Josef's, except that the Kaiser's was forked in the middle while Gedalia's was all of one piece.

Though Gedalia had much on his mind these days, he could not bring himself to say it. Despite his satisfaction with Hirshl and Mina, he was a more and more worried man. Sooner or later, if not today then tomorrow, the Creditor would call in His debt and expect to be paid with back interest.

Tsirl popped in, as was her custom, to see what the children were having for supper. "There *is* one more thing that you need," she observed, overhearing Mina. "A new lock on your pantry to protect it from your maid and all her lovers!"

Just as Gedalia was about to leave, in walked Hirshl and Bertha. Why not, Hirshl suggested, ask his in-laws to have supper with them? Why not, suggested Mina, ask her in-laws too? Boruch Meir was sent for, and they all sat down together. From then on, whenever the Ziemlichs were in town they were joined at the young Hurvitzes' by Tsirl and Boruch Meir and a good time was had by all.

These meals were truly enjoyable. When they sat chatting around the round table in its new chairs, both Hirshl's and Mina's parents felt that, although their houses had grown emptier, their families had grown larger. And though the upholstered chairs in Boruch Meir's house may have been more comfortable to sit in than the wicker ones in Hirshl and Mina's, wicker did have the advantage of being easily moved about the room.

"Just look at the niggardly times we live in," said Boruch Meir, wiggling his fingers through the back of a chair. "They make chairs nowadays with more holes in them than straw. I wouldn't be surprised if one day soon they make them with no backs at all."

Gedalia Ziemlich nodded. There was nothing in the world that Boruch Meir did not have a clever opinion on.

Hirshl lit a cigarette and smoked it like a grandee in front of his elders while Mina drove its smoke away with her hand. Boruch Meir asked Hirshl for a cigarette too, lit it, took several puffs, stubbed it out, scoffed that he never could see what the pleasure was in smoking, and inspected the hairs of his beard to make sure that they had not turned black from the smoke.

"How is the count's brother?" Tsirl asked Gedalia.

Gedalia gave her a puzzled look, as if it escaped him what there possibly could be to ask about.

"The one who has his cigarettes made in Paris," Tsirl prompted.

"He and the count had a quarrel," said Bertha.

"What, counts quarrel too?" asked Tsirl.

"Brothers do," said Bertha. "It seems that the count's brother lit one of his cigarettes from Paris with a match when there was already a lit candle on the table, and the count cursed him out for being wasteful. The upshot is that the count has sworn to bequeath his whole estate to the Church when he dies."

Boruch Meir wiggled his fingers through the back of his chair again and said, "I'll bet these first were made of solid straw and had the holes cut in them afterwards."

"Leave it to Boruch Meir," said Tsirl. "Do you mean to tell me that if the two don't make up, the whole estate goes to the priests?"

"The priests will get their share whether they make up or not," said Bertha. "You needn't worry about them, my dear."

"I have worries enough of my own, thank God," said Tsirl. "Tell me, Mina, when is that maid of yours serving supper? I think I'll go see what she's making."

The maid was making potato pancakes, and though this was a dish that Tsirl must have eaten a thousand times in her life, she stared at it as if there were no greater delicacy, asked for the recipe, and hung on every word with her mouth wide open as if in anticipation of a rare treat.

"These pancakes," said the maid when she had finished describing them, "are a favorite of Mr. Gildenhorn's."

Tsirl sighed. "That Gildenhorn travels so much that he must eat new foods every day." Her eyes had a far-off look. The world might be full of fine things, yet not everyone had the luck to enjoy them.

Boruch Meir looked lovingly at Tsirl. Her round, rosily tinged face with its head of dark hair seemed suddenly changed to him. Indeed, each time he looked at her he discovered something new. His glance passed to Hirshl, who had not put on weight and was as thin as on the day of his wedding.

Bertha seemed to read Boruch Meir's thoughts. "If Hirshl would come stay with us in Malikrowik," she said, "we'd fatten him up for you."

Hirshl reddened. Had his mother-in-law really kept tabs of all he ate in her house? He glanced at Mina and declared, "I know someone who was born in Malikrowik and still weighs less than a spider leg."

"The automatic spoon has yet to be invented," said Boruch Meir with a smile. "But anyone not too lazy to lift his spoon to his mouth is in no danger of going hungry at your mother-in-law's."

"Your maid," said Tsirl without stopping eating, "is a wonderful cook and human being. Keep a good, good eye on her, Mina, because human beings have a way of walking off with things."

Mina was startled. All her life she had been watched out for by others, and now she was being told to watch out for someone herself.

The maid came back into the room. Tsirl regarded her genially and said, "Have you come to bring us more good things to eat?"

"There's a Mr. Kurtz at the door," said the maid.

"Goodness me!" cried Tsirl happily. "Come in, Mr. Toyber, do come in."

"I believe the girl said Kurtz," Bertha said.

"I'm so glad it's Toyber," said Tsirl loudly. "If it weren't, I wouldn't let him in, because this is strictly a family occasion. But Toyber is like one of the family."

"I'll come another time," Kurtz was heard to tell the maid as he departed.

"The poor fellow," said Bertha. "How humiliating for him."

"But how can you say that, my dear?" Tsirl asked. "Didn't I say how glad I was that he was here?"

"That Toyber was here," said Hirshl. "But it wasn't Toyber, it was Kurtz."

"You can't tell me that you wouldn't have been happy to see Toyber," Tsirl said.

"But we're talking about Kurtz!" exclaimed Hirshl.

"Oh, you mean the young man who danced beneath the handkerchief," said Tsirl. "Whatever became of him?"

"Do you think I remember if it was under the handkerchief or over it?" Hirshl asked.

"Well, I thought he was marvelous," said Tsirl. "I doubt if you'll find another like him."

In the end Bertha too was glad that Kurtz had gone away. Being together was nicer without the presence of strangers, especially on a mid-October night when it was already cold out, though the fireplace had not yet been lit. As long as they were inside together the cold was barely noticeable, but an outsider would have brought it in with him.

Gedalia cocked his head. "I hear our horses," he said.

"Why is that Stach in such a hurry?" asked Bertha, smothering a yawn with her hand.

"I don't hear anything," Tsirl said.

"Nor I," said Boruch Meir. "Not a hoofbeat. Wait, just a minute: yes, that's a horse whinnying."

"But whose horse?" asked Tsirl. "How do you know it's yours, Gedalia?"

"Father and his horses know each other," said Mina.

Gedalia gave her a fond nod.

"That," said Tsirl, "is when they can see each other. But how can he recognize them by the sound they make when he's in here and they're out there? You can't expect me to believe that, Mina."

Stach curbed the horses, climbed down from the carriage, and struck his hands together to warm them. Not that it was winter yet, but it was time to get ready for it.

Indeed, winter was soon upon them. The warm, bright sun grew pale and cold, and the merry outings of summer gave way to long, somber hours of sitting at home. Rain and snow followed one another, driven by strong winds. If one was lucky enough to have them, it was a time to be with one's friends before a roaring fire in a brightly lit home.

Hirshl seemed like another person. He enjoyed having company, and company felt comfortable with him. Even people who did not seem to be his type grew accustomed to dropping in on him and Mina, whether singly or in groups. Even Kurtz, whom Hirshl did not especially like and Mina could not abide, was a frequent visitor. Surely it was not just his habit of pinching off bits of bread and rolling them between his fingers that made Mina dislike Kurtz, who had been, after all, the first to congratulate her on her engagement; since dislike him she did, however, Hirshl felt obliged to go out of his way to be nice to him.

So transformed was Hirshl that he was now even on first-name terms with Sophia Gildenhorn, who called him Heinrich. Sophia was at Mina's constantly. She liked to be with what she thought of as young people, for though she was only two years Mina's senior, she seemed to herself, having been married first, much older. Nevertheless, she still always left as soon as Hirshl returned from the store. God in heaven knew why. Perhaps it was to give Hirshl and Mina a chance to be alone together.

Sometimes Mina snuggled close to Hirshl and whispered in his ear. Not that there was anything wrong with what she said, but it did make him feel cornered, and no music is sweet to a cornered man. Do I mind her? he asked himself. No more than I mind anyone. It's just that she's always around. It's like having to wear a coat all the time that never keeps you warm.

19

GOD IN HEAVEN knew what was the matter with Mina. Her
mood was sometimes better and sometimes worse, but better
or worse she gave Hirshl no peace. Suddenly, even if he was
on his way out, or in the middle of a book, let alone simply
standing about, she would interrupt him by saying things like,
"Swear to me that you'll never breathe a word of it and I'll tell
you something that happened to me before we were married."
Hirshl would swear and Mina would tell; yet just as it baffled
her how her and her ex-girlfriends' secrets could leave him so
cold, so he failed to grasp what point she saw in such trivia. In
the end she would accuse him of not loving her, since if he did
he would care about her past.

The mornings were worst. No sooner did Mina awake than
she had to tell Hirshl about some dream of hers, which would
be forgotten before she ever told it. Just as he was about to
leave for the store, however, she would remember it—or
rather, not it but them, for she had had, it seemed, a whole
slew of dreams, each single one of which, between one yawn
and the next, she felt compelled to relate. Not that her dreams
were that long; it was more her manner of telling them. If she
dreamed of ants, for example, she would insist on describing
them ant by ant until Hirshl could feel his skin crawl with
them and even detect their odor, which was like that of Mina's
bath lotion. He was sure that, when he rolled up his sleeve in
the synagogue to bind his tefillin to his arm, everyone would
smell it.

It was hard to say if Mina was getting heavy or wasting
away. Though she had never been especially robust, she now
looked quite delicately frail. She could no longer stand her

favorite foods, yet sometimes she had cravings for dishes she had never tasted in her life, and she had spells of fainting and nausea and suffered from headaches and toothaches. At the same time, although she fought it and corseted herself more tightly than ever to prevent her pregnancy from showing, her stomach was swelling and her limbs were filling out. The plump, good-natured maid now slept by her side, made her hot drinks all the time, gave her frequent little baths, and hovered over her constantly while talking in low tones so as not to excite her, since too much emotion was bad for both mother and child.

Tsirl was exuberant. Only yesterday, it seemed, she had been nursing a child of her own, and here she was soon to be a grandmother. Bertha too could not get over that her baby daughter was about to have a baby, while as for Sophia, she sometimes clapped her hands and said things that Mina had never heard her say before. Sophia too wanted children; yet as long as her husband kept gallivanting about, how could she expect to have them? Once she had imagined she was pregnant and once she actually had been, yet the chicken she was counting on had failed to hatch. Mina, on the other hand, was growing round as a sachet bag from day to day.

Bertha all but moved in with the young couple and lived more in town than in the village. She spent most of her days with Mina and often slept at night in the spare room that had been set aside for the infant that Mina was carrying. If anything, however, this gave Hirshl more breathing room, for now, when Mina awoke in her bed, where she passed much of her time drowsing, she reached out not to him but to Bertha, who came running at once as if her daughter's yawns were the most eloquent of appeals for assistance. Indeed, when a bundled-up Mina lay sleeping amid her mountains of quilts and pillows in the overheated room that smelled of toilet water, her mother and maid awaiting her beck and call, she resembled a sickly infant herself being treated with potions, vapors, and incense by two witch doctors, who attended her every waking word as if it were a pagan oracle's.

Mina was far from blind. Though she had never been in love, she knew what love was not. Once, when the two of them were waiting for Sophia to arrive, she said to Hirshl, "I know what's on your mind. You're thinking about Sophia."

"What makes you think I'm thinking about Sophia?" asked Hirshl.

"I just know you are. You wish she were here already."

"Why should I wish she were here?"

"So as not to have to be alone with me. I bore you."

"Do you think I'm bored?" asked Hirshl.

"What do you take me for? You wish I were dead."

"Why should I wish you were dead?"

"You just do."

"Nobody just wishes his wife were dead."

"Nobody who loves her," said Mina.

"And somebody who doesn't love her does?"

"That's just what I was waiting to hear from you, dear."

"What were you waiting to hear?" asked Hirshl.

"That you don't love me."

"I don't?"

"Didn't you just say that if you loved your wife you wouldn't wish she were dead?"

"Supposing I did," said Hirshl. "Does that mean I don't love you?"

"If you loved me you wouldn't have said it."

"What would I have said?"

"If you loved me," said Mina, "you wouldn't even have thought it. Or would you say I'm wrong and that you do care for me a tiny bit after all? You're a smart boy, Heinrich: you know I'm no worse than other women and that you won't find another wife like me even if I do die. Do you hear me, darling? But I have no intention of dying, not even for your sake, because your next wife won't make you any happier. Do you think Sophia's better than I am? Well, she's not. Oh, she seems likable enough, but if you knew her as I do you'd realize that's just on the surface. She learned to get on people's good side helping her father sell lottery tickets, which is lower than

I'd ever stoop, because I come from an honest family that's earned its keep by hard work, not by flattery. Why, when I think of how my father started out as a milkman with a route, I feel proud of him! And my own children won't go looking for an easy living either but will support themselves like he's done without bowing and scraping. Oh, how miserable I am! Come here, Heinrich, give me a kiss. No, not on the forehead, darling, I'm not a dowager queen. On the mouth. Or was that the last kiss you had left? Looking at you, a person might think every kiss cost a fortune."

Like any well-bred Szybuszian, Hirshl was proud of his family. It may not have been descended from the celebrated Yeshaya Leib Hurvitz, but it was highly thought of nonetheless, and though until now he had refrained from boasting of it, Mina's reference to her father made him do so. It was doubtful, however, whether he made much of an impression on her, perhaps because he soon got onto the subject of his mother's brother, whom his surprised wife had never heard of, so that he said to her:

"If you ask me, my uncle was perfectly sane and just pretending to be crazy, because otherwise his father, that is, my grandfather Shimon Hirsh, whom I'm named after, would have married him off to some woman he didn't love and made him waste the rest of his life on her, raising a house full of her little darlings, and making lots of money, and getting filthy rich, and being disgustingly respectable. There may be nothing wrong with all that, but I tell you, it would have left him an empty shell of a man. If my uncle had managed to make something of himself on his own, everyone would have said how clever he was. Since he didn't, everyone thought he was crazy. Nothing ever turns out the way we'd like it to. Our lives aren't our own, Mina, and others do what they please with them. You can be the same person you always were, and yet suddenly you can do nothing right, even though you're doing what you've always done. The fact is that nobody cares who you really are. One day you're told to do this and the next day that, and in the end you just do whatever it is and lose all respect for yourself, which everyone else has already done long ago. I've thought a lot about this, Mina, and there's a lot that I could tell you, only it's already past your bedtime. I will say this, though, and that's that if I feel empty inside, what does anything else matter? You look so sad, Mina. I swear I didn't mean to make you feel that way. It makes me sad to think of my uncle too, even though it happened years ago. Well, let me tell you something funny, then. Do you see that fat volume in the bookcase? It's a Hebrew dictionary. The man who compiled it was married off when he was young to some woman he didn't even know, as was the custom in those days. Do you know what he did? When he grew a little older and decided to get rid of her, he took the cat one morning and put his tefillin on it. Just imagine it, Mina: his wife and her parents were so frightened that they agreed to a divorce at once. After that he married a woman of his choice and lived with her happily ever after. I don't know if he still puts on tefillin every day, but I'm sure he leaves the cat alone."

Hirshl was wrong if he thought this story would cheer Mina up. Unlike Hirshl, Mina had been educated in a boarding school, and before that by Polish tutors in the village, and had no interest in Hebrew dictionaries. One day, in fact, when the dictionary fell by mistake while she was taking down a book from the shelf, she nudged it along the floor with her foot until it vanished beneath the bookcase.

Hirshl was fed up with so many people dropping in. Though for a while after his wedding he had welcomed having guests, he no longer was glad to see them. He had liked entertaining because he had enjoyed having a home of his own to play host in; now that his home had lost its charms for him, so had playing host.

The fact of the matter was that even in his entertaining days Hirshl had been of two minds about it, since Mina and he had never liked the same people. Indeed, he had liked whom he did less for themselves or their good qualities than for their being disliked by Mina, which made liking them

128

seem an obligation. This annoyed Mina, who felt that he was groveling before them, so that she treated them even more coolly. Hirshl, for his part, retaliated by snubbing her friends—apart, that is, from Yitzchok Gildenhorn, whom the two of them made an equal fuss over, Mina seeing to it that his favorite pancakes were prepared by the maid and Hirshl breaking out his best wines and cigarettes for him. Hirshl was cordial to Sophia too. Not that he was all that keen on her; yet he did not want Mina to accuse him of slighting her best friend, who, together with her husband, as he was generous enough to remind them, deserved the credit for his and Mina's marriage.

And so people stopped coming, until whole weeks passed with hardly a single visitor. It started with Leibush Tshortkover. Since he only talked about eating and drinking, Leibush might have been expected to keep frequenting a house where he could do as much of either as he pleased, yet he was the first to abandon it. Human nature is unpredictable: though Leibush Tshortkover came from the west of Galicia, while Szybusz lay in the east, and from a family of Bobov Hasidim, a sect that was unknown in the town, where he had felt rejected and frightfully lonely at first, so that, when he was taken up by Gildenhorn, in whose house there were always card games, drinks, and lots of fun, he became his fast friend, he had never cottoned to Hirshl. Evidently it was less the drinks that mattered than the conversation between them.

The next to make himself scarce was Mottshi Shaynbart. "Mind you, Hirshl," he said, "I'd come more often, but the old crutch can't take the stairs anymore." Clearly this was a pretext, the truth of the matter being that, since they made one complete human face between them, Leibush's beard and Mottshi's mustache were inseparable and always went everywhere together.

Kurtz too was seen less and less. As long as Hirshl and Mina's house had been full of guests, being one of them had not made him self-conscious. Now that he was the only one left, he felt out of place and vanished.

Kurtz came from a well-to-do home and would have been well-to-do himself had he not left it for the poems of Schiller. German poetry, however, proved a poor provider, so that, if not for the religious studies that he remembered from his childhood, which enabled him to obtain a teaching post in the local Baron de Hirsch School, he would have been left high and dry. As it was, the position was unenviable, for since Kurtz knew as well as anyone that religion was taught only so that the school could not be accused of opposing it, what importance did it really have? Seeing his subject considered a waste of time made him feel like a waste of time too, and seeing him feel that way convinced others that he was. Had he bothered to hold his head higher he might have been more highly regarded, but since he would not have topped five feet even then, it hardly seemed worth the effort.

Apart from their parents and Sophia, no one came to Hirshl and Mina's anymore. A silent world could be glimpsed through the triangular parting of the curtains. Sometimes Hirshl stood at one window and Mina at another. It was hard to say if they were looking out or in.

"If you wanted them to come, they would," Mina would reply when Hirshl accused her of driving away their friends. Though he knew she was right, it was easier to blame her than to try winning them back. To make up for the loss, he found himself liking Sophia more than ever, as if she now came only for him. And yet, though it irked him when she too failed to appear, he still sat reading a book when she did.

Sophia was worth having over. She knew what went on in Szybusz as a housewife knows what is cooking in her neighbor's pot. As long as she gossiped in her normal voice there was nothing very lively about her, but as soon as her voice dropped to a whisper both she and Mina became the very soul of animation.

Hirshl stared over his book at Sophia. Though two years older than Mina, she looked two years younger and resembled a still-growing adolescent. As if her sole motive in talking were pleasing her friend, she went on and on as long as Mina let her. Mina's lips were parted and there was a veiled look in her eyes; a pink flush tinted her ears and her earrings glittered in the lamplight. It was uncanny how she could listen.

It was uncanny too how Hirshl could be annoyed by what so recently had given him such pleasure. Barely half a year ago, when he sat talking to Mina in Sophia's house, it had made him glad just to look at her, whereas now the opposite was true. In fact, looking at her was becoming harder and harder. Sometimes her face seemed as white as cotton wool to him; other times still cotton-woolish but crimson; and in either case, such comparisons were not flattering, though whom they flattered less, the husband or the wife, was debatable. Whichever, it was bad for both of them.

Not that Hirshl spent all day with Mina thinking of unpleasant comparisons. Most of the time he was in the store, while each morning he went to pray in the Great Synagogue. He had a great fondness for this high, handsomely decorated building that was vaulted like the heavens inside. He liked its cool stairway that led up to the prayer hall; even more, the hall's ceiling, which lacked supporting columns and seemed to float on thin air; more yet, its stained windows, one for each of the twelve tribes of Israel—and especially its eastern one, which threw a gleaming prism of light on the curtain of the Holy Ark; but most of all, the stone bimah on whose lectern lay an ancient prayer book written on deer vellum that had once long ago, in times of persecution, been handled by men who had martyred themselves in God's name, and which was still prayed from today with the same punctilious, unchanging adherence to each word and melody of tradition. Though Akavia Mazal had written an entire chapter about this synagogue in his book, Yona Toyber knew even more about its history; yet Hirshl no longer sought out Toyber's company. He preferred to be alone with his thoughts and was not looking to share them with anyone. Indeed, he had so many of them that only God in heaven knew them all.

20

HIRSHL HAD NOT SEEN Blume since she left his parents' home. Though each day he hoped she would appear in the store, where the Mazals shopped regularly, she never did. Yet while Blume did not come, Hirshl did not stop thinking of her. He pictured her in the breaks between customers and sometimes, when selling them some item, even imagined making her a present of it. Months went by and still he did not despair. If she won't come by herself, he thought, I'll have to make her.

How could he make her? Hirshl believed that if he thought very hard of someone, concentrating his utmost, that person would be bound to come. No matter how hard he thought of Blume, it was true, there was still no sign of her; but rather than give up, he told himself: I must not have been thinking hard enough, from now on I'll think even harder. It reached the point that he could not abide having his mind taken off her by anything. He waited on customers as though at gunpoint and could hardly bring himself to say a civil word to them.

The Hirshl who had changed so after his marriage had reverted back to type. No one can be who he is not for very long. His once full home was empty. Its only visitor nowadays was young Mrs. Gildenhorn, and since she came to see Mina, Hirshl felt no need to amuse her and sat by himself with his thoughts—one of which, on the day of Blume's birthday, was: A single person was created perfect in this world, and I am not allowed to see her. Though he was about to be a father, Hirshl was still a mere boy.

Tsirl saw that Hirshl was out of sorts and spoke to Boruch Meir about it. Never suspecting that their married son could

132

be pining for Blume, they decided to send him to Malikrowik for a rest.

Being in Malikrowik with Mina, however, did Hirshl no good at all. Indeed, the tranquillity of the village and his mother-in-law's meals bored him to tears and made him even more sluggish and flaccid. If he did not spend his time in front of the fireplace leafing idly through a prayer book, he spent it yawning in front of Mina. A walk in the snow might have worked wonders; yet as the snow fell outside and Hirshl remained within, there was little chance of his taking one.

The winter days were short and the winter nights long—and in the village, where even the days could seem endless, the nights were doubly so, especially as Hirshl had nothing to do with himself. His parents saw that it was a mistake to have sent him to Malikrowik, which, though a lovely spot, was not for him, and, bringing him back to Szybusz, encouraged him to lead a more social life there.

And so Hirshl began again to frequent the Society for Zion clubhouse, which had been renovated in his absence and now had two rooms instead of one, the first for reading and the second for conversation and chess playing, so that the talkers no longer bothered the readers. A small buffet at which one could order a quick snack had been added too. Before one could even say "Yossele," Bendit the carpenter's son of that name would arrive with the coffee, tea, or beer, the sweets or peppered chickpeas that one had asked for.

Hirshl's friends at the club welcomed him back warmly. He may not have been a Zionist, but since when did only Zionists belong to the Society for Zion? People came to it for all sorts of reasons, among them not wanting to pass their evenings in the study house or among the socialists instead.

Once more Hirshl was a member in good standing. As before he paid his monthly dues, to which he added a special contribution when asked for one. Indeed, he was asked often, for war had broken out between Russia and Japan, and the depraved government of the Czar was sending Jewish boys to be killed at the front. Those who could flee the draft or desert

133

did so with nothing but the shirt on their back, and there was not a town in Austrian Galicia without its young Jewish refugees. Anyone whose heart was not made of stone was eager to help; yet not everyone who was eager to help had the means to. Hirshl had them and helped. He was not about to turn down old friends for the first time now. Whatever was asked of him, he came up with.

Hirshl had another sterling quality too, which was that he had no interest in high office and was not competitive about it, so that when the Society had its annual Hanukkah party, for instance, he did not insist on being seated on the dais. Indeed, his modesty was apparent even in his reserve; for whereas his grandfather, Shimon Hirsh Klinger, rarely talked to anyone because there was no one to whom it was worth talking, Hirshl's silence was more a matter of feeling that he himself was unworthy of being listened to.

One way or another, Hirshl was again surrounded by the companions who had sat with him in the schoolroom and the study house until they had put away their books and gone into business, some with their parents and some for themselves. Most of them had put away their traditional black garb too and now went about in modern dress. Once a small town of millers and moneylenders, Szybusz had become a commercial center surrounded by nearly a hundred villages whose prolific growers of wheat, barley, oats, and beans had come to realize that, rather than stay up all night at the spinning wheel, they could just as well buy their clothes in town. In fact, people came from other towns to shop in Szybusz, which was almost a small city by now and attracted merchants even from Germany—who, when they arrived, did not bother to tour the Great Synagogue with its sun, moon, and signs of the zodiac, the old study house with its Bible glossed by a cardinal, or any of the other leading sights, but spent their time doing business, eating and drinking in the taverns, and sitting in the Society for Zion clubhouse, where they glanced at the headlines and advertisements in the newspapers while skipping over the political columns and the parliamentary reports that were perused by the local intelligentsia. Several youngsters in Szybusz had even taken to aping these foreigners—and indeed, anyone not hopelessly narrow-minded might well have been proud of the fact that, whereas once all of Szybusz had bought tickets for the performance of a single chanteuse, there were now young men in town with their own private harems of such performers, a night with one of whom cost more than the money raised in a year by the Needy Brides Charity Fund or the cigarettes ordered from Paris by the Count of Malikrowik's younger brother. Why, even the "nebbichlach" of Sebastian Montag, the town's leading citizen, were so much beef on the hoof compared to these artistes, some of whom had even been written up by the press!

It would be too much to say that Hirshl enjoyed the Society for Zion clubhouse, but it did give him somewhere to be besides the store and his home, so that, on evenings when Mina was not expecting him, he went there straight from work. In this he was not alone, for the membership of the club had changed. Not only had it grown larger, it was now for the most part composed of married men like himself, whether because Zionism had made further inroads or because the members of former years had aged. Whichever, there was much less singing than there used to be. The youngsters who had once spent their evenings pouring out their hearts in song now had too many cares and children, while the new generation did not appear to be musical and preferred to talk politics or play chess.

Sometimes Yona Toyber dropped in at the club. He would remove his hat, place it on the chair in front of him, lay half a cigarette that he had carefully divided in its crease, insert the other half in a holder, and sit watching the young men play chess. Not that he himself was a chess player or even (though he knew practically by heart the whole of Ya'akov Eichenboym's Hebrew chess manual *Sefer ha-K'rav*) a kibitzer, but his method of doing business had changed. Once, when a young man came of age, his father had told Toyber what girl he had in mind and Toyber had taken care of the rest; now, however, it was the young man himself who Toyber had to hear from and the parents who had to be convinced.

(And yet when Hirshl was engaged to Mina, the reader may ask, did not the idea come from Tsirl? Indeed it did. Either the world was changing very quickly, or else Hirshl's engagement was already passé when it took place.)

As in the past, Hirshl borrowed three books from the librarian's unlocked bookcase on Monday and Thursday nights. He did not, however, read them but let them lie gathering dust in his home. And though four candles burned at his parents' on Sabbath eves, one for Boruch Meir, one for Tsirl, one for Mina, and one for himself, none burned in Blume's old room, for Blume now lit her candle elsewhere and the new maid stepped out as soon as the dishes were done. Like the marriage of many an educated young man, Hirshl's had put an end to his reading days. Even if Mina picked up one of his books, he never discussed it with her. Hirshl was as silent as was Blume's room without the sound of her footsteps.

He soon grew tired of the clubhouse. There was something rather odd about seeking out company yet making no effort to talk to it, which was what Hirshl, who sat lost in thought, chose to do. Indeed, when spoken to by anyone he gave a guilty start as if caught doing something he should not have been.

Yet talk was everywhere: in the store, at home, at the club. The only sensible way to avoid it would have been to go to the study house, wrap his prayer shawl around him, and sit there saying nothing all day long.

Sheer force of habit kept Hirshl going two or three times a week to the clubhouse, where he sometimes glanced at the newspaper without realizing that he had already read the same news. And the next day in the store, listening to some customer tell it again, he would wonder, Now where have I heard that before?

Gradually he went to the club less and less. Sometimes he set out for it and turned back halfway there. In the end he stopped going altogether.

21

IT WAS THE OPINION of Tsirl's sensible friends that while there were people who liked to be with people, there were others who preferred to be by themselves and needed to take regular walks. The mother of the town's new doctor, who was one of Tsirl's customers, agreed. In fact, she said to Tsirl, a young man of more or less Hirshl's age who had come to consult her son was told by him: "No prescription that I can give you will be half as good for you as a bit of fresh air." Tsirl mulled the matter over and finally broached it to Hirshl.

Hirshl was neither for nor against it. Although in theory it seemed a fine idea, in practice he was not quite sure what it meant. On a wall of the Gildenhorns' home was a picture of a slim young man in a colorful jacket, the tails of which were flapping in the wind; he wore a pink top hat, carried a rattan cane, and was in the act of striding forward with one leg, beneath which was written, "The Walker." If that's what my mother has in mind for me, wondered Hirshl, when and where does she expect me to do it?

Tsirl kept after him, though. "Hirshl," she said to him in the store one evening, handing him his walking stick as it was getting dark out, "why don't you go out for a walk? Put on your jacket and get some fresh air so that you'll have an appetite for supper." Hirshl put on his jacket, took his stick, and stepped out into the street. From then on, a little before closing time each day, his mother handed him his walking stick and said, "Here, put on your jacket and take a nice walk."

At first Hirshl found these constitutionals tiresome. The exercise was dull and made him sore all over. No sooner did he set out than his feet, shoulders, side, or even whole body began to ache. It was difficult to adjust to a street beneath his feet when he was used to a roof above his head, especially when that street led nowhere.

Eventually, however, Hirshl found a destination for his walks in an outlying section of town. Sometimes he would reach it in a roundabout manner and sometimes he headed straight there. If he met someone he knew on the way he would do his best to get rid of him, while if this proved impossible, he would walk with him back to the marketplace, take his leave of him there, and set out again. As soon as he arrived, like an alcoholic sneaking a drink and afraid of being discovered, he looked for a place to hide.

Though it had no synagogue, the street that Hirshl was on was known as Synagogue Street, there being a local tradition that the first Jewish house of worship in Szybusz had stood on the spot where the Catholic church was now situated. In fact, one sagging wall of the church, which was older and lower than the others, was said to have belonged to the original structure. This wall, legend had it, was bent in sorrow over its fate and, on the night of the Ninth of Av, the day of mourning for the destruction of the Temple, shed real tears like the Wailing Wall in Jerusalem.

Szybusz was an ancient site and had been lived in by Jews from the earliest times until its destruction in 1648 by Chmielnitsky's Ukrainians, who burned the synagogue to the ground. When the town was rebuilt by the Polish Count Potocki, the Jews were not only permitted to come back but were exempted from all duties and taxes for a period of twelve years, after which they were to pay a levy of a thaler per household and half a thaler per hearth every year, as determined by a Jewish assessor. Their butchers too were excused from the slaughter of pigs, in lieu of which they were required to bring a bucket of tallow and a side of beef to the castle of the count every Friday. These obligations met, the returnees were declared free to buy houses, to manufacture salt, beer, brandy, and wine, and to engage in any trade that they desired, and were subject only to the personal court of the count, which conferred on them the right to elect their own rabbis and leaders in accordance with their own laws.

It stood to reason that Synagogue Street, bounded as it was at its upper end by the ruins of the count's castle, which had been subsequently sacked by Tatars, and at its lower end by the river, had once been inhabited by Jews. In fact, it was the fear of a Tatar raid (against which the castle protected them on the land side and offered them refuge if it came by water) that had caused Jews to build their homes there in the first place. Nowadays, however, not a single Jew lived on the street except for Akavia Mazal. Its few, low thatched houses, small and scattered amid clumps of trees and greenery, were lived in mostly by government clerks, only some of whom Hirshl knew—and even those but slightly, for though they shopped at his parents', he took little notice of them. Perhaps this was because they were not sent large gift packages at Christmas but were paid off in person, bribing a lowly official being a much simpler affair than bribing a superintendent or department head. After spending all day in an office they came home at night to Synagogue Street and shut themselves up once again, so that, apart from one of their wives stepping out to draw water, or one of their daughters slipping off to meet a beau, Hirshl never saw a living soul there.

Although the profound silence of the night might have seemed scary to a city boy like Hirshl, he was hardly even aware of it. If he saw a pair of lovers approaching, he turned his head away and so did they, neither party wishing to be seen. Even the dogs, which at first had barked at him, now merely growled in acknowledgment when he passed.

As quiet as a mouse, Hirshl walked down Synagogue Street. What was he thinking of? Indeed, there was much he might have thought of, for much had happened to his ancestors in this place. Not long before the birth of his great-great-grandfather, for example, a local landowner had cast a wagonful of Jews on their way to Szybusz for the penitential prayers of Elul into the river, whose unappeased waters were said to rise so high each autumn that only the Tashlich service said on

139

Rosh Hashanah kept them from flooding the town. In the forest across the river, on the other hand, stood a ruined Catholic convent in which the miscreant Chmielnitsky's troops had raped six hundred nuns in one night, so that the grass grew red there to this day. Yet though Hirshl was not unmindful of such events, they were far from uppermost in his mind. He was not, after all, a chronicler of human misery, which was something that he gladly left to Akavia Mazal, in whose house Blume lived. How was she making out there? Since the day she left his parents he had not spoken a word to her.

Hirshl could not have spoken a word to Blume, because the two of them had had no chance to meet. Now that he stood facing the house in which she lived, though, what was to keep him from doing it?

Every evening before closing time Tsirl handed Hirshl his walking stick and urged him to go for a walk. No longer were these excursions odious, for they had become second nature to him. Sometimes he made a circuit of the town before coming to Synagogue Street, and sometimes he went straight to Akavia Mazal's house, which he scrutinized from every angle. Though he had never been inside it and did not know its layout, something told him that the light in the northernmost window was Blume's. Like a man waiting for the heavens to open so that he might beg them for mercy, Hirshl stood facing that window. What did he wish to beg for? For Blume to look out and see him.

It felt good to be out-of-doors by himself on a quiet summer night and to forget about the store with its cartons and crates that were everywhere; about its customers who breathed all over him while vying obsequiously for his attention; about his mother who sat by the entrance buttering them up; and about Mina waiting for him to come home at closing time. Of course, he could have gone to the Society for Zion club too, where one could read the newspapers and chat, but Hirshl preferred to walk down the peaceful street while the stars shone down on its houses in their setting of trees, the night breeze brushed his face, and the water flowed gently in the river, from whose far bank came the good smell of the forest. Not even the rain could spoil his pleasure. The harder it fell, the longer he stayed out in it.

It seemed odd to Tsirl that Hirshl should insist on walking in the rain. Yet since she knew that he was a creature of habit who might stop his walks entirely if he missed even one of them, she said nothing to him about it. On such nights Hirshl donned his overcoat, turned up his collar, took along an umbrella, and set out. He liked the steady drumming of the raindrops that kept time with his thoughts and allowed him the privacy of them by drowning out all other sounds. He still believed that will power could bring two people together. If I keep thinking of Blume, he told himself, she will have to appear. Of course, this method had failed him so far, yet it had done so, Hirshl was convinced, because the customers in the store kept distracting him. Out in the rainy street there was nothing to spoil his concentration.

At this point, however, a fresh obstacle appeared in the person of Getzel Stein, whom Hirshl twice spied standing by Akavia Mazal's house. Though he did not think that Getzel was following him, he betook himself elsewhere and refrained from coming back.

22

GETZEL STEIN, THE SUBJECT of this chapter, worked in the Hurvitzes' store and dreamed of Blume. Yet his dreams, like any that fail to come true, were unhappy.

Although a mere shopboy, Getzel was officially called a salesman, the word shopboy having fallen into disrepute. (Not that being a salesman was any different from being a shopboy, but in the time it took to realize as much a shopboy's stature could rise.) Getzel himself, though, needed no such titles, for even without them he was an active young man with ambitious plans for the future—and though none of these had as yet been fulfilled, he had already played a role in one historical event, namely, the founding of a local chapter of the Workers of Zion Party, of which he was a charter member. Not a few students and even some of their parents supported this party—the parents because, if their children had to be socialists, better the Workers of Zion than the Polish PSP, and the students because, had they joined the PSP, they would have had their parents' servants for comrades.

Most of Szybusz had no use for historical events and simply laughed at the new group. Not everyone made fun of Getzel and his friends, however. A new generation had arisen in town that believed in changing the world. Some of these young people joined the Polish socialists, while others wavered but did not, saved for the Jewish camp in the end by either the religious training of their childhood, the respect still felt for their parents, teachers, and elders, or the wondrous tales about the Land of Israel that had been told them when they were little. Many talked in favor of the Workers of Zion, and some even signed up for it. God in heaven had kept their dreams from leading them astray.

The pro–Workers of Zion faction in Szybusz did more than just talk; it elected a steering committee and invited as its guest speaker the head of the regional organization, a cousin of Sebastian Montag's who could have easily been the chief of all the Zionists in Galicia were it not for his proletarian conscience. Nor was his speech the sole event planned. A gala evening was scheduled along with it, since while a speech could reach only the handful of people who turned out to hear it, a gala evening provided other opportunities as well, such as ushering, decorating, and singing in the choir, all of which, once tasted, created a lifetime appetite for political activity.

Between the store and the Workers of Zion, Getzel led a double existence: if he shirked his work as a shopboy he would anger the Hurvitzes, who were Blume's cousins, while if he neglected the party, what would become of it? Indeed, in honor of the gala evening he had even learned by heart several poems concerning the plight of the Jewish people and the exploitation of the working class. Yet though Getzel had bumbled about like a mooncalf for years before discovering that his true vocation lay in the reciting of poetry, no sooner was this revealed to him than he was forced to give it up, it being pointed out by his comrades that declaiming in public was an honor traditionally reserved for the young ladies. And even then, finding the right young lady was no simple task. If she was well-off enough to be educated, her parents would never allow her to appear before an audience of socialists; while if she was not, what sort of impression would she make? And so, on Getzel's recommendation, the steering committee invited Blume Nacht, who had read a lot of books for a housemaid.

God in heaven knew why Blume turned down the offer. Although Getzel must have asked her a thousand times, she refused to take him seriously even once. And in general, what made her keep a presentable young man like himself, and one who earned an honest living besides, at arm's length? Many a housemaid in Szybusz would have been glad of his company, whereas Blume not only failed to encourage him but actually drove him away. Could it be that her heart was still pledged to Hirshl, even though he was married and no longer free? And yet she had not even come to Hirshl's wedding, at which Getzel had been an honored guest. Worse yet, each time she turned him down it was with that extraordinary smile of hers that could make everything seem of no account, including one's own self.

If Getzel was of no account, however, the fault was not his own but his family's. His father was an ex–chicken slaughterer—that is, a man with a license to slaughter chickens but no chickens willing to be slaughtered—who went from house to house looking for work, which meant pulling at his long sidelocks, chewing on his beard, and coming home in the end without a penny. Getzel's mother had a notions stand in the market and hardly fared better, while the house was kept by his hunchbacked sister, a spiteful creature whose whole body was warped from sheer malice. Besides her there were two other sisters, but these were the bane of Getzel's life, for each of them was as empty-headed as she was pretty. "Where are the girls?" Getzel would ask upon coming home from the store every evening; yet before the hunchback could so much as snap at him, "Where do you think?" he knew what the answer would be, since each day when the sun went down they went off to visit Viktor, the Singer sewing machine agent, a bachelor who lived in rented rooms. Still, Getzel went on asking, for if he did not, who would? Certainly not his father, who saw nothing wrong with his baby daughters getting some enjoyment out of life. Getzel would have liked dearly to enjoy life himself, but he knew the facts of it only too well. A Singer sewing machine agent was here today and gone tomorrow. Just try suing him for breach of promise when you couldn't even find him—and supposing you could, how could two women sue him at once?

Growing up poor without a carefree day in one's life was no pleasure. Though Getzel earned enough in the store to set up house for himself, he was forced to contribute every cent of it to his parents' home, which was sheer hell for him to live in. When his mother was not fighting with his father she fought with his sisters, who fought with each other or with Getzel when she was not around. How he envied his two older brothers who had escaped to America, from where, when implored by their father to have pity and send home a remittance, they had replied that Columbus did not discover the New World for them to bear the old one on their backs.

Getzel sat with a suffering look, eating his supper and reading a socialist tract. He was self-conscious about his lack of education and wished to acquire a better one. As he had never learned much in the schoolroom and had forgotten what little he had, whatever he read seemed new to him. And though the literature he possessed was meager, there was still much he could glean from it.

The small lamp, whose wick was bent and sooty, gave hardly any light. The hunchback sat at her sewing machine, making herself underclothes. It was enough for her to ruin her eyes slaving for others all day; at night she was her own boss and could sew what she pleased. The machine seemed on the verge of giving out. The flywheel creaked and groaned; yet when his sister saw Getzel cover his ears in an effort to concentrate, she jiggled her leg to make it creak even louder. Meanwhile his mother, having finished banging about with her pots, struggled noisily into her boots and began mopping the floor with a wet rag until the whole house felt uncomfortably damp.

She was not yet done when Getzel's father came home in unusually high spirits and declared, "Well, well, if it isn't my socialist! Tell me, why don't you make me a brand-new world in which the chickens will line up to be slaughtered? Only I suppose that in any world that you made, no one would know a kosher chicken from a pig."

It was intolerable for Getzel to have to endure such torture. He would have given anything for a quiet corner to share with people like himself who wished only to read a book or newspaper in peace with a modicum of mutual respect.

Getzel had a vision of the good days to come when he and his friends in the Workers of Zion would sit talking like human beings in a club of their own. He rose, went to his corner of the room, and drew back the curtain that hid his clothes.

"Are you looking for your new tie?" asked his sister.

"As a matter of fact," said Getzel, "I am."

"Well, you needn't bother."

"What do you mean, I needn't bother?"

"Not," said the hunchback, "that you aren't welcome to look for it if you'd like to."

"Where is my tie?" shouted Getzel.

"It's at Viktor's. Saltshi wore it there to show him what good taste you have. She dresses like a man anyway."

By now Getzel's father had sat down to eat at the head of the table. His mother, who consumed only medicines, stood at the stove brewing some potion while looking wrathfully at her husband enjoying his food and, to her great annoyance, ignoring her completely. She would have liked to let out a great scream. Of all possible livelihoods, God had given her the one with the smallest profit and the biggest aggravation, namely, selling buttons, bows, bangles, needles, and hairpins in the marketplace—and yet as bitter as she felt, she knew that if she started to scream she would never be able to stop and that her voice must be saved for hawking her wares. Angrily she stirred her brew in silence, waiting in vain for it to get done, for the wood in the stove was still green and sputtered like potatoes in hot oil.

The hunchback sat by her machine on the windowsill and regarded the wood that refused to burn for her mother with an odd satisfaction. Meanwhile Getzel's father, seeking to head off the scream that had formed on his wife's lips, said to Getzel, "Why don't you study a page of Talmud instead of reading that rubbish?"

He pawed Getzel's books as he spoke, dribbling food and liquid on them from his beard while glancing at his wife as if to say, See, I do everything for your sake.

Getzel's mother, however, declared, "You're afraid that when you're dead and buried he won't know enough Talmud to intercede for your soul, eh? Well, whether he does or doesn't, you won't get any further in the next world than you have in this one. Getzel, it's high time you left this den of murderers and ran away to America like your brothers instead of wasting your life here like I did. Just look at him, will you! The man pretends to slaughter chickens, but all he's ever slaughtered is his own wife and children!"

Just as Getzel's mother knew what it was like to sit in the marketplace all day, so she knew how it felt for Getzel to stand in the Hurvitzes' store until he was falling off his feet and then

146

to come home to a father and sisters who only rubbed salt in his wounds. Mother and son understood each other. Each day Getzel passed her in the marketplace, huddled in her old rags while she waited for the customers to come. A wretched sight when they did not, she was hardly less so when they did and she had to contort her wrinkled face into a smile for them, even her laughter sounding like a groan. Were he not so sorry for her, he would have taken her advice and made off to America long ago. But what would the poor woman do without him? If only with God's help he could find a wife, set up a house of his own, and have his mother come live with him.

Yet what peace could Getzel's mother have even then as long as her daughters were not married? The hunchback was no cause for concern. She was mean and ugly enough to stay out of trouble, although an old widower or divorcé asking for her hand would not be getting a bad bargain, since her chest was full of the clothes that she had made for herself at night and the money that she earned by day. What about his other two sisters, though?

Such was Getzel Stein, whom Hirshl saw standing in front of Akavia Mazal's house. And though Hirshl did not suspect him of having been sent by his mother to spy on him, he was wise to betake himself elsewhere. Getzel may not have been there because of Tsirl, but he was not there by accident either, for he was sweet on Blume himself. It was just as well for Hirshl that Getzel did not see him keeping vigil by her house.

23

BEFORE MANY DAYS had passed, though, Hirshl returned to his old haunts. His world had shrunk so that almost nothing was left of it but the street on which Blume lived.

Once more he circled Akavia Mazal's house, his eyes on the candle burning in the north window. God in heaven knew whose light it was. Most likely it belonged to Akavia, who sat up nights writing at his desk. Yet Hirshl's heart told him it was Blume's, and there is no way of reasoning with a broken heart.

Hirshl walked up and down, up and down, his steps growing shorter and shorter the longer he waited. Blume could not stay shut up in her room forever. Sooner or later she was bound to come out.

Yet when God in heaven saw to it that she did Hirshl had no reason to be glad. He was on one of his circuits of the house when he heard the garden gate swing open. It had been blown by the wind, which was followed by Blume, who had stepped out of the house to close it. "Who's there?" she asked when she saw someone standing in the street.

"It's me," Hirshl said.

Blume recoiled and retreated into the house.

Hirshl felt utterly crushed, utterly mortified. What am I doing, what? he moaned again and again, seizing his head with his hands. Rain began to fall, striking his face; his whole body was drenched with sweat; yet he remained where he was. Not that he expected Blume to come out again to comfort him. Having come this far, however, he refused to abandon his post.

The rain fell noiselessly. Through a curtain of mist so thick that he could not see his own self the image of Blume appeared as brightly before him as it had on the day she had stroked his head in her room after walking out and returning. Hirshl rested his head on the latch of the gate and began to cry.

The tears kept coming. Rain collected in his shoes. He let the umbrella slip from his hands and soon was wet all over. Then the rain stopped and the moon came out. Hirshl wiped his eyes and prepared to go home. Yet still he did not budge.

Dejected and soaked to the bone, he stood outside Blume's house. It shimmered in the moonlight, and in its north window, which Hirshl mistook for Blume's, a candle burned. It did not burn all night, though, for when he glanced at it again it was gone. He thought of the candle that had gone out at his wedding and of the Hindu sect that lit candles at a divorce, one for the husband and one for the wife, and made the man or woman whose candle went out first depart forever. He had not felt as sad then as he did now thinking about it.

Never since his walks to Blume's house began had Hirshl been so downcast. His throat had a lump in it, and his lips felt puffy. Though he was not sure if he felt hot or cold, he was certain that he was coming down with something. The thought of being ill upset him less than the thought of being it in a bed next to Mina's.

Though the sky had cleared, the air, earth, and grass still had a good rainy smell. At last Hirshl went home. A rooster crowed and the clock inside chimed twelve as he reached the front door of his home. He paused on the doorstep to consider what to tell Mina should she ask where he had been. I'll tell her I was at Blume's, he decided.

—Who is Blume?

—What, you don't know who Blume is?

—Not your ex-housemaid?

—Yes, our ex-housemaid.

—But what were you doing there?

—Why, she's my love.

—How odd that no one told me before.

—No one told you?

—No one.

—Well, I had better start from the beginning then.

—The beginning doesn't interest me. I want to know what she is to you now.

—You want to know what she is to me now?

—Precisely. What is she to you now?

—But I told you that I'm coming from her house.

—You are?

—Yes, Mina, I am.

—Is this the first time you've been there?

—Really, Mina. I go there every night.

—Every night?

—Yes, every night. When I'm awake I walk, and when I'm asleep I'm transported.

—Heinrich, aren't you confusing yourself with Rabbi Joseph de la Reina, who was transported every night to Queen Helen of Greece by the Devil?

—No, Mina, I'm not confusing myself with anyone. Joseph de la Reina is a totally different case. But as long as you've asked, suppose I ask you how you know about him. You certainly never learned any Jewish history in that boarding school of yours.

—How do I know about him? Do you really think that just because my headmistress became a Catholic I don't know the first thing about being Jewish?

—Your headmistress became a Catholic?

—Yes. That's why I was taken out of school.

—And is that why you were married to me too?

—I really couldn't tell you.

—But you can tell me, Mina. You just don't want to.

—I'm not keeping anything from you. If someone isn't telling the whole truth around here, it's not me.

—Meaning that?

—That it's you, Heinrich. You never tell me anything.

—Are you referring to Blume?

—Blume? Who is Blume?

—How can you ask who Blume is when all this time we've been talking about her?

—I'm not one to pry, Heinrich.

—You're not one to pry?

—No, I'm not.

—Then maybe you can tell me what made me start telling you about her in the first place?

—I suppose you felt you had to.

—I felt I had to? What is that supposed to mean?

—That's something you know better than I do.

—Isn't it strange that you know that I know when I don't

150

know that I know myself? But I believe I'll go to sleep now, because I can see that you want to sleep too.

Hirshl took off his shoes and wet socks and tiptoed to his bed. The windows were shut tight, and a warm, somnolent smell came from Mina. As she was fast asleep, his whole conversation with her must have been a dream. God in heaven knew what it meant. Hirshl undressed, curled up beneath his blanket, and fell asleep at once.

He could have slept a thousand years. God in heaven had melded his body with the bed. Even when a sound woke him he kept his head on the pillow, luxuriating in the sensation of his bedclothes and quilts. He felt as if he must have been lying there since the Creation of the World—nor, having gone to sleep after midnight, was he at all inclined to get up. It was only because of the mirror on the wall across from him that he saw the face of Mina's mother smiling at her sleeping son-in-law.

Hirshl felt in fine fettle. The events of the night before seemed far away and forgotten. His sleep had been so delicious that a wondrous sense of well-being pervaded his whole body. If only he could sleep one more hour, he would be a new man.

In the end he caught Mina's eye and Mina made a sign to her mother. Bertha stepped out of the room and Hirshl rose, washed, and put on fresh clothes in place of his wet ones. Then he drank a cup of coffee and went to the synagogue to pray. Since Mina had found out she was pregnant, Hirshl had taken to praying there daily, it being a way of spending less time with her.

The answer to a man's problems, he mused to himself as he walked, is to sleep as much as he can. All the way to the synagogue he thought of sleep until, remembering how Blume fled at the sight of him, he suddenly grew sad.

What a pitiful thing human life was. A man slept all night in order to rise in the morning, and looked forward all day to sleeping again at night. And between sleeping and waking, what a lot of guff he had to take.

Blume generally wore a gray dress whose snug bodice kept her beauty well confined. What had made her choose it for herself? The heart that it confined had chosen it.

Yet gray though her dress was, it took no great wisdom to realize that not everything gray on the outside was gray on the inside too. Within its snug bodice Blume's beauty was as unconfined as ever. God in heaven knew why she was not Hirshl's wife. For all that she denied being like her father, she resembled him in many ways. She had in her a great deal of Hayyim Nacht, the difference being that when things looked black for her father he had simply sat and complained, while Blume never uttered a cross word. She had managed to land on her feet, and the mute blue look in her eyes that were neither happy nor sad made one notice something special about her.

Getzel Stein tried writing Blume letters and gave up. This was not because of his handwriting, ragged scrawl though it was, but because, losing heart when he pictured her, he tore up the paper each time. Even Dr. Knabenhut, if he happened to run into her, did not speak to Blume as he did to other young ladies. Indeed, though Blume, despite having every reason to be one, was not a socialist, Dr. Knabenhut saw to it that he ran into her often—whereupon he put aside the public welfare and found some rather private things to say to her. For a while she would listen intently; yet suddenly, with a shake of her head, she seemed to shrug off everything he said. At such times she suggested a drowning man fished from the river who, coughing up the water from his lungs, gets to his feet and walks away from his astonished rescuers. Having turned down Getzel Stein, she did not seem particularly interested in Dr. Knabenhut either.

Whom did she think she was waiting for? Did she really believe some wealthy young man would still come along and marry her? The fact was that, having been unlucky with one once, Blume wanted no more mother's or father's boys, whether they dreamed of Zion or of the millenium. Once, long ago, she had given her heart to a young man named Hirshl

Hurvitz, not because either of them planned it that way but because, one day when she grew up, there he was: Hirshl, who could have been her twin. Anyone knowing the two of them might have wondered—as indeed Tsirl did—why they should have been meant for each other; anyone less clever than Tsirl, however, must have felt a twinge of pity at seeing the two cousins parted. And while we know what this did to Hirshl, what it did to Blume is something else. Still, anyone talking to her could only have been impressed by the shadow of a smile around her lips that seemed to say: I may have been unlucky, but I managed to land on my feet.

24

THE SCHEDULED ARRIVAL of the draft board kept being postponed each week and each month. God in heaven knew whether this was to give Szybusz more time or to drive it frantic with uncertainty.

Hirshl felt a change of attitude toward him. No longer was he everyone's darling. His own family seemed to take pleasure in his distress. His mother-in-law, who used to boast to the world of what a fine fellow he had grown up to be, now looked at him as coldly as if she wished he had never grown up at all. Indeed, no one could look at him these days without making him feel like a burden. A year or two ago Hirshl would have had nothing to fear from the army. Now, however, there was a new draft board that refused to take bribes. It was almost certain that he would be called up.

His nerves were shot. He hardly ate what was put before him and had trouble sleeping at night. And even if he slept, he would awake in the morning feeling that he hadn't.

He suffered from aches and pains. Each day he rose exhausted: his head hurt, his arms and legs were heavy, and he shivered as if with a chill although he felt hot all over.

Yet as bad as it was to sleep poorly, it was worse not to sleep at all. Whole nights found Hirshl wide awake in bed. Often he did not even shut his eyes. Listening to Mina's every breath, he lay on his side without moving so as not to awaken her, since if he did she was sure to want to talk. The sound of her voice at night was like a nail being driven into a wall.

His first night of insomnia was a strange one. It seemed to go on and on while he lay tense and rigid, his thoughts coming and going sporadically. Several times he had the feeling that something important had happened, yet when he tried to recall what it was it turned out to be nothing at all. Hearing a rooster crow, he got out of bed to see if it was midnight; before he could look at the clock it crowed again. The whole world is asleep and resting, thought Hirshl, except for me. Tomorrow the shopboys will see me yawning in the store and think I spent the night making love.

In the morning he rose pale and tired. Though he could easily have stayed in bed, he felt too on edge, and the bed itself refused to let him get comfortable. Outside in the street he was amazed by the broad, well-rested expanse of sky and earth. Men were on their way to the synagogue with their prayer shawls and tefillin, their faces refreshed and aglow. Automatically he trudged after them.

The early risers had finished praying and a second prayer group was forming. A morning breeze blew through the open windows of the old study house. Hirshl opened a volume of the Talmud and noticed a fold in the corner of one page. It was the same fold he had made on the day he first began to work in the store. He tried reading the text but got nowhere. A few years ago no intricacy of the passage would have escaped him, while now he could not even remember the simple meaning of the Aramaic words.

Hirshl did not bother consulting a doctor. Insomnia was not an illness or a medical problem. But though he did not look for a doctor, the doctors came looking for him. Whoever he ran into had some advice to give him. If one person told him to drink sweet tea with brandy before going to bed, another recommended straight rum. Sometimes he tried the first, sometimes the second, and sometimes both together by taking the tea with brandy on retiring and the rum when he woke in the night. The next morning he would be sick from them both. If not for the coffee he drank with his breakfast, he could not have kept on his feet.

When one stayed awake at night, one heard all kinds of noises. Dogs barked, drunks sang, wagons rumbled down the street, men coming home from the tavern spoke in loud voices. Eventually all of these sounds vanished, leaving only the crowing of the cock. But though Hirshl could crawl into bed feeling more dead than alive, the mere thought of that outrageous squawk was enough to banish all prospect of falling asleep.

He would stare up at the ceiling, feeling the minutes and the hours go by. At last he would shut his eyes as hard as he could in the hope of dozing off; yet just then the roosters would bristle their combs and break into their horrid screech, while the warm smell from Mina's bed, which should have had a soporific effect, only reminded him that she had taken all the sleep for herself and left not a wink for him. Perhaps she had studied sleeping at boarding school.

Mina lay on her back in a pink nightgown with satin straps like the ones worn by her friend Sophia when her husband was in town, her chest rising and falling above her distended stomach. One would think that Hirshl had every reason to be content with her. Yet when the feeling was missing, thinking did not help very much.

And the Lord saw that Leah was hated. Jacob had two wives, one of whom he loved and one of whom he did not. Well might one ask, If he already had found a woman to love, why did God give him one to hate? And why did he have to marry the hated one first? Was it just in order to hate her, which is something he would never have done otherwise? In the end, of

155

course, he prevailed, and when his seven years were up he was given his beloved too. Yet what did she do then? For the price of a mandrake root she sold him to her sister, whom he hated.

And to Hannah he gave a double portion. Elkanah too had a wife whom he loved and gave twice as much as to Peninah. But what was a man to do who could not give his beloved anything, having already given all away to the woman he hated?

Such thoughts had their good and their bad side. If they were bad for Mina, they were good for Hirshl, since they kept his mind off other things. Even then, however, he was not to have a moment's rest, since no sooner was he occupied with the Bible than the cock began to crow. No matter how much blanket he pulled over his head, there was no keeping out the sound of it. Hirshl turned to look at his wife, whose chest rose and fell, her warm smell of no avail because she had already taken all the sleep for herself and left not a wink for him.

Mina slept in perfect silence. Her narrow bed was right next to Hirshl's, and he could hear her every breath. She may not have kept him from sleeping, but her sleeping kept him from thinking. He had hardly thought of one thing when the sound of her breathing made him think of another, such as a story he once had heard about two business partners who went on a journey in the course of which one was killed.

No one knew who the murderer was. The surviving partner, being both pious and rich, was above suspicion. One day, however, while he was writing to his wife from an inn where he had stopped, a rooster hopped on the table and defecated on the letter. The wrathful man leaped to his feet and tore the bird apart limb by limb. A police inspector who happened to be present seized him and cried, "It's you who murdered your partner!" The case was reopened, and the man was found guilty.

When a man lost his temper, he was not in control of himself. Why, he might suddenly leap to his feet and kill all the roosters in the world! It was just as well that Hirshl put away his pocketknife at night. In fact, when sometimes he forgot, he rose from bed especially to do it. There was no point in looking for trouble.

In a word, neither the brandy in Hirshl's tea nor the straight rum helped him to sleep. He could have drunk them from a dropper or swallowed the whole bottle in one gulp: it would not have made any difference.

But while his eyes were shut, his mind was open, and while his body lay still, his thoughts could roam where they pleased. Whatever he saw or heard that day came up for review at night. Things he had never understood before were suddenly clear to him. Though he had never, for example, seen a photograph of his mother's crazy brother or of her grandfather who drank tea through a hole in a sugar cube and wore a chamberpot instead of a skullcap on his head, he saw them as clearly in bed at night as if they were standing before him.

It was storming violently outside. The trees swayed in the wind. The birds and beasts of the forest hid as best they could, and not even a bug showed its face. One man alone was out on such a night, because he had no home to call his own. Who was he? Why, Hirshl's uncle, who had been banished by his parents for disobedience.

Yet Hirshl did not bring storms upon the forest every night. Sometimes the trees stood quietly at peace while a mild sun shone down on them and the birds flew chattering among their branches. A good smell of grass and mushrooms filled the air, and Hirshl's uncle lay on his back, happy to be alone and unbothered. When he was hungry, he picked and ate berries. When he was thirsty, he drank from the spring. Not for him the houses, shops, customers, and women of mortal men.

When Hirshl tossed, turned, and moaned that his head was killing him, Mina dabbed it with cologne. Though the remedy helped, he could not stand the smell of it. Napoleon, he would try telling himself, actually bathed in cologne water, yet not even his admiration for Napoleon could make him like it any better.

When Bertha and Tsirl saw that Hirshl was not sleeping, they personally took charge of his bed. No one who failed to see them fussing over its sheets and pillows with their own hands could know what true mother love was. None of this, however, did the least good. The one person who might have made a proper bed for him was Blume, since Hirshl had slept well enough in the days when she had made it.

There was one other thing that Hirshl tried, which was dipping absorbent cotton in oil and stopping his ears with it. If this made them less sensitive, however, it made the rest of his body more. Whenever a wagon went by, or a rooster crowed, the noise sent shock waves running through his knees, as if that was where his auditory nerves were.

His arms and legs were so sluggish that he hardly could lift them. The slightest movement took a great effort. Not even the smallest joint in his body obeyed him anymore. His head felt full of thorns.

After suffering like this for many days, Hirshl went to see a doctor.

25

THE WAITING ROOM of the doctor consulted by Hirshl was shaped like a long corridor. Within the broken frame of a boarded-up window hung a large illustration of a gouty patient being treated by a physician and his aides. In the middle of the room stood a round table on which, smelling of disinfectant, lay some brochures put out by German sanatoriums. Seated alongside Hirshl were three women who talked among themselves in whispers and a thin, irritable-looking man who pinched an extinguished cigarette between his fingers while spitting into a handkerchief. He appeared to be afflicted with every disease that Hirshl had ever heard of, and, after taking out a cigarette to dispel the fetid air, Hirshl immediately replaced it in his pocket for fear the man might ask him for a light.

The thin man belched. Hirshl shut his mouth, exhaled through his nostrils, and twisted his neck so as not to have to breathe the fellow's germs. Yet the belcher stared at him steadily, as if to say, If you think you have seen human misery before, you had better take another look at me.

The door of the office opened and out stepped an attractive woman with a relieved look on her face, as if she had been cured of a serious illness. If he cured her, thought Hirshl, he can certainly cure me. The doctor removed his eyeglasses, wiped them on the edge of his white smock, and inquired who was next. The three women stood up together. "Which of you is first?" asked the doctor. "I am," said the thin man testily, getting to his feet and pointing with a finger to his heart.

Now what was it I wanted to do? Hirshl asked himself when the door of the office had closed again. Ah, yes: to smoke a cigarette. Since the one in his pocket was crushed, he took out paper and tobacco to roll himself another. Just then, however, it occurred to him that the smoke might bother the three women, who must have scolded the thin man for smoking in their presence and made him put out the cigarette that he held. Or had he simply run out of matches? Yes, one should always take extra matches, because one never knew when one might need them. How strange I must have looked at the Gildenhorns' that night when I went about looking for a match. If Mina had not arrived when she did . . . but where was I? Oh, yes: a modern man should never be without a match. The cavemen never let the fire go out, and neither must we. A match is our fire in the cave.

The office door opened, and the sickly man emerged with a constipated expression. There was nothing relieved about it, which must mean that he was incurable. Could not the doctor have found something hopeful to say nonetheless? But no, clearly this was a doctor who refused to lie even to the most desperate cases. It was better for a sick man to know the truth. I've come to the right person, thought Hirshl: if anyone can straighten me out, it's him. Ai, how much longer will I have to wait? There are still three women ahead of me. If he spends ten minutes with each one, that means at least half an hour.

He was in the middle of this calculation when the doctor came out of his office, wiped his glasses once more, and asked who was next. The three women jumped up again; but now it turned out that they really were together, only one of them being a patient while the other two were members of her family.

The doctor smiled at Hirshl and invited the women inside. Before long two of them returned to the waiting room, leaving the third in the office. Suddenly she screamed. Either the doctor had pressed her too hard where it hurt or else he had told her the truth. No woman could stand too much truth, especially from a doctor. Though if a doctor were to tell me I had only a year to live, reflected Hirshl, would I be any calmer about it? How hard it is to sit here. It's so stuffy I'm falling asleep. I don't mean falling asleep, because I can't fall asleep, but I can't keep my eyes open either. Is there something in this room that's drugging me? I am not sleeping. I am not sleeping. I just have to close my eyes.

Hirshl let out a light snore. He awoke with a start and shut his eyes again. A good doctor can put you to sleep just by making you wait. Is there such a thing as dreaming in the middle of the day? There is if you can sleep, but I can't. I must have been thinking. I must have thought that I dreamed what I thought.

What did I think that I dreamed? That a button came off my jacket and Mina sewed it back on and I was chewing on the thread. But what made me think that was good for the memory? I'd better spit it out. That's not a thread, though, that's a

160

snore. I must have fallen asleep and not noticed that another patient came. They'll keep coming and coming until the doctor goes home and never even knows I was here. I'd better make a sound so that he does.

When Hirshl tried making a sound, however, it came out like another snore.

The doctor listened to Hirshl as if he had never heard of such a case before, without interrupting him even once. Then he advised him to go for long walks and to get lots of fresh air, which would brace his body, soothe his mind, increase his appetite, help his digestion, and guarantee him a solid night's sleep. He also urged him to take a cold bath and a cup of hot milk before going to bed and not to use sedatives, which became so habit-forming that they poisoned the system and sapped a man's will and strength.

The doctor's advice made Hirshl's condition no better. As if he had not taken enough walks and cups of hot milk already! I do believe, he thought, that sitting in that waiting room was the best medicine yet, because it at least put me to sleep.

In the end Mina's obstetrician was apprised of Hirshl's problem and prescribed a sleeping powder for him. Sometimes, he explained, the body simply forgot how to sleep and had to be retrained. Once Hirshl grew used to sleeping again with a sedative, he would be able to sleep without it. A sleepless night did the body more harm than any drug.

Just as he had listened to the first doctor, so Hirshl listened to the second. At nightfall he quit the store, went straight home, and prepared himself for sleep, so that by nine o'clock he was already in bed. His mother came by to see that he was tucked in and that he had taken his powder. Then she wished him a good night and left, leaving Mina to blow out the candle.

The curtains on the window were drawn all the way, and the room was as dark as a grave. Hirshl shut his eyes. I am falling asleep, he told himself. I am sleeping already. Tonight nothing will keep me awake. Yet suddenly it occurred to him that the room was so dark because he had gone blind. He opened his eyes in a fright. Pitch-blackness was everywhere. Panic-stricken he sat up and looked all around until, making out the glimmer of the windowpane and the glint of the metal lamp stand, he was satisfied that he still had his sight. The sudden movement upset him, however, and left him wide awake.

The fact is, thought Hirshl, that someone in an impressionable state like mine should not be allowed to sleep in the dark: I had better get out of bed and open the curtains. Yet before he had even set foot on the floor every object in the house began to glitter wildly. And not just in the house: whatever was in the street outside—people, lights, horses-and-buggies—impinged on his consciousness too.

The two sleeping powders that he had swallowed felt as if they were stuck in his throat. At last they dissolved there. Mina climbed into bed and lay as still as she could so as not to disturb him, while he lay wondering when the drug would take effect and what should worry him more, having taken it against the first doctor's orders or the fact that it was not putting him to sleep. If he had not swallowed the two powders, he could pick up a book now and read. How long did they need to do the job? Well, they were down the hatch: there was nothing to do now but wait.

Half an hour went by without his dozing off. Evidently the drug was not working. Or could he already be asleep and only dreaming that he was awake, as he had done at the doctor's?

It did Hirshl good to recall that he had fallen asleep at the doctor's, since that proved he still could. To sleep to sleep to sleep: that was the one thing he wanted. To sleep and to forget everything. But he could not. Eyes shut, the clock ticking away, the hours coming and going, he was sure to stay awake again all night. If he were not drugged he would get up and stop the clock's ticking, which was playing havoc with his nerves.

The one good thing about the sedative was that it kept

Mina quiet. The clock chimed. Look how another hour has passed without my noticing, thought Hirshl. I should be happy that the clock won't chime again for sixty minutes, which is enough time to sleep and get my strength back. Who says a man needs more sleep than that? The few minutes I dozed at the doctor's did me more good than a whole night of it.

Hirshl had barely shut his eyes when the first cock crowed.

His arms and legs weighed a ton and his throat felt lined with a mixture of cake dough and sand. Either some of the sleeping powder was still stuck there or he had caught cold from sweating in bed. What he needed to put him back on his feet was a good cup of coffee. The thought of it made him imagine its smell; the smell of coffee made him picture a hot cup of it, and the beans before and after being roasted, and the sacks of them on the shoulders of the porters who brought them from the station to the store; and the sacks of beans brought to mind the mice that sometimes scampered inside them. Suppose one were inside a sack, and he were to open it, and the mouse were to jump into his mouth, and he were to close it, and the mouse were to remain there half in and half out, with its long tail protruding and tickling the tip of his nose until he fell asleep. . . .

Hirshl rose in the morning feeling like an opium eater. A heavy caul enveloped his head and descended over his eyes. He could hardly make out what was said to him, which sounded like a distant echo in his ears. A cup of strong coffee was his one hope of recovery—yet where was he going to get it? What passed for coffee in his home was merely coffee-colored milk. Once after his marriage he had been to Stanislaw and had drunk real coffee in a coffeehouse. Of course, there were such places in Szybusz too, but no self-respecting citizen would be caught in one.

Here it is time for morning prayers, thought Hirshl, and all I can think of is coffeehouses. Yet what was so sinful about a coffeehouse? It was simply a matter of local custom. Perhaps no decent person would frequent one in Szybusz, but there were towns where this was not at all the case.

As a matter of record, Hirshl was quite mistaken about what was served in his home, for Sophia Gildenhorn, who could brew a cup of coffee whose aroma alone was enough to wake the dead, had taught Tsirl, Bertha, Mina, and Mina's maid to make coffee just like her own, which Hirshl could enjoy for the asking.

The piping hot, deep-brown beverage put before him cleared his head at once. A cup of it made Hirshl, whose limbs had been heavy as lead, feel light as a bird. Blume should only have seen him now! Yet Blume was not like Hirshl and did not sit thinking of him, much less of how she might see him. Not that she had forgotten him. She had simply put him out of her mind—and the rest of the Hurvitz establishment with him. Even the letter she received from Getzel Stein had gone unanswered. Indeed, when Getzel ran into her one day and asked her for her answer, she told him there was none.

Did Blume expect to be carried off by a prince on a white charger? In fact she did not, not even if his name was Dr. Knabenhut, who was always inquiring about her. In any case, Dr. Knabenhut had no more romantic interest in Blume these days than Blume had in him, for so great was his devotion to the public welfare that he was about to marry a rich woman solely in order to continue his political career without being dependent on his father. Not that he was any more self-denying than Blume—the proof being that Blume had come to the conclusion that not every woman had to marry, by which she meant herself as well.

Mina lay in bed. The bigger grew the child in her womb, the bigger Mina grew too. It cannot be said that she was ecstatic over the prospect of having it. Ecstasy was too much to expect from a woman with a depressed husband like Hirshl. And though Mina was reduced by now to being little more than a walking hotel room, she and Hirshl seldom talked about the infant. Nor did Hirshl think about it when he was alone or wonder what it would turn out to be like.

Since he had started drinking coffee à la Sophia Gildenhorn, Hirshl was on his toes all day long, let alone a good part of the night. Indeed, he was so much on his toes that it was all he could do to keep himself from jumping right out of his skin. He had given up going to bed early and resumed his habit of late walks, though he no longer took them to the same place. Their one purpose was to keep him out of bed, which was the least restful place he could imagine. He had despaired of ever being able to sleep and wished only to make the nights as short as possible.

Mina lay in her clothes, half awake and half asleep. She had felt so weak that evening that she had not even bothered to eat supper. Hirshl ate by himself and said the grace. Then he rose, put a glass of water by his bed, covered it with a plate, laid a double dose of sleeping powder on top of it, put on his overcoat, turned down the wick of the lamp, and prepared to step out.

"Where are you going?" Mina asked him.

"Where am I going? As if you didn't know I was going just where you and all my well-wishers keep telling me to go: for a walk."

He was already at the door when Mina said, "Enjoy yourself. But I want you to know it can't go on like this. I promise you I'll outlive you. That isn't my way of wishing you a short life; it's just that you had better realize you're not going to get rid of me so quickly. And what I'd like to know is, exactly how do you envisage spending our life together in the meantime? I don't care what you say to me, but for God's sake, say something! Your silence is killing me. You're a sensible enough person to understand that we can't go on like this anymore. I've been meaning to talk to you for a while, but I kept hoping that something would change. Well, it hasn't, so I've come out with it. You want to take a walk? Go right ahead, you'll have plenty of time on your way to think about what I just said. And please tell the girl, Heinrich, that I don't need her anymore tonight. I'll undress by myself. Why do you think my mother didn't come today? Good night, Heinrich. You needn't tiptoe when you get back, and you can turn up the lamp all you like. You don't have to worry about waking me. I only wish you slept as well as I did."

26

HIRSHL ROSE AS USUAL for the morning prayer. He felt unusually alert, and his eyes shone exuberantly. As is often the case when one's spirits are high, he did not stop to ask why they were, yet his good mood was evident even in how he washed and dressed. Nor was it affected by the headache he had, which merely proved to him that, while he might not feel well physically, there was nothing the matter with his mind. Indeed, a sound mind was needed to realize that there was something wrong with his body.

He was on his way out when Mina awoke. Seeing there was no chance of slipping away unnoticed, he halted. Mina opened her eyes, yawned, and said, "Did you sleep any, Heinrich?"

His good mood vanished all at once and his eyes went red with a rage that would have struck her aghast had she seen it. Immediately, however, he fought to contain it and did his best to be friendly.

"Does your head hurt, Heinrich?" asked Mina.

"Come, Mina," he answered. "Where would I be if my head didn't hurt? It's my way of knowing I'm alive."

She reached for her cologne bottle and asked, "Would you like to rub a little of this on your forehead, Heinrich?"

"It might help," said Hirshl, regarding her approvingly, "but I'd better not now. I'm going to synagogue, and the men who pray there aren't used to eau de cologne. They would think that I was the strangest-smelling creature they had ever smelled. Is there anything I can do for you before I go?"

"Thank you, Heinrich," said Mina. "I don't need anything right now."

"Then I'd better be off," said Hirshl.

"Goodbye, Heinrich," said Mina.

"Goodbye, then," Hirshl said.

"Goodbye," said Mina. "On your way out, Heinrich, please tell the girl that I'm up."

"You see, Mina," said Hirshl, "first you said you didn't need anything and now there's something you want. Who knows what else there might be if you let yourself think of it. But I'm talking so much that I've already forgotten what you said. Please don't be angry with me for asking, but what was it you wanted me to tell the girl to do?"

"Just be so good as to tell her that I'm up," Mina said.

Hirshl regarded her with a queer animation, as if he had heard an intriguing bit of news. His eyes gleamed with an extraordinary light and he said, "You are up, Mina? You really are? I swear I'll tell the girl, though I must say it surprises me to see you up so early. Not that that's any reason not to tell her exactly what you said. I may have forgotten once, but I won't forget again. Just look at me, though, promising you not to forget when I nearly forgot to take my prayer shawl to synagogue with me! And while we're on the subject of forgetting, let me tell you something I just remembered. Mr. Coocoo kept me up all night again. I do believe it's time we got rid of him. Don't you think we might take him to the throat-slitter? He just has to go *whisht* and there's no more cock-a-doodle-doo."

Hirshl ran a finger over his throat and laughed.

"Do you want to slaughter the rooster?" asked Mina.

"That, Mina," said Hirshl, "is the most marvelous idea."

"But it was your idea," Mina said.

"My idea, Mina? Why, I never said a word about a rooster. How can you call it my idea when I never said any such thing? And even if it was, no one could have read my mind but you.

Well, I have to go now. You don't happen to know what time it is, do you? My watch has stopped. It was tickety-ticking along, and suddenly it just went and stopped."

"It's half past seven," said Mina.

"Half past seven? Then it really is time to go. You know, I'm amazed by people's optimism. If they have to be somewhere on time they trust their watches, though you see for yourself how a watch can take a notion to stop running. You look at it and it doesn't say a word. You turn it every which way—still no answer. Even when you shake it, it doesn't wake up. It couldn't care less how you feel. Why, you come to depend on it as though it were your own father and mother, you carry it around in your pocket, you even make it a gold chain—and it just stands there and laughs at you. Do you suppose being tied to a gold chain all day long isn't good enough for it? Of course, this is all in a manner of speaking, since a watch has no mind of its own. It isn't a rooster that crows whenever it wants to. I suppose you'll tell me that a person should have two watches, one to tell the time by when the other stops, but believe me, two watches are too much for anyone. You'll just forget the second one anyway. It's not as if we had two brains in our heads to keep track of them both. Well, goodbye, Mina. I'll tell the maid you want to get up. If you ask me, though, you're better off sleeping. If I could sleep myself, I'd do it until hell froze over."

Hirshl recovered his good mood on the way. Whatever he saw—the servant girls gossiping to each other in the market, the children washing their faces in the doorways of the houses—only heightened it. A dappled dove perched on the back of a horse pleased him in particular.

Yona Toyber passed and greeted him. Hirshl flushed and said with a slight stammer, "I'm on my way to synagogue. It's a fine day, Mr. Toyber, isn't it?"

Yona Toyber cast him a sideways glance and extracted a rolled cigarette from his pocket. "Where's your father-in-law these days?" he inquired.

168

"He doesn't often come to town because my mother-in-law is here so much. Someone has to mind the farm, isn't that right, Mr. Toyber?"

Toyber nodded, shook Hirshl's hand, and went his way.

I suppose it was indecent of me, mused Hirshl when they parted, to have wanted to kiss his hand when I shook it. Now what was I thinking about? Yes, about whether that dove was so free with that horse because it knew it was tied. How smooth Yona Toyber's hands are.

Not only did Hirshl forget to tell the maid what Mina had asked him to, Mina forgot to do it too. She kept dozing off and waking up with a start each time she recalled their conversation. Since the day she had known her husband, she had never seen him in such a state. Not that anything had happened—yet she had a sense of foreboding all the same.

Bertha found her daughter feeling low. "Is something the matter?" she asked.

"Not really," Mina said. "Heinrich just seemed very strange today. Everything he said was strange."

Bertha was alarmed. "How do you mean, strange?"

"It's hard for me to explain, Mother," said Mina. "He had this strange, happy gleam in his eyes. In general—"

"But what can be on your mind?" interrupted her mother. "In general, he's happy he's going to be a father."

"That isn't it, Mother," said Mina. "That's not the kind of happiness I meant."

"Ach, Mina," said Bertha. "You make too much of things. A man has his moods. Even a stone isn't always the same. If it's in sunshine it seems happy, if it's in shadow it seems sad. It's the same stone, it just doesn't look it—and a human being is no different."

As Mina kept the rest of her thoughts to herself, Bertha sighed and went on, "All these troubles come from not having faith. People are so taken with themselves nowadays that they forget all about God. If a young woman isn't primping in the mirror for her husband, she's asking him if he likes how she

169

looks, or else she's back in front of the mirror to see what it was he liked. Between him and the mirror she has no time left for the Lord. Why, she doesn't even realize that a man's mood can change! One day he's like a willow tossing in a storm and the next he's as quiet as a sparrow in a nest. I ask you, what difference does it make how your husband looked at you? You're a married couple, God joined you together, why make so much of every look? If I had made so much of every look of your father's, we'd never be where we are today."

Hirshl stepped into the Little Synagogue, donned his prayer shawl and tefillin, and joined the prayer. Though he had intended to pray in the Great Synagogue, where he could have stood unnoticed in a corner, his meeting with Toyber had unnerved him and caused him to come here instead.

Midway through the service he felt a jolt in his head as if it had been banged against a wall. A moment later he felt another jolt as if it were being blown right off. He bent to look at the floor, then felt his forehead to see if his tefillin had been knocked to the ground. As soon as he could pull himself together, he drew his prayer shawl over his head and resumed his prayers. A thousand thoughts raced through his mind, but he was unable to concentrate on even one. A draft riffled the pages of his prayer book, which he began to turn backward and forward. He smelled snuff and heard the snuff taker sneeze and mutter something against the evil eye. Two men who had prayed already were discussing a Talmudic text that dealt with the head feathers of slaughtered birds. Suddenly everyone fell still and rose for the silent prayer.

It was the day of the New Moon, and the Torah scroll was taken out to be read. As it was carried around the synagogue, Hirshl pushed back his prayer shawl and stepped forward with the other men to kiss it. Idly he pinched a bit of wax from a candle and kneaded it with his fingers while rehearsing the Torah blessings under his breath in case he was called upon to recite them. After a while he stuck his hand in his pocket to knead the wax there unseen, and when it slipped from his fingers he continued kneading himself. The discovery that he was squeezing his own flesh without feeling it alarmed him. Had his fingers gone numb or was he dead? He gripped his head with both hands and thought, I can't be dead as long as my head hurts. I'm glad I'm not screaming, because if I was I might crow like a rooster and seem crazy. Perhaps someone can tell me why it is that a man's a poor devil when he screams like a man and crazy when he crows like a rooster, but a rooster that crows isn't crazy at all, it's just talking rooster talk. I suppose that a rooster barking like a dog would be as crazy as me crowing like a rooster. It's a good thing I'm screaming like a man then and not going cock-a-doodle-doo.

27

HIRSHL LEFT THE study house feeling as light as a feather. He could have reached the forest with three steps, yet he made himself walk slowly, for a man in full possession of himself, he thought, should do nothing that might appear unseemly.

He made his way with a modest air of deliberation, clutching the velvet bag that contained his prayer shawl and tefillin. Anyone happening to see him just then would have thought he had much on his mind; yet no one saw him at all, and anyone seeing him would have been wrong. Soon he reached the cattle market, where he paused to rest for a while before cutting through the vegetable gardens behind it. Then, after resting once more, he entered the forest.

The forest was perfectly still. Not a leaf stirred. The ground gave off a mixture of good smells. Holding his bag in his left hand, Hirshl tipped his hat with his right as if passing before a reviewing stand, though there was no one there but him and the trees. Let them think you're saluting, he told himself, and there won't be any trouble. What a fool you were, Hirshl, not to have thought of that in front of Blume's house. There's nothing like tipping your hat for staying out of trouble—unless it's taking off your shoes so that Mina won't hear you when you come home late at night. I had better take them off right now.

As he was about to remove his second shoe, though, he stood up anxiously and thought, Why, I said I couldn't feel my own body, but now I see that I can. Or is it just something I imagined, as I did that the trees were officers of the Kaiser when they're really nothing but trees? Because even if the Bible says that a man is a tree of the field, that's not at all what it means. A man can't grow on a tree. He can hang himself from one, though. Would he hear the rooster crow if he did? Oh no oh no, he would hear the frogs croak in the river. Suddenly Hirshl struck his head and cried aloud, "I am not crazy, I am not!"

He looked about and thought, You said I was crazy because I cock-a-doodle-do, but now you can see that I cock-a-doodle-don't think that I'm gaga that I'm ga ga ga ga ga a crazy man crows like a rooster but I go ga ga ga ga.

Father in heaven, wondered Hirshl, glancing up at the sky, what time can it be? He took out his stopped watch and studied it, then lay down in the grass with it hanging out of his pocket, one shoe off and one shoe on, happily laughing and ga-ga-ing to himself. He could not remember ever having felt so at peace. Oh nice oh nice, he thought, staring joyfully up at the sky with a hallucinatory smile on his lips. All at once he leaped up in dismay and exclaimed, "Half past seven!"

In an instant his smile vanished and a turbid froth appeared in its place. He spat it into the air and it fell back into his eyes. Again he spat it upward and again it rained down on him. Then he turned and ran, the hat toppling from his head. The sun beat down on him. The veins stood out hotly in his brow. He drummed on them with his fists, then removed his other shoe, placed it on top of his head, and began to hop on one foot until a stone sent him sprawling.

As bizarrely as he was acting, Hirshl had his wits about him. He knew that, unlike his mother's grandfather who wore a chamberpot on his head, he could not make a hat of a shoe, and that, unlike his maternal uncle who ran off to the forest for good, he would have to go home in the end. Why didn't he, then? Because he had lost his hat, and one did not go hatless in the hot sun.

"I wonder what's kept Hirshl from the store today," said Tsirl when eleven o'clock had come and gone. She went to his apartment to investigate and found her daughter-in-law in bed with a hot compress on her head and Bertha standing by her side.

"Where is Hirshl?" Tsirl asked.

The two of them turned white with consternation.

Tsirl was equally alarmed. "We had better go look for him," she said.

"Please do," said Mina tremulously. "Oh, please do." Tsirl gave her an approving look. "He's probably in the store by now," said Bertha, adjusting the compress. Yet one look at Mina was enough to know that Hirshl was probably not.

Mina was beside herself with worry. Coming on the heels of her talk with him that morning, Hirshl's disappearance left her stunned. Though several times she tried telling Tsirl what had happened, she was too distressed to talk.

Another hour went by with no sign of Hirshl. By now they had searched the whole town for him. At first they did not advertise his absence. Yet before another hour had passed, all Szybusz knew of it.

Though various sightings of Hirshl were reported from different places and times of the day, no one knew where he was now. Even those who had seen him disagreed among themselves, some saying that he had been behaving strangely and some that he had not. The same held true of the men who had prayed with him in the study house: half claimed to have known at a glance that something was wrong, while the other half insisted nothing was.

Boruch Meir questioned everyone composedly, yet he was pale and his beard was disheveled. Though nothing of the sort had been said aloud, something told him what it did not yet tell Tsirl, namely, that the matter was far from simple.

At sundown Hirshl was found in a field with one shoe on one foot and the other on his forehead, an expression of great anguish in his eyes. It was hard to look at him, though he himself stared straight back at his finders without saying a word. At last he cried out to them, "Don't cut my throat! I'm not a rooster! I'm not!"

"What are you talking about, Mr. Hurvitz?" they asked.

"I won't say a word," said Hirshl. "Not one. Do you know Blume Nacht? Of an evening in the marsh grass I'll sit like a froggy and go ga ga ga."

They brought him home and sat him down there. He looked about and could not understand why everyone seemed so sad. When Mina approached him he smiled at her, yet he burst into tears when she reached out to stroke his hair with her cold hand. At last he pulled his head away and said, "Blume, I didn't go cockle, I just went ga ga ga."

Mina fainted dead away and was put to bed at once. Hirshl raised his hand in a military salute and said, "Ga ga ga."

"He should be taken to Olesk," remarked someone.

This gave the family a new fright. Though no one had dared mention the word, the holy tzaddik of Olesk was known for his cures of crazy people. Gedalia alone took it calmly. All his life he had been waiting for disaster to strike, and now that it had he was not at all surprised.

Szybusz was agog with the news all night and by morning had settled down again. If someone asked someone else the next day, "Did you hear that Hirshl Hurvitz has gone crazy?" the answer was sure to be, "If anyone has gone crazy, it's you and your great-grandmother. What did you want him to do, cut off a finger? Or perhaps you would rather he put out an eye?"

What possessed Hirshl's townsmen to talk like this about

him was simply the fact that he was soon to be examined by the draft board, which was the strictest ever, and that he was perfectly fit. Hirshl, it was the considered opinion in Szybusz, was feigning madness to get out of the army.

A year or two previously there would have been no need to worry: when the draft board arrived one simply went to the right person, who fixed things with the members of the board, who gave one a medical exemption, the Kaiser having no use for an army of invalids. True, it could not be stated with any accuracy that all of Szybusz avoided service in this way. On the contrary, there were genuine invalids who were drafted, though they too were soon sent home, the Kaiser having no use for them either. God in heaven knew what had changed, but this year's board no longer took bribes. And while at first it was thought in Szybusz that this was just a rumor started by the fixers in order to jack up their prices, reports were not long in arriving from other towns of people being shot for bribery.

A doctor was brought to see Hirshl. To test him he asked how old the Kaiser was.

"Half past seven," Hirshl replied.

"And what is your name?" asked the doctor.

"Half past seven," said Hirshl.

The doctor thought the patient might not know any German and asked him again in Yiddish. "Half past seven," Hirshl said. It was his answer to every single question.

The doctor checked Hirshl's eyes, took his pulse, wrote out a prescription, and declared, "If this doesn't work, we'll try something else."

The second and third prescriptions made Hirshl no saner than the first. Nor did the medicines given by any of the other physicians who were consulted yield better results. In the end it was decided to take him to a specialist in Lemberg.

And so two days after the onset of Hirshl's illness his parents set out with him for Lemberg, taking along a paid companion to watch over him.

The companion proved unnecessary. Hirshl bothered no

one and neither croaked nor crowed. He simply sat and said nothing the whole trip. God in heaven knew what he was thinking. Though his parents pointed out to him each station they pulled into, he didn't even trouble to look up. From time to time Tsirl offered him food from a basket. If his hand was closed, he did not open it to take it; if it was open, he did not close it to grasp it; and when she tried sticking it into his mouth, he simply refused to chew.

As they entered Stanislaw, Tsirl redoubled her efforts. "Look, Hirshl, look, we're in Stanislaw," she said, hoping to get a response to the name of the town in which Mina had studied. Hirshl, however, showed no more interest in Stanislaw than he had in any other place he had passed through.

Tsirl felt despondent. And thinking of the store just made it worse. Since the day she stopped nursing Hirshl she had hardly missed an hour's work in it, and, on the rare occasions when she had, she had left it in the hands of her husband and son. Now all three of them were away. It was not that she was worried about pilfering. Getzel was as good as gold and would keep an eye on Feyvel. Still, a store should not be left without an owner, to say nothing of a house. Had Blume still been the Hurvitzes' maid, Tsirl would not have been concerned. But how could she not be with Blume's replacement? Indeed, Tsirl thought of a great many people on the way to Lemberg, of whom Mina did not happen to be one.

At a station not far from Lemberg, Getzel Stein's father boarded the train. He was coming from seeing the Rabbi of Belz, whose intercession he had sought with the chicken eaters of Szybusz, and his beard was unkempt and his shirt open at the collar in the manner of the Belz Hasidim. Not that the Rabbi of Belz had the least influence in Szybusz, where most Jews were not Hasidim at all and the few who were owed their allegiance to the courts of Tshortkov, Husatyn, Sadigora, Vishnitz, and Utynja. Yet as the rabbis of these places had turned Getzel Stein's father down flat, he had gone in the end to Belz. He was telling the Hurvitzes of his adventures there when into their car walked Sebastian Montag.

176

Sebastian Montag was on his way to see what could be done about replacing the draft board that was about to visit Szybusz with another, more amenable one. Though he had been traveling first-class, a sudden craving for a Jewish conversation had made him leave the first-class carriage to explore the rest of the train. "Your Polish gentleman," he explained, "is fine to drink and gamble with, but talking to him is a waste of breath. In the time that it takes him to understand what you've said a Jew can say his prayers twice. The only difference is that, when a Jew prays, God sometimes answers to the point, which is more than can be said of your Pole."

Sebastian Montag was sorry to hear about Hirshl. He patted him on the head, bent down to kiss him, and recited two verses from Psalms, one against illness and one against possession by spirits, before going back to the first-class carriage for a gentlemanly game of cards.

28

THEY ARRIVED IN Lemberg and went straight to Dr. Langsam, an elderly neurologist who had treated many of the mental patients in Galicia. It was said of him that he had studied in his youth to be a rabbi, but that, hearing a Jewish patient once abused by a Polish doctor, a not uncommon occurrence in those days when Gentile physicians treated Jews' bodies while damning their souls, he had resolved to go to medical school instead. Before long he acquired a reputation as a first-rate practitioner whom people came to see from all over, while eventually he stopped treating physical complaints in order to specialize in nervous ones, which could lead to hopeless dementia if not dealt with in time. Never one to give up on a case, he had nursed many of his patients back to health.

Unlike the doctors before him, Dr. Langsam did not seek to test Hirshl with puzzles or by asking him how old the Kaiser was. He simply said hello and inquired, as if unable to understand what such a healthy-looking young man was doing in his sanatorium, "Well now, what seems to be the matter with you?"

After he had examined Hirshl he gave him a bed, had food and drink brought to him, and attended to all his needs as if he were a guest needing to recuperate from a long, tiring journey.

Dr. Langsam did not put many questions to Tsirl or Boruch Meir either. It was immaterial to him whether or not they told him the whole truth about Hirshl, since neither the patient's history nor his previous course of treatment struck him as particularly important. What was crucial, he explained to Hirshl's parents, was to keep their son out of the lunatic asylum and away from Szybusz—out of the asylum because it could make even a sane man crazy, and away from Szybusz because he would never get well if the children there called him names and threw stones at him. The combination of meekness, resignation, and sadness that he saw in Hirshl's face made the old doctor take an instant liking to him.

Dr. Langsam made no effort to sound either hopeful or discouraging. "I have never kept anyone here who was not sick," he told Boruch Meir and Tsirl, "nor turned anyone out who was. When your son is ready to return home, I'll write to inform you." He told them what the treatment cost, asked for three months' payment in advance, and promised to give Hirshl kosher food.

Dr. Langsam was sparing in his use of drugs. He had long forgotten most of the old ones that he learned about in medical school and did not bother keeping up with the new ones. Since some medication was expected of him, however, he sometimes mixed five drops of a ten percent tincture of opium into a liquid and gave it to his patients to drink. This solution, which he had come across in an old medical journal and grudgingly prescribed for the sole purpose of distinguishing his method of treatment from that of the tzaddik of Olesk, was administered to Hirshl twice a day in a small glass containing equal parts of water and brandy. The dosage was decreased after the second week, and the only other medicine received by Hirshl was a laxative every Monday and Thursday, the opium having a constipating effect.

Hirshl took these preparations uncomplainingly. He no more objected to the bitter taste of the opium than he did to the nauseatingly sweet laxative, whose yellow emulsion looked like insecticide. Now and then Dr. Langsam substituted castor oil, or gave him all three remedies together.

Boruch Meir and Tsirl returned disconsolately to Szybusz. As long as they were occupied with Hirshl, there had been no time to feel their disgrace; now that they were homeward bound without him, the full extent of it began to dawn on them. They sat alone in their compartment, Boruch Meir in one corner and Tsirl in another, heaving a sigh now and then. For years they had waited for their son to be born, and now they had raised him and married him off for calamity to single him out. The ancient rabbinical curse on Tsirl's great-great-grandfather had not yet run its course. Perhaps it might have had Hirshl remained in the study house and become a rabbi himself.

In Stanislaw they changed from the express to the local. The journey to Szybusz was a slow one. The train stopped at every station, and passengers got on and off. Some were Boruch Meir's fellow townsmen, who knew more about his own life than he did. Though he pulled his coat up and his hat down so as not to be recognized, they noticed him at once and shouted hello at the top of their voices. Not that his downfall made them happy. Far from it. Their happiness came rather from having been away from Szybusz, for a few days' absence from home did wonders for a man.

Boruch Meir and Tsirl crept abjectly into town. Every street and streetcorner bespoke their ignominy. Here Hirshl had been led home from the forest. Here he had crowed like a rooster. Here he had quacked like a duck. Here he had croaked like a frog.

A short while later Bertha arrived.

"You certainly gave us a good scare," she exclaimed. "Why, Mina is in her eighth month. Did you ever think what all this excitement could have done to her and the baby, God forbid?"

Tsirl stared at her and said, "I swear to you, Bertha, I don't know what you're talking about."

"Well, I do," said Bertha. "I just don't know why you kept it from us."

"Kept what from you?"

"About Hirshl."

"We didn't tell you about Hirshl? Do you mean to say that you don't know where he is?"

"Of course I know," said Bertha.

"Then what did we keep from you?"

"Don't you think we should have been told?"

"We didn't tell you that we were going to Lemberg?"

"Of course you did, you just didn't say why."

"Oh my God, Bertha. I thought all Szybusz knew why."

"Tsirl," said Boruch Meir, "let me talk to Bertha."

"I wish you would, Boruch Meir," said Bertha. "I'd like an explanation."

"An explanation of what, Bertha?" Tsirl asked.

"How can you have pulled such a trick on a young girl like that? It's not as if she were something that the cat had brought home, God forbid."

"What kind of a trick?" asked Boruch Meir.

"Do you think I don't know the whole thing was staged?"

"What was?" Tsirl asked.

"Why, Hirshl's madness."

"Staged?" asked Boruch Meir and Tsirl in one breath.

"Oh, come now," said Bertha. "Don't you think I know that it was all just a stunt to get out of the army?"

"A stunt to get out of the army?" repeated Boruch Meir.

"The whole world knew except me. We were half dead with worry until they came along and told us."

"Who's 'they'?" asked Tsirl.

"Why, everyone and his uncle. Yona Toyber and Sophia Gildenhorn and that short little what's-his-name fellow."

"Kurtz," said Boruch Meir. "She means Kurtz."

"Right," Bertha said. "Kurtz, that's his name. The little dwarf who danced at the wedding. Even he knew Hirshl did it to keep from being drafted."

Boruch Meir stared at Bertha flabbergasted. Tsirl leaned toward her and whispered, "Mum's the word, mother of the bride. Does Mina already know about it?"

"I'd hate to think of what might have happened to her if she didn't."

God certainly works in mysterious ways, Tsirl thought. Boruch Meir said aloud, "Don't be upset with us, Bertha. The whole thing called for the utmost discretion."

"Bertha doesn't have to be told," said Tsirl. "She knows perfectly well that the less said about it, the better. Now let's go see Mina and bring her regards from Hirshl."

On their way they met Yona Toyber. Yona, who was the first to see Hirshl on the morning of the day he was found in the field, had perceived right away that he was not fully in his senses.

"Well, Mr. Toyber," said Bertha, "what do you think of the latest developments?"

Yona Toyber let out a sigh and said, "Not everyone has the good fortune to live in a country with no draft."

When he was gone Boruch Meir remarked, "What a clever fellow that one is. Nothing he says seems to make sense, but when you look at it more closely, it's as if he's read your thoughts. Has anyone heard news of his wife? They tell me she's terribly ill."

29

AFTER THREE DAYS of sleeping off his fatigue in bed, Hirshl no longer replied "half past seven" to every question. On the contrary, he gave long-winded answers to whatever he was asked, forgot the names of things and had to describe them in a roundabout fashion, and often lost track of what he was saying and was forced to start again from the beginning.

Although it was commonly assumed in the profession that a neurologist who had not known a patient when he was well could only diagnose his ailment by a battery of tests, this assumption was not shared by Dr. Langsam. In fact, he never bothered testing Hirshl at all. He simply talked with him to stimulate his mind.

No matter how well-off a man is in a big city and how dirt-poor he grew up in his native town, he will always remember the latter with nostalgia. Although forty years had passed since Dr. Langsam had left his birthplace, he still talked about it all the time, and while the town itself had changed greatly in those years, one would never have known it from his descriptions. Every day he came into Hirshl's room and sat down by his bed to chat with him, and each of these conversations began and ended with Dr. Langsam's hometown. Sometimes he reminisced about its market street, whose shops, flanked by tiny houses hardly larger than chicken coops, stood empty all week long. If a shopkeeper had a bit of education he would study a page of the Mishnah, while if he did not he would sit reciting Psalms—until, that is, Thursday arrived, when the whole town came to life, the peasants poured in from the outlying villages to do their buying and selling, and the local merchants circulated frantically among them trying to earn a few pennies for the Sabbath. And sometimes Dr. Langsam told Hirshl about his study house, which had glowed with the light of learning even though its walls were falling down and its ceiling was as black as tar.

What did his fellow Jews eat and drink in those days, and when did they find time to rest? "If someone were to tell me that human beings cannot survive like that," said Langsam, "as a doctor I would have to agree. But the fact is that they survived for generations and didn't even know what they were missing—except, I must say, for our local rabbi, who longed all his life to buy a copy of *Mahatsit ha-Shekel*,

182

Rabbi Shmuel Halevi of Cologne's commentary on Rabbi Yitzhak Alfasi's commentary on the Tosefta, and never had enough money. He had all week to study without interruption, because litigation was seldom brought to him in such a small place; and since there was nothing to eat but bread and onions, even questions about the dietary laws rarely arose. The one exception was Thursdays again, when a Jew who slaughtered a calf or a chicken for the Sabbath might bring him a perforated lung or a malformed crop for his opinion. Then he would place his handkerchief in his Talmud for a bookmark, take out a little penknife, and begin poking about at that crop's membrane like a doctor performing an autopsy. Why, no surgical instrument I have ever seen since seemed to me the equal of that dull knife with which he kept scraping away in the hope of being able to pronounce some poor Jew's meat kosher! The only other implement that he owned was a goose quill for writing his scholarly annotations. He made his own ink from candle smoke, and sometimes, when his quill was broken and he couldn't get hold of another, since geese were not slaughtered every day, he simply made a mark with his fingernails to remind himself to write his thoughts later. But God," concluded Dr. Langsam, "did give us Jews two good gifts, the Torah and the Sabbath. I don't know what we would have done without them."

Had anyone asked Hirshl how Dr. Langsam was treating him, he might have replied in surprise: What? Is he a doctor? Still, he could feel that he was being healed. The firm hand that casually shook his own each time the doctor came and went was not soft like Yona Toyber's, nor did it make him want to kiss it. Often, when Dr. Langsam sat chatting with him as one chats with a friend, Hirshl would wonder, Does he really know that I crowed like a rooster and sang that it was snowing on the green, green grass? That's hard to believe, because he would have locked me up in a cage and doused me with cold water if he did. Indeed, although Dr. Langsam spoke with Hirshl about many things, he never mentioned his illness; just as Hirshl, though he spoke of many things to Dr. Langsam, never mentioned Blume Nacht.

He had in fact stopped thinking of her. Yet while he no longer invoked her image, it still sometimes hovered before him—and when it did, and he felt her mute blue glance upon him, the smile that played faintly over his lips was very much like her own. There was nothing really surprising about Hirshl seeing in Lemberg what Blume was doing in Szybusz, for he had grown up with her in one house and was familiar with her every movement; as implausible as such clairvoyance might seem, it was true.

One day Dr. Langsam came to see Hirshl. He shook his hand, asked how he was feeling, and, without waiting for an answer, sat down on the edge of his bed and began to chat as usual while taking his pulse. Upon leaving he asked Hirshl if he would like to go out to the garden.

Before long Schrenzel, the fatherly orderly, came by, helped Hirshl to get dressed, and took him to the garden, where he sat him down in a chair while standing a short distance away. After a while he returned him to his room, helped him to undress again, and put him back into bed. From then on Hirshl was taken outside for an hour or two, or sometimes even three, every day.

The sanatorium's attractive garden was planted with trees, bushes, and flowerbeds, and had chairs and benches for the patients. Often when Hirshl was sitting there he saw an old man scratching at the ground and talking to himself. This was Pinchas Hartleben, who had owned a house and property in Borislaw, where one night he had seen the earth open up and swallow his wife and children. Not knowing that this land, which seemed accursed like Sodom and Gomorrah, was in fact floating on underground deposits of oil, he went and sold it for a song to a man who was soon a millionaire, while he himself was left practically indigent. Eventually he took to wandering from place to place, scrabbling for oil in the dirt with his fingers, and talking to his dead wife and sons. "Just wait," he

184

would tell them. "Soon I'll discover a whole bunch of oil wells and you and I will be rolling in gold." He was already an old man when some people who had pity on him sent him to Dr. Langsam.

Another patient of the doctor's, who came from a long line of Hasidic holy men, was named Rabbi Zanvil. His father and brothers were well-known rabbis, and he too had attracted a camp of followers; yet being by nature an unworldly recluse, he had refused all their honors, stopped eating and drinking, and begun speaking of himself as though he were already dead and no longer living in this world. Indeed, anyone coming to ask him for his blessing was accused by him of practicing necromancy. This, however, only attracted more disciples, who were convinced that such abnegation was for the greater glory of God. After giving up food and drink Rabbi Zanvil next renounced sex with his wife and all the other commandments, citing the statement in the tractate of *Nidah* that the dead are absolved of their debts. At first, when rumors started that he was not in his right mind, attempts were made to hush the matter up; but as his case seemed more and more hopeless, he was brought to Dr. Langsam in the end. Of course, he might just as well have been taken to Rabbi Shloymeleh of Sassov, the son of the tzaddik of Olesk, a great wonder-worker like his father and every bit as good an exorcist. Rabbi Zanvil's father, however, had been feuding with Rabbi Shloymeleh for years and wanted his son to see a proper doctor in order to prove to the world that doctors could cure crazy people too.

Yet another frequent figure in Dr. Langsam's garden was Feibush Vinkler, a tall, thin, uncommunicative man who, when he was not looking for water to wash his hands with or cursing the well-known Jewish Spinozist Shlomo Rubin, preferred to be left to himself. The mere mention of Rubin, however, made Feibush spit angrily on the ground, for the man had invented a mechanical dog with a gauge in its mouth that could register one's every thought. In fact, this animal, which was controlled by Rubin from afar, had only to bark and the entire contents of one's mind tumbled straight into its jaws and were brought by it to its master, who did with them what he pleased, sometimes restoring them to their rightful owner, sometimes giving them to someone else, and sometimes keeping them for himself and leaving the thinker's head empty. Feibush Vinkler's thoughts had been exchanged for another man's, and he could not abide the new ones given him.

(Not that Feibush had ever met Shlomo Rubin in his life, for the two of them lived miles apart and their paths had never crossed. Nor, of course, did such a dog exist outside of his own imagination. If there was any truth to this story at all, it was simply that a book of Shlomo Rubin's had once come into his possession and indeed changed many of his thoughts.)

Feibush Vinkler had dealt in salt. His tiny, low-ceilinged shop was full of blocks of it piled one on top of another, their whitish-gray surfaces glittering like a world without end, like a vision of eternity, like a covenant of salt from the first unto the last of days. Indeed, who could get along without salt? When a man was born he was sprinkled with it, and when he died salt tears were shed for him. Each time he sat down to eat he salted his food, and each time his wife cooked she salted it too, for nothing could taste good without it, not even sweets or pastries, not even dishes fit for kings. It would seem far from certain whether salt was given the world as an analogue of retribution, Lot's wife having been turned into it, or of consolation, the sacrifices in the rebuilt Temple in Jerusalem being destined to be offered with it; yet in any event, whereas kings had once sowed conquered lands with it, they now made of it a royal monopoly and took a stiff share of its profits; and as there was no arguing about the price of it with the Kaiser or haggling over it with one's customers, Feibush Vinkler had plenty of free time to stand in his shop by a table, his hands in the folds of his caftan and his eyes on such mysterious texts as the *Yalkut Re'uveni* or the *Midrash Talpiyot*, in which the secrets not only of the Torah but of the entire universe were expounded. Feibush even found time to read Christian and pagan philosophers, though he was a strictly observant Jew and a great devotee of religious tradition—on account of which, despite his being a man of few words, the repute that he was held in was considerably higher than the income from his shop. Why waste time talking, after all, when all the arcana of heaven and earth were an open book before one?

There was in Galicia, in a place called Wieliczky, a vast underground salt mine sixteen miles by four that resembled a subterranean city—or rather, many such cities, one beneath the other, with streets of salt and houses of salt and stables of salt and statues of salt in doorways and in rooms of salt, from which hundreds of thousands of tons of salt were extracted every year. It was in Wieliczky—whose known reserves, according to Abraham Mendel Mahr's volume of European geography *Shvilei Olam* (which was not to be confused with Shimshon Bloch's book about Africa by the same name), were still increasing after six hundred years of continual operation—that Feibush bought his salt, which he resold in his shop as his mind was soaring to celestial pinnacles that few other men even dreamed of. The fact is that he could have lived his life out in honor were it not for a certain bookcase in the local study house that contained, alongside the books of Shlomo Rubin, many other nineteenth-century Hebrew volumes, in which Halakhah, Aggadah, Kabbalah, and the humble beginnings of modern scholarship were all jumbled hopelessly together. One day Feibush put a match to this case, the fire from which burned down the study house and a good deal of the rest of the town. Had he not been quickly bundled off to Dr. Langsam, he no doubt would have been thrown into prison.

Hirshl behaved toward these men as their guest, looking politely at whatever they wished to show him and listening to whatever they had to say. With Pinchas Hartleben and Feibush Vinkler he hardly exchanged a word, both men being preoccupied, one with finding oil and the other with barking dogs. Moreover, Schrenzel, the fatherly orderly, had cautioned Hirshl to keep away from Vinkler, who had a nasty temper and, when in one of his depressions, was perfectly capable of spitting in your face without giving a hoot who you were.

Rabbi Zanvil, on the other hand, befriended Hirshl and even took to calling him "cousin" in the mistaken belief that Hirshl was like himself a direct descendant of the renowned Yeshaya Leib Hurvitz. In his head Zanvil kept a long list of the death dates of famous holy men, on each of which he told Hirshl all about the tzaddik in question, not omitting his own self, the anniversary of whose passing he observed every year. In fact, he never referred to himself without immediately adding "may God rest his soul" or "may his memory stand us in good stead."

For hours on end, his stooped body bent toward Hirshl beneath its large white skullcap and a modest smile on his face, whose beard and sidelocks had been clipped short by the sanatorium, Zanvil spun his necrologies, which once a year were about him. Hirshl had never heard such wonderful stories in his life, every one of them brimming with the love of God and of His chosen people. Until now all he had known about the Hasidim and their rabbis was pejorative, for he had grown up in an environment where the very word Hasid was pronounced with a sneer—and while scholarly books about Hasidim and collections of their legends that showed them in a better light were available, no one in Galicia even bothered to read them, for the Hasidim considered them sacrilegious, while their opponents imagined a Hasidic anthology to be simply a kind of Jewish jokebook.

Even though Dr. Langsam treated him as if he were healthy, Hirshl knew that he was an inmate of the sanatorium and was not allowed to leave its gates. Still, he neither complained nor brooded about this. If anything, he felt grateful, as a homeless child might be expected to feel toward someone who has taken him in.

Indeed, Hirshl had good reason for feeling this way, because he never had been better off. He had a fine room that faced out on the garden and he could sleep all night long without being bothered until seven o'clock in the morning, when Schrenzel came to give him a cold rubdown and a cup of milk, coffee, cocoa, tea, hot chocolate, or fruit juice, along with a light breakfast that did not burden his digestion. At noon, on the other hand, he was given a glass of wine to spur his appetite. Then, if it was raining outside, Schrenzel returned to play chess with him, after which Dr. Langsam returned for one of his stimulating talks. These chats must have stimulated the doctor, too, for the more he said, the more he had to say. In fact, though he had spent only the first twenty years of his life in his native town, a thousand years seemed not long enough to tell about them. Sometimes he repeated old stories to Hirshl and sometimes he related new ones. Though he had studied in famous universities, lived in great metropolises, and frequented celebrated theaters and opera houses, all these places might as well never have existed: nothing had remained in his memory, it seemed, but the little town he grew up in, with its merchants saying Psalms in the marketplace, its rabbi making bookmarks with his fingernails, and its students struggling to decipher them.

"I have no doubt," Dr. Langsam told Hirshl, "that there are many unsolved problems in this world, and many scientists working on them, whose importance is greater than my rabbi's. After all, they are dealing with the secrets of the universe, while he was studying things that are of no interest to anyone today. And yet I must say that while the scientists are always baffled in the end, there were at least times when we understood what our rabbi was saying. Well, he's in the world to come now, writing his annotations with the gemstones of Paradise and no longer using goose quills—while as for that copy of *Mahatsit ha-Shekel* that he always wanted to buy, I can promise you that he and Rabbi Yitzhak Alfasi are sitting and studying it together. There was a time when I felt guilty for never having sent him the money to buy it with. Do you think I couldn't have spared the two or three kroners that it cost? But I kept putting it off, and once he was dead he no longer

189

needed them. Anyway, I sometimes think that, even if we never pay back those we owe the most to, it's enough that they suffer no harm from us. That may seem like a cynical thing to say, but it isn't. We can do good to someone and never be repaid by him, but someday he will do good to someone else, and that person will do good to someone else. And so good gets passed on and the world remains halfway livable."

Sometimes Dr. Langsam told Hirshl about the blind musicians who sat on empty sacks in the marketplace of his town and coaxed from their instruments such boundlessly sweet music that it could put one into a trance. And though the doctor's voice was that of an old man, Hirshl was as entranced by the sweet, gruff sadness of it as he might have been by a lullaby, had he ever heard one when he was a child. Tsirl, however, had never sung to him because she knew that her voice was unmusical, while the old housemaid whose husband had run off was too busy with the housework or with sewing the shrouds for her funeral to have any time for such things.

Sometimes Dr. Langsam brought Hirshl books of fiction to read and quizzed him about them with jesting questions, such as what color horse was the hero riding when the lovelorn maiden saw him through the window, or what kind of flower did she give him after he had been blinded in a duel. He himself never read these novels, which had been left him by his wife, a woman much younger than he who, in a moment of madness, had taken her own life. "What's in them?" he once said to Hirshl. "Mostly a lot of descriptions of ladies' fashions. That's all very well if you're a tailor or a jeweler, but what do you do if you're not?" Still, he seemed to enjoy the sight of Hirshl reading the same books his wife had read.

There were even times when Dr. Langsam turned his face to the wall and sang Hirshl the songs he had heard from the blind beggars in the marketplace.

Hirshl knew nothing about the real world. Had anyone asked him, he would have said that it was divided into the rich and the poor, and that the rich had it better. And though his own unhappiness had nothing to do with being poor, he still could not understand how as rich a man as Dr. Langsam could have such a suffering face.

God in heaven knew what made people do what they did. Here was a doctor who had healed many a mentally ill person in his life and yet had been powerless to prevent his own wife from killing herself. The poor woman had committed suicide after an unhappy affair with a rogue whom God had made different from other Jews and given a wooden leg, which the scoundrel still hopped about on with the help of his crutch, twirling his mustache and carrying on like a conquering hero.

30

THOUGH GRIEF, worry, humiliation, and other emotions could easily have endangered Mina's pregnancy, she overcame them all and gave birth to a baby boy.

Hirshl received the news in a ten-word telegram from Szybusz in which he was informed that both mother and child were doing well. At first he failed to grasp what need there was to tell him that Mina was well, or what she could be doing with a child. Then he laid his hand on his heart, which was pulsing oddly as if gripped by pincers.

Hirshl felt neither happy nor sad. When he himself was born, his own father had been happier. What joy Boruch Meir had felt then! How lavishly he had celebrated the occasion! He had been twenty-six years old at the time, a mere youngster and a newcomer in Szybusz, yet already better known in the town than Hirshl was even now.

It would have been natural had Hirshl tried picturing his wife and new son. Instead, he pictured his father, who seemed very big and made him, his father's son, seem very small.

During the first part of his stay in the sanatorium Hirshl tried not to think of the past. Anything that reminded him of Szybusz he quickly put out of his mind. He did, however, dream of the town, and some of these dreams kept recurring. Later on he stopped dreaming of it and began thinking of it while awake. Although his thoughts were not as frightening as his dreams, they angered him every bit as much as had the reality of Szybusz itself. And while Hirshl no more believed in metempsychosis than did any other educated young man of his age, having to return to his parents' store seemed to him a worse fate than any possible reincarnation.

It was a long way from Lemberg to Szybusz by train, which stopped at many stations, yet Hirshl's imagination covered the distance in no time and showed him all of Szybusz at a glance. Although he didn't know all his fellow townsmen by sight, he certainly knew most of them, if not by their real names, then by their nicknames, so that, like the ants dreamed about and described to him by Mina, he found himself remembering every one of them. Worse yet, just as the thought of so many ants had made his skin crawl, so did the thought of so many Szybuszians. Dr. Langsam, who had been away from his hometown for forty years and had no intention of returning, could feel as nostalgic for it as he pleased. Hirshl, who had been away for only a short while, could not bear hearing Szybusz mentioned.

Once again Hirshl had trouble sleeping. After not missing a single night of sleep since his arrival in the sanatorium, he suddenly could not catch a wink of it. And as bad as his insomnia had been in the first place, its reappearance following a long absence drove him to the verge of despair. Why, he had all but forgotten what a sleepless night or the morning after were like, and here he was tossing and turning once more and unable to enjoy a moment's rest! Despite there being no Mina to have to listen to breathing or talking, her voice like a driven nail, no barking dogs or crowing roosters, not even any people in the street, he still lay in bed like a broken watch that could not keep the right time. All kinds of visions passed before his sleepless eyes. Held in the fingers of a Szybusz whose hills, dales, and valleys had shrunk to the size and shape of his own hand sat a tiny blind beggar, who sang a song about the snow that fell on the ground where the froggies grazed. Perhaps the Angel of Dreams knew when it would end, but to Hirshl the song seemed interminable. It was still going on when a cloaked woman appeared, bent low before him, and sliced him a piece of cake. Yet before she could give it to him a man came along and threw a pocketful of coins at him—or rather, into his eyes, which soon were covered with two mountains of them. Though Hirshl screamed and sobbed, carriage wheels kept drowning out his voice. He uncovered his eyes and saw Sophia Gildenhorn, slender and attractive, sitting in a buggy with a friendly smile and smelling of something good.

Hirshl was a nervous wreck again. His nights passed without sleep, and his head hurt all day. A great sorrow haunted his dazed eyes, which ached with an inner feeling of devastation. Though he no longer crowed like a rooster, croaked like a frog, or sang about the snow in the grass, his existence was pure agony. Yet Dr. Langsam, though he saw all this, gave no sign of having done so.

"Could all those books be having a bad effect on him?" Schrenzel asked the doctor.

"A few reams of paper," scoffed Dr. Langsam, "or even all the yards of satins and silks described in them, are harmless enough. But just so you don't think I'm neglecting him, here's what I'm going to do."

What Dr. Langsam did was to put Hirshl on iron pills and arsenic salts and to have Schrenzel give him lukewarm baths. Hirshl swallowed the pills dutifully and let himself be washed three times a day in tepid water. Before long his eyes regained their healthy luster, his headaches went away, and he began to sleep again at night. He also resumed his games of chess with Schrenzel, did his exercises, ate and drank with a hearty appetite, and went for walks in the garden, where he helped Schrenzel to weed, water the flowers, and chop firewood.

Hirshl liked the hours spent with Schrenzel in the garden. The trees and shrubs gave off a good smell, the work tools shone in the sun, and little winged insects flew all around. Schrenzel went about his work while keeping one eye on Hirshl, who wiped the sweat from his face without a sound. Though he was working hard and had every right to grunt now and then with the effort, he did not. True, a woodcutter could have done in an hour what would have taken Hirshl a week, but woodcutters worked in the winter and not in the hot summer sun, and they were paid for their work, while Hirshl was paying Dr. Langsam. Not far away from him Pinchas Hartleben was scratching at the ground while talking with his dead wife and children. He had yet to strike oil, which was not something that one did every day, but his faith that he would was worth all the earth's treasures. Rabbi Zanvil and Feibush Vinkler were nowhere to be seen. Either they were all better and had been released, or they had acted up and had been confined by Dr. Langsam to their rooms. Hirshl did not ask, and Schrenzel did not volunteer to tell him.

31

ELUL WAS THE LAST and best month of the Jewish year. Even when the weather was hot it was not as hot as Tammuz, and even when it was cold it was not as cold as Tevet or Shvat. The days were longer than winter days but shorter than summer ones, the clouds that sometimes hid the sun were warm and cool by turn, and the trees in the garden were bathed in an orange light. Though Hirshl had been in Lemberg for two and a half months, he still had seen nothing of the city. Once, upon hearing how Yona Toyber had been kept from reaching Lemberg by a geography book, he could not keep himself from laughing. Yet now that he had been in Lemberg all summer, had he seen any more of it than Toyber?

Perhaps, thought Hirshl as he sat by himself one day, I will be a prisoner here until I die. Perhaps I will be one even after I die, like that corpse they found chained in irons in that peasant's cellar in Malikrowik. And the proof that I am one already is that no one pays me any attention or brings me any news from home. Why, one would think there was no draft board to appear before, no son to bring up, no store that needed looking after!

Hirshl pictured the long, narrow store with its scales and counters, its large balance that his mother liked to sit next to, its little office where his father kept the books, and its customers being waited on by Getzel and Feyvel. He suddenly was overcome by a hatred for Getzel such as he had never felt for anyone before. Could it be that he envied him his activity in the store while he, the owners' son, did nothing all day but eat, drink, play chess, and listen to the tall tales of Dr. Langsam, who kept talking circles around him and refused to let him go? Indeed, Hirshl was beginning to doubt whether there was any chance of being released in Dr. Langsam's lifetime. How old was the doctor, and how much longer could he live? And yet even if he would die and be buried some day, so would everybody he had cured. Never in his life had Hirshl felt so close to the reality of death. Nor was it just his parents' store that he kept imagining. It was their home too and everything in it, even its abandoned dovecote, even its unused room with the pile furniture in which Mina had dabbed herself with cologne before their engagement. It was not necessarily his favorite spot, yet being away from a place made a man think of it.

Hirshl felt that he was back to normal. If he regarded the other patients, he really did seem to himself more like a visitor in Dr. Langsam's sanatorium. He didn't scrabble in the earth for oil, tell stories about his own death, or curse Shlomo Rubin for inventing a mechanical dog that stole thoughts. And yet while one had to be crazy to believe in such an invention, Hirshl wondered what, if a dog like that existed, it could tell him about the things that people were thinking of him back in Szybusz. He himself no longer thought about his mother's brother and grandfather. Since coming to the sanatorium he had not even dreamed of them. Perhaps they had purged their souls in limbo and did not have to wander about there anymore and haunt him. He too felt purged and fit. He hoped his wife and son were well too.

Mina could not nurse her baby, for the nipples of her breasts were inverted. Of course, the condition could have been corrected before she gave birth by coating the inside of a perforated zinc cup with olive oil and placing it over her nipples to draw them out, but Hirshl's hospitalization had left everyone too stupefied to think of it.

Bertha brought a sturdy wet nurse from the village who had never been sick a day in her life. In fact, upon giving birth herself she had disproved the medical opinion that alcohol was bad for parturient women by downing a whole quart of vodka, after which she had devoured the light repast permitted by the doctor and gone on to eat a huge meal. Besides nursing the baby, she helped Mina a good deal around the house. Bertha and Tsirl were more than satisfied with her. They would have liked to be as satisfied with the baby.

Meshulam was so frail at birth that he was not circumcised until the age of a month instead of the usual eight days. Being a firstborn son, he also had to be redeemed by his father from a kohen, a descendant of the priestly class, in accordance with the biblical rite. As Hirshl was not there to perform it, however, the child had a copper amulet with the letter *heh*, the fifth letter of the Hebrew alphabet, hung around his neck to indicate that his father owed the kohen five gold crowns.

32

ONE FRIDAY BEFORE Rosh Hashana a letter arrived from Dr. Langsam saying that Hirshl could come home. So that he should not have to travel alone, the doctor suggested that someone come to Szybusz to get him.

As soon as the Sabbath was over Tsirl packed a bag for Boruch Meir, who took a cab to the train station.

It was the first night of the penitential prayers of Elul. The train station was deserted. No one apart from the station workers was to be seen. Boruch Meir bought a ticket and boarded the waiting train. He found a seat by a window, put down his bag, and sat down.

It was a moonless night. A dark sky and earth loomed toward each other and merged, blackly blotting out the silent world. The train stood on its tracks, peering with a nervous tremor into the endless night, then took a deep breath and set out. Boruch Meir was glad to have a compartment to himself in which to stretch out and sleep, though he had trouble deciding on which bench to do it. In the end he chose the one he was sitting on and placed his bag beneath his head. No sooner were his eyes shut, though, than it occurred to him that he had no business sleeping on a night when Jews everywhere were awake and at prayer. He sat up, wet his fingers on the frosty window in lieu of washing his hands, and took out his prayer shawl, tefillin, and prayer book. He was about to open the book when the train came to a halt.

Boruch Meir stood up and peered out the window to read the name of the station. As he was trying to make it out a soldier returning to his base sat down with his bag on the bench facing him.

197

"Well, the summer is over," said Boruch Meir.

"Yes, sir," said the soldier.

"It will be winter soon," said Boruch Meir.

"Yes, sir," said the soldier.

"But not as soon as all that," said Boruch Meir.

"No, sir," said the soldier.

"We still have some summer days ahead of us," said Boruch Meir.

"Yes, sir," said the soldier.

"And how, Nikofer," asked Boruch Meir, "are you yourself these days?"

"Just fine, sir," said the soldier. "I can't complain, sir."

"Nikofer," inquired Boruch Meir, "aren't you curious to know how I knew your name was Nikofer?"

"Yes, sir," said the soldier.

"Because, Nikofer," said Boruch Meir, "it is strange that I should know your name is Nikofer when I've never seen you before in my life, isn't it?"

"Yes, sir," said the soldier.

"Yes sir, no sir, yes sir," said Boruch Meir. "Aren't you going to ask me how I knew your name was Nikofer?"

"How did you know my name was Nikofer, sir?" asked the soldier.

"Aha," said Boruch Meir. "I guessed it."

"You guessed wrong, sir," said the soldier.

"Then what is your name?"

"If you're so good at guessing, sir," said the soldier, "you may as well guess again."

"You're a funny boy, Ivan," said Boruch Meir.

"It's not Ivan, sir."

"Then what is it? Stefan?"

"Keep guessing, sir."

"Do you think, Petri," said Boruch Meir, "that I have nothing better to do than to sit here guessing your name?"

"Yes, sir," said the soldier.

"Then you have another guess coming yourself, Andrei," said Boruch Meir, opening his prayer book to begin the penitential prayer. The soldier stretched out on his bench, shut his eyes, and began to snore at once.

It's a rare gift these Christians have, thought Boruch Meir, to be able to fall asleep the minute their heads touch something solid. He took out his watch, mouthed "twelve" to himself, yawned, and put it back in his pocket. Midnight was the hour when his fellow Jews assembled in the synagogue and the cantor donned his prayer shawl and launched into the *ashrei*.

A great sadness descended on Boruch Meir. Had he waited to take the next train he could have been praying now with the congregation, yet he had all but forgotten what night it was in his eagerness to see his son. And even as he told himself this the feeling of sadness yielded to one of shame that brought a blush to his face. The thought of sitting in a railroad car when so many Jews were begging God for forgiveness made him feel like an outcast.

The train stopped at another station. Boruch Meir rose and peered outside again. The darkness was so great that he could not tell if it was coming from above or below. Not a single passenger boarded the train. The Kaiser is not doing very good business tonight, thought Boruch Meir.

The train breathed in, breathed out, and gave a lurch. Boruch Meir and the soldier were still alone in their compartment. Boruch Meir stifled another yawn with his hand and began to recite his prayers. Not being a learned Jew, he was uncertain whether or not when praying by himself he was supposed to recite the adoration beginning "O Lord, O Lord, God merciful and gracious." In the end he compromised by standing up and reading it to himself from the prayer book as if it were not really a prayer. Just as he finished, the train stopped again. He turned the page of his prayer book and wondered which would come first, the next station or the next adoration.

The train started up. Boruch Meir looked at the sleeping soldier and thought, I should have asked him what station to wake him at so he won't miss it and be punished for being absent without leave.

A conductor entered the compartment, checked Boruch Meir's ticket, and woke the soldier, who took out a chit and handed it to him. The conductor held the paper up to the light and left.

Before the soldier could fall asleep again Boruch Meir asked, "Well, do you like serving the Kaiser?"

"Yes, sir," said the soldier.

"But you'd like to be home too," said Boruch Meir.

"Oh yes," said the soldier. "I would."

Hirshl had come close to being a soldier himself, thought Boruch Meir. In fact, if not for what had happened to him, he might have been sleeping tonight in a uniform too. Though the thought had not crossed Boruch Meir's mind until now, the soldier's reply made him realize how lucky Hirshl was not to have been in Szybusz over the summer when the draft board arrived. "Justice is thine, O Lord," he whispered, vindicating God's ways.

He had barely finished the penitential prayer and was seeking to sleep when several passengers entered the compartment. One of them resembled his brother Meshulam, or at least reminded him of him. It had been twelve years, mused Boruch Meir, since he and Meshulam had last met or—apart from the New Year's card and rhymed poem they exchanged once a year—even written each other. Why, I do believe his sons are old enough to be married, thought Boruch Meir. And there's a daughter to find a husband for too, if I'm not mistaken. Who does he expect to get for her, some young *Rabbiner?* He's a queer bird, Meshulam. Someone even told me he had joined a Zionist organization in Tarnow and was planning to become a farmer in Palestine. Some farmer he'll make! He'll end up a charity case there. But why am I thinking about him? That man doesn't look like him at all.

Boruch Meir leaned his head against the window and dozed off. Noisily the train rushed on through the night, stopping, starting, and stopping. By the time he awoke it was daylight and he was already in Lemberg.

Hirshl had passed the whole summer in Lemberg. A little beard ringed his face, which had grown fuller and tanned. The fear and bewilderment were gone from it, as was the nervous fatigue. He was his old self again, and his movements flowed normally too. Three months of healthful living at Dr. Langsam's, with its exercise in the sun every day and its long hours of sleep every night, had put him back on his feet. And yet he felt ill at ease, especially facing his father, who walked in smelling of Szybusz, which made Hirshl's spirits sink at once. He shrank in Boruch Meir's presence as if apologizing for causing so much trouble while hoping in his heart to be forgiven.

Boruch Meir threw his arms around his son, hugged and kissed him, and asked him a few commonplace questions as if nothing out of the ordinary had happened. He was equally tactful on the train ride home, until Hirshl became so conscious of this that he seized his father's hand to thank him. Afraid of crying, though, he restrained himself and said nothing.

Boruch Meir had told the doctor how everyone in Szybusz was convinced that Hirshl's madness was staged to dodge the draft. "It's an ill wind that blows no good," Dr. Langsam had replied. "Now, when Hirshl goes home, at least he won't need to feel ashamed."

Szybusz was a long way from Lemberg, and much had happened there in Hirshl's absence. Looking at his son, Boruch Meir wondered where to begin. Should it be with the druggist who had sought a court order against him and Tsirl to prevent them from selling smelling salts without a license? Boruch Meir was uncertain who would win the case, the druggist or the firm of Hurvitz, but even if he had to drop the salts, he was doing a brisk business on a much faster-moving item, namely, paint—for Schleien, the master painter who had left for America, had unexpectedly returned to Szybusz, and the whole town was repainting its houses and shop signs. Indeed, so great an artist was Schleien that some shopkeepers had actually bankrupted themselves ordering new billboards from him. He had also redone the interior of the Great Synagogue, much to the displeasure of Hayyim Yehoshua Bleiberg, who had led a furious protest against the painting over of the old walls and ceiling. It was a token of Boruch Meir's modesty, however, that he chose not to mention the Bleiberg affair to Hirshl, as this would have also obliged him to mention who had donated the paint to the synagogue. Boruch Meir did not like to boast of his own generosity, especially when its sole object had been to coax heaven into making his son well.

In any event, there was no need to entertain Hirshl on the way, for a train ride to Szybusz, especially in the month of Elul, was entertainment in itself. The passengers, it turned out, were divided into four camps. The first of these, a party of esrog dealers on their way back from Greece, was in a bellicose mood. Why, to think of the weeks they had just spent running around that land of unscrupulous cutthroats without tasting a Jewish meal or hearing a Jewish prayer in order to bring Jews esrogs for Sukkos—and here the local Zionist press had the gall to attack them and blacken their names! The Zionists in the car shouted back that any Jew buying or blessing citrons from Corfu when Jewish farmers were sweating blood to grow the same fruit in Palestine was an out-and-out anti-Semite. At this point the fray was joined by a band of Hasidim, some of them returning from taking the baths and others on their way to their rabbis for the High Holy Days: anyone purchasing an esrog from Palestine, they yelled, was himself doing business with anti-Semites, which was what the irreligious Jewish farmers there were.

There were also ordinary Jews on the train who were neither esrog dealers, Zionists, nor Hasidim. At every station they bought apples, pears, and plums from the vendors on the platform, which they both ate themselves and passed around to their fellow passengers. True, none of these fruits was a match for an esrog, which came all the way from the isles of Greece and had a special blessing all its own; yet God had made them fragrant and juicy, and had not put any restriction on eating them. Slowly the car filled with the aroma of autumn fruit and the bitter quarrel subsided. The train stopped and started, its passengers getting on and off. Why, one still had half an apple in one's mouth and here was Szybusz already!

33

HIRSHL ARRIVED HOME to be met by Mina with a baby in her arms that, cuddled in its white pillow, made him think of a bawling red beefsteak. He greeted his wife and ignored the child, feeling as unmoved by the sight of it as he had been by the news of its birth. Two blue droplets sparkled in its face, and he knew that it was looking at him. His lips trembled. He felt the need to apologize for having brought it into the world without loving it, without even the capacity to love it.

A greater Father than Hirshl, however, had other ideas. As much as Hirshl tried not looking at the child, as much as he tried not even thinking of it, tender feelings for it began to creep into his heart. Before long he was hugging and kissing the same infant he had been certain he could never love. Whereas only yesterday he had grimly told himself, Well, I have to put up with him because I'm to blame that he's alive, his own life now seemed to him to exist solely for the sake of his son. (So God in heaven plays the father with us. As busy as He is making and unmaking cosmoses, He still finds time even for a small-town storekeeper, even—just as Hirshl did—for a baby in the cradle.)

What indeed made Hirshl leave the store and not only run to see his son but clap hands, hop like a frog, and whistle like a bird for him? Perhaps the joy of seeing the first beginnings of a smile on his face. All that a man really needs, Hirshl thought, is a little joy in his life. If I can't be happy myself, at least my son can be. And while I never had the childhood I wanted, at least I can see to it that he does.

But what happiness could there be without love, and what child would want a childhood in which its parents did not love each other? Hirshl wondered whether it was possible for a Jew to hate his wife—and yet, though he did not really hate Mina, not loving her was almost as bad. Had his heart not been another's, he might have been happy with the woman he had. More than one man who failed to marry the wife of his choice had shared a contented life with someone else in the end. But Hirshl had given his heart away and no longer had it to share.

Blume was still not married. God in heaven knew who she was waiting for. Having turned down Getzel Stein, she showed no interest in anyone else. Could she have her eye on Yona Toyber, whose wife had recently died? Yona was still a young man. Barring war or cholera, anyone with habits like his was sure to live to a ripe old age.

But Blume's eye was not on Toyber, and Toyber's eye was not on Blume. What Yona wanted was a capable housewife to light the stove, make the beds, do the wash, and take care of his tender orphans while he looked after his business. When he went and married the hunchbacked daughter of the ex–chicken slaughterer Stein, therefore, it was wrong of some Szybuszians to consider it God's punishment for all the mismatches Yona had made. The fact of the matter was that Yona Toyber knew exactly what he was doing when he overlooked the ugliness of Getzel's sister in favor of her many virtues, for not a day had passed since their wedding without proper meals served on time, a well-heated house, fresh sheets on the beds, and clean shirts to wear. Indeed, the bride's own mother could not believe her eyes when she saw her monstrous shrew of a daughter washing Toyber's children, dressing them in clean clothes, making them breakfast each morning, and trotting them off to school like little scholars. She even began to visit her regularly, not because her daughter needed help, but so as not to be accused of not giving it. Besides, it was a welcome opportunity to rest from her own housework, which had become too much to cope with, for though Getzel's sisters had dreamed of getting rid of the hunchback for years, they were sorry now that they had. Not that they had regularly dined on caviar before. Yet at least there had been hot meals on the table, whereas now what food was infrequently served was always cold—nor was there anyone to complain to but their mother, since Getzel spent all his time at the new Workers of Zion club and their father was still on the road, soliciting the aid of Jewry's leading lights in his chicken wars. No one knew when to expect him home. He was indeed making little progress, for it was difficult to cross a tzaddik's threshold without first crossing his secretaries' palms, and Getzel, the old man claimed, had stingily hid all his savings and refused to lend him a cent.

Actually, Getzel had put his savings in the bank—and while his account there was a small one, it was big enough to earn him a reputation for being a hardheaded fellow who knew all about such things as capital, compound interest, and putting one's money to work. No longer did he waste his salary from the store on such frills as colorful ties, which his sister Saltshi had in any case stopped wearing to Viktor's or anyone else's. Either some-one had put a hex on Saltshi or the love potions she had con-cocted to keep Viktor's affections were having a bad effect on her, for she lay in bed surrounded by poultices and herbal remedies, turning greener by the day. As for Viktor, he had left town, while the Singer agent who had taken his place had found other girlfriends. Tastes vary. Even Viktor's: sometimes he had liked Saltshi better than her sister Beiltshi, and sometimes he had liked Beiltshi better than her sister Saltshi.

A mournful silence hung over Getzel's home. Were it not for Saltshi's groans and Beiltshi's attempts to comfort her, one might have guessed it was deserted. The sewing machine had moved out with the hunchback, as had the angry creak of its wheel. Not that it had any reason to be angry these days, for its mistress was treating it well: she did not overwork it, oiled it often, and even sang to soothe its jangled nerves. And while generally speaking the younger generation in Szybusz had for-gotten the old songs, the new Mrs. Toyber sang the same sad, sweet ballads of love and death that her mother and her mother's neighbors had sung, even though the mere mention of dying was enough to make her gray eyes glisten with tears. Could she be worried that Yona Toyber was not long for this world when he was still in the prime of life and had the habits of a man intending to live to a hundred and twenty? Having experienced so much misery in her life, perhaps she simply could not believe she had seen the last of it.

And yet the hunchback did not sing to complain about her fate but simply to pour out her soul—after which, sweetly solaced, she went back to finishing the new *kittel* for her husband, the fringed *tallis koton* for her stepson, or the blouse for her stepdaughter that she was working on. The children's mother, God rest her poor soul, had been ill toward the end of her life and had let the house chores go untended. Yet what the good Lord took with one hand He restored with the other, and what Yona Toyber's first wife never got done his second wife more than made up for.

34

HIRSHL WAS WHOLLY OCCUPIED with the store. Though he was not especially creative, he did his job well. True, he had done what was expected of him before his marriage too, yet then he had his mind on other things, while now he kept it on his work. No longer did he compare the woman customers with each other or wonder which attracted him most. If, as the old legend has it, God first created man half male and half female, with two heads and one back, and then sundered him, so that all men and women were born separate forever after, Hirshl had once stared at every woman as if it were his mission in life to find his other half; now, however, he had come to the realization that he was as complete as he ever would be and that the missing part of him would not be found. And though the thought of this sometimes saddened him, he slowly got over it as does someone who has lost something precious and must learn to make do with something else in its place.

Tsirl no longer urged him to go for walks. Anyone as busy as Hirshl had no time for them. The place for a walker was the Gildenhorns' wall, on which hung a picture of a slim young man with a rattan cane beneath his arm and one foot poised to set out. Hirshl had better things to do. Like most other Szybuszians he stepped out once a week, on Saturday afternoons, for a breath of fresh air—and never in the direction of Synagogue Street. Variety was good for a man, and too much of one thing led to boredom. Unlike Akavia Mazal, whose passion was the study of antiquities, Hirshl had seen enough of that street, each stone and building of which, from the Catholic church that stood on the site of the old synagogue to the ruined convent whose grass came up red, was familiar to him. His whole life was ahead of him—why spend it walking down the same street? Nor was the fact that it was also lived on by Tirza Mazal, who had no more interest in ancient history than Hirshl, any reason for him to change his mind, for Tirza lived on Synagogue Street only because of her husband, just as Blume Nacht worked there only because of Tirza. Once Blume had had a job in the center of town; now she had one on the edge of it.

When a man was preoccupied, he was best off being by himself. Once his worries were over, however, he belonged with others, especially if he could take his wife along with him. Not every day did a man have time for his wife.

The Sabbaths after the Sukkos holiday were delightful. The rained-on ground was no longer hard on the feet, the low sky seemed almost near enough to touch, the sun was warm without being hot, and the dust was gone from the streets. The clouds had wrung themselves out over the holiday, and soon it would be time for snow. If the good Lord was putting off the cold weather, this was only for the last potatoes to be dug and the last logs to be split for firewood.

Hirshl and Mina strolled side by side. Once Hirshl had liked to walk with Toyber; then he had walked by himself; now he was walking with his wife. It was to Yona Toyber's credit that he had brought Hirshl and Mina together even though it had cost him a walking partner.

Hirshl was wearing his Saturday-afternoon clothes that were neither too dressy for a casual stroll nor too casual for the Sabbath. As shrewd as it had been of his mother to have such an outfit made for him, however, it now fitted him too tightly, for the days spent at Dr. Langsam's had put some flesh on his bones. Not even his father could complain anymore that he had gained no weight since his wedding.

Mina too had filled out and was no longer so aristocratically thin. Though the automatic spoon had still not been invented, her waistline had grown by at least a fraction of an inch. Perhaps it was the aftereffect of her pregnancy, or perhaps she had become less chary of lifting her spoon to her mouth. In any case, only a misanthrope could have failed to enjoy seeing her with Hirshl.

The two of them were far from alone. Many husbands were taking the Sabbath air with their wives, some of them businessmen and some of them workingmen, since while the former did not choose to pass the whole day in the synagogue, neither did the latter spend it all listening to Dr. Knabenhut preach. Not that it would have done the burghers of Szybusz any harm to sit one day out of seven with a holy book, which was something they were too busy making money to do the rest of the week; yet if anything held true of the middle-class Szybuszian, it was his greater concern for the needs of the body than for the needs of the soul. And the same went for the working class. Though it might have learned something from Dr. Knabenhut, it liked the sound of its own small talk better than any of his big ideas.

Hirshl promenaded with Mina through the streets of Szybusz, stopping often to chat with people he knew. The sight of Hirshl Hurvitz being so sociable when he had been written off by everyone as a recluse just went to show how wrong public opinion could be. Even the town's greatest snob, its resident newspaper correspondent, Vovi Tshortkover, who had been the first to accuse Hirshl of snobbishness, now admitted that he was a pleasure to talk to. Although Hirshl was not really interested in everything that was said to him, he knew how to be a good listener.

Hirshl and Mina passed a house that was under construction and Hirshl stepped into it for a look at its new walls, rooms, doorways, and window frames. Having been born in a house that was finished, he was curious to see one that was not. Once, he reflected, when the world was young, men had built whole cities, whereas today the building of a single house was considered an event. He was still in the middle of this thought when more people entered the skeleton of the house to inspect and discuss it. Now that Dreyfus was finally acquitted and no longer the sole subject of conversation, Szybuszians could talk of other things, such as local and state politics, the health of the Kaiser Franz Josef, who was a great friend to the Jews, the Catholic priests who were said to waylay Jewish girls and entice them into convents, and the Alliance Israelite, which had recently opened an office in Vienna. While most Jews in Szybusz were enthusiastic about this organization for the advancement of their people, which was run by Jewish barons and plutocrats who, while thoroughly at home in the royal houses of Europe, were not ashamed of their origins, there were also unabashed dissenters like Hayyim Yehoshua Bleiberg who claimed that it did more harm than good. Why, Bleiberg declared, just look at the anti-Semitism in Rumania! Had not the House of Rothschild floated the Rumanians a loan, their government would have collapsed long ago instead of persecuting the Jews—which just proved that the Rothschilds of the world valued their profits more than their people.

Bleiberg was a queer duck and had queer opinions. When the whole of Szybusz was ecstatic over the repainting of the Great Synagogue, he alone had raised a rumpus over the disappearance of the moon and the twelve signs of the zodiac from its ceiling, which Schleien had painted over with something that looked like an open umbrella. After all, the drawings that Bleiberg was up in arms about were two hundred and fifty-six years old and had not been retouched since the synagogue was built; with justice the imperial representatives who came to pay the Kaiser's respects on Yom Kippur eve could have accused the Jews of Szybusz of lacking even the piety to maintain their own house of worship. It was a lucky thing that the synagogue sextons had been able to get hold of Schleien, even if he did paint the interior walls with gold and silver polka dots like those in the buffet of the railway station. And besides, the buffet was done in cheap watercolors, whereas Schleien had used real oil paint donated by Boruch Meir and Tsirl, thus ensuring that his work would endure for generations to come.

Saturday afternoons were short in autumn. The town was still walking and talking when the evening mail arrived.

The clipped notes of a bugle sounded, heralding a yellowish carriage that drew up in the courtyard of the post office. From it emerged the postman, who strode to the street with his pouch slung around his neck, his eyes as hard as a charity warden's. Yet though his was the power to deliver or withhold the fates of men, he was only too glad to get rid of his load and let everyone have his mail.

Silently the townsmen stood facing him, each of them waiting to hear his name called. Sometimes, if the postman was in the mood for a joke, he might call someone's name, then say, "Sorry, there's nothing for you today, better luck tomorrow," then hand him a packet of letters just as he was turning disappointedly to go. Yet the letters were sealed; one had no way of knowing what was in them, or, if one could guess, of knowing it all; there was no choice but to wait for the three stars in the sky that meant that God had put away his Sabbath; and God was in no hurry to light stars. Either He was fonder of the last wee hour of the Sabbath than of all the six days of Creation combined, or else He was piqued with His children for being so eager to get on with the new week.

Still, if the sealed letters could not be torn open until the Sabbath was over, there were postcards and newspapers that could be read right away.

Many different newspapers reached Szybusz, some in German, some in Polish, and some in Yiddish, several of which were sent to their families by emigrants in America. There, thousands of miles away, sat encyclopedically knowledgeable men who wished only to transmit their knowledge to Szybusz, so that every Szybuszian could know what his great-grandfathers had never guessed at and be far wiser than they. His own father might have studied each page of the thirty-six volumes of the Talmud seven times; his grandfather, seven times seven; yet what had they known in the end? A whole lot of fairy tales, whereas after an hour of reading the newspaper one was an encyclopedia on two legs oneself.

Besides the German, Polish, and Yiddish papers, there were Hebrew ones too. Yet while once many Hebrew newspapers were subscribed to in Szybusz, there were now only two, one for the Society of Zion, and one for a certain young man who wrote Hebrew poems. God in heaven knew what made a young fellow like him care for Hebrew. Did he think it was a ticket to riches or fame?

Times had changed. For centuries Jews had loved the Hebrew language and made it the jewel in their crown. Indeed, not only Yona Toyber, but even Sebastian Montag, our town's leading citizen, had written an article in it in his youth. Even now he beamed when recalling this piece that had appeared in the journal *Hamaggid* under the title, borrowed from the prophet Isaiah, "By His Magnanimity Shall a Man Stand." But who in the younger generation still knew the holy tongue at all? Nowadays one studied only what was practical, even if one was a Zionist or a socialist.

In any case, Zionism was spreading and its popularity was on the rise. Still, it was far from a tactical error on Sebastian Montag's part to have clung to his universalist views, for supposing even that in fifty or a hundred years there might be Zionist politicians as powerful as himself, one of whom was sure to be his own second or third reincarnation, what room did Zionism allow for his talents in the meantime? None of which, of course, kept him from fraternizing with the Zionists, drinking Carmel wine from Palestine with their leaders, and joking with them in his fashion—or from telling better jokes than they did, since his were steeped in Jewish learning and delivered in a sonorous voice. So musical was Sebastian in fact that he occasionally served as the cantor of the Great Synagogue—something, it was rumored in Szybusz, that gave him more satisfaction than all his "nebbichlach." In a word, if Sebastian had reason to fear anyone, it was not the Zionists but the socialists.

As small and spry as a leprechaun and as smoothly shaven as a matinee idol, Dr. Knabenhut darted about town organizing the workingmen. Ever since his arrest by the authorities for spreading illegal propaganda, he was brimming over with confidence. Once, running into Sebastian Montag, he said to him, "There are two honest men in all of Szybusz, and both of us belong in jail. The only difference is that I should be locked up for making a better world, and you for cheating at cards."

The whole of Szybusz felt Knabenhut's knout and lucky was the man whom it spared, though if it came down hard on the well-to-do it seemed soft as a caress to the poor. When he had finished his Saturday lectures at the socialist club Knabenhut liked to go for a walk, followed by a peripatetic crowd of his students who never took their eyes off him. His own eyes took in a good deal more, for while keeping one of them on his entourage he let the other rove freely. Sometimes indeed, spying a certain young lady walking by herself, he even left his disciples to join her. One might have thought that she should have been his follower also, since being a housemaid was proletarian work. One would, however, have thought wrongly.

Hirshl gazed straight ahead, his animated conversation with Mina suddenly forgotten. Six months had passed since last he saw Blume—and now there she was. Mina too, though generally not in the habit of staring at strangers, stopped to look. Something about the girl with Dr. Knabenhut made her want to ask who she was, but her lips trembled too hard for her to speak.

Hirshl stood as perfectly still as if the Angel of Dreams had waved his magic wand before his eyes. And indeed, just as one dreams of one's beloved without seeing her, so one sees her and thinks it is a dream.

Sophia Gildenhorn, who had joined Hirshl and Mina on their walk, saw Blume with Knabenhut too. Ordinarily she would have made some comment, but she was feeling too low to take notice. What made Sophia so low? Not knowing which was worse, her loneliness when her husband was away or all the hoopla when he was home. Not every woman could go from one extreme to the other without hysterics. Mina did all she could for her former counselor, who now needed counseling herself, and Sophia spent long hours in Mina's house, where she no longer feared intruding, as Hirshl and Mina had been married for over a year. Yet neither did she spend her time there anymore whispering gossip that left Mina wide-eyed. All she wanted to do was to be with Mina's baby. Though God in heaven had not given her a child of her own, He had at least given her best friend one that she could play with.

At last the stars come out and the shops opened. Mina and Hirshl went home, and then Hirshl went to the store to bring his father the mail from the post office. There was lots of it: business letters, bills, personal letters, charity appeals, official letters, wedding invitations, and two more letters besides, one from Szybusz and one from abroad. In addition, there was a letter to Hirshl written in Hebrew. This came from the town's former rabbi, who now had a position elsewhere and had written a book on Jewish law, a copy of which he had sent to Boruch Meir with a request for a donation to help defray the cost of publication. Seeing the book at his father's, Hirshl had ordered another copy for himself, enclosing a contribution of his own, and now its author had written back to thank him for his love of learning and support of its practitioners. Not that Hirshl had needed another book on Jewish law. He could not even remember what was in the books he had already read. He had simply wanted to help a worthy cause, which the appearance of a new legal commentary was.

As for the letter from abroad, it came from Gedalia's cousin Arnold Ziemlich, who, not knowing if there was a post office in Malikrowik or even how to spell the village's name, wished Boruch Meir to tell Mina's father that he was planning to come for a visit during the winter holidays. Although Tsirl doubted whether he really would, Boruch Meir was sure of it, for a German always kept his word and could be counted on to do what he said.

One last letter remained, that sent from Szybusz to Szybusz. Never before in the history of Szybusz had one Szybuszian written another, but as the crazy druggist now demonstrated, there was always a first time. Just a few months ago he had taken the Hurvitzes to court for selling smelling salts without a license—and here he was informing them by mail that he had decided to withdraw his complaint! Perhaps Sebastian Montag had gently hinted that he should, or perhaps he had given up hope of winning the case. In any event, it was one less worry for Boruch Meir, who had every reason to be pleased.

Besides having one less minor worry, Boruch Meir had one less major one. After all he had been through, including his fear that Hirshl would never be the same again, here was his son wholly occupied with the store once more. In fact, Hirshl made the most of every day: he knew when to be in the store and when to be with his wife, when to do business and when to put it aside for the sake of a friendly conversation.

35

ONCE MORE HIRSHL'S home was full of guests. Yet if once he had invited them in order to be hospitable, now it was for the pleasure of their company.

Not all of the old crowd had returned. Once, when Hirshl had asked Mottshi Shaynbart why he had stopped visiting, Mottshi had replied, "The old crutch can't take the stairs anymore." That had been a joke, of course, but now Mottshi's real leg was acting up too. He still frequented the Gildenhorns, who lived on the ground floor, but Hirshl's stairs were too much for him to climb.

Life could go on without Mottshi Shaynbart, however. A town of over fifteen thousand people, more than half of them Jews, had more legs than one. And while Leibush Tshortkover no longer came to see Hirshl either, his son Vovi, the resident newspaper correspondent who had put Szybusz on the map, had taken his place. What was Szybusz doing on the map? It was, after all, a town like any other, with geese waddling in its streets and poor folk going barefoot beside them. But Szybusz had a man named Knabenhut, who made first-rate newspaper copy, so that not a month went by without a story by Vovi about him. Vovi's new friendship with Hirshl worried Tsirl. One might have thought that she feared her son turning into a dangerous radical. Boruch Meir, on the other hand, treated Vovi with respect, not because he was afraid of being written up in the newspapers, but because he believed in getting along with everyone.

Once a week Hirshl's friends all dropped in on him. The large lamp was lit, a clean cloth adorned with a diagonal strip of embroidery lay on the table, and the wet nurse and Mina served coffee that was more than half cream along with heart- and crescent-shaped pastries. Seated among friends, one's coffee cup in one's hand, a person felt cozy all over. Though the men all wore hats or skullcaps and might have talked about godlier things, they preferred such mundane topics of conversation as the new shop opened by the local Catholic priest who wished to undercut Jewish business or the newly appointed judge Mr. Szmuelowicz, a Karaite who took bribes like a Christian but went to the Jewish bathhouse once a week.

The wet nurse's coffee was not as strong as the brew that

Hirshl had drunk before his stay in Lemberg. On the contrary, it had a soothing, pleasantly lethargic effect. One was free to talk or to listen, to try a crescent-shaped cake or a heart. Not that Blume's cakes had not been delicious. These, however, were too.

When Gildenhorn was in town he came to see Hirshl also. Hirshl would break out two or three bottles of his best wines in Gildenhorn's honor and Gildenhorn would sip from a little glass of each without finishing it. Men's tastes are said to follow the seven-year itch. (True, seven years had yet to go by since Gildenhorn began hitting the bottle, but most likely he did not do so for the taste of it even then.)

Gildenhorn no longer seemed so tall to Hirshl either. Perhaps he had only looked big next to Kurtz, whose leaving town had shortened him by several inches. It takes a dwarf to make a giant, as the old saying goes.

What had happened to Kurtz? He had taken a fancy to the Hurvitzes' latest housemaid, who was a wonder in the kitchen, and had married the woman. One day, when some officials of the Baron de Hirsch arrived to inspect the school that bore his name in Szybusz, which was on the verge of firing Kurtz, Kurtz's new wife invited the delegation head to dinner and so impressed the man with her cooking that right then and there he appointed Kurtz headmaster of the Baron de Hirsch School in his own city. Though not everyone in Szybusz believed in miracles, the skeptics were hard-pressed to explain how Kurtz, who was the worst teacher imaginable, had been made a headmaster solely on the strength of a dinner served by his wife.

After closing time Boruch Meir and Tsirl occasionally stopped by Hirshl and Mina's to see how Meshulam was doing and to hear what was new in the world. Boruch Meir sat in a wicker chair, holding his watch chain. Whether it was from constant mental concentration or from the palsy he had developed in his hand, he now gripped the chain all the time. No longer did he rub his two hands together when feeling pleased. Was the world no longer treating him right, or had Boruch Meir changed with time?

Boruch Meir had changed with time. He had grown heavier and rounder, and, though not a native son of Szybusz, he had Szybusz written all over him. Sitting in the store all day long was fattening. Boruch Meir was so busy with his books that he had no time to stretch his legs. Besides which, neither he nor Tsirl liked walking. When the shopboys and Hirshl went home, the two of them exercised by counting the contents of the cash register. At such times, no walk in the world could have enticed them.

In silence they sat as one person, not troubling to talk. Nor did God in heaven trouble them to thank Him for having given them back a healthy son. A store was not a synagogue in which one prayed and said Psalms all day long. It was enough that they had given the paint for Schleien's renovation and that God had signaled His acceptance of their offering by making Hirshl better. Why, even Dr. Langsam had said that there was no danger of a relapse. And the proof of this was that when it said in the newspaper one day that the police were searching for a dangerous escaped mental patient by the name of Feibush Vinkler, Hirshl read the item as though it did not concern him in the least, even though his parents were afraid that it would bring back upsetting memories. What concerned Hirshl was the store. He was wholly occupied with it and did his job well.

The shopboys grew used to Hirshl's ways and no more raised an eyebrow over them than they did over Boruch Meir's or Tsirl's. Nothing in the world remains the same. Whereas once Hirshl had stood lost in thought while the shopboys did their work, now he went about his work while the shopboys stood around thinking.

Or rather, one shopboy did: Feyvel, the assistant clerk. As though it were not bad enough in this world, he reflected, that the rich had it over the poor, some poor had it over others. Not only did Getzel act a cut above him, though the two of them worked in the same store, but he had gone and started his own Zionist club and had himself elected president. Even the fact that the owner's son, Hirshl, treated Feyvel better than Getzel could not make up for what Feyvel believed Getzel to have that he himself did not.

Getzel paid Feyvel no attention. He had other things on his mind. After all, Boruch Meir Hurvitz had been a shopboy like himself and had married the owner's daughter in the end. Getzel knew, of course, that history never repeats itself—but then it was not the owner's daughter that he wished to marry but only the owner's cousin. Socially speaking, indeed, he was not sure he did not outrank her. He, for instance, had been invited to Hirshl's wedding, whereas Blume either had not been or had been made to sit with the other housemaids in the kitchen. Life had no end of puzzlements.

And yet though Getzel earned more money than she did, had a savings account in the bank, and was president of the Workers of Zion Society of Szybusz, Blume would not even look at him. She was certainly a strange one: the more anyone ran after her, the less interested in him she became. When it was Hirshl who had wanted to marry her, she had turned a deaf ear, and now that it was Getzel, he could not get a kind word out of her.

When autumn came and the students went back to school, managing the Workers of Zion Society fell entirely to Getzel. The clubhouse could not run itself: if he was away for a single night the chairs would be thrown all over in the morning and the newspaper would be crumpled on the floor. Yet while Getzel had his hands full, he still found time to visit his hunchbacked sister. The devil they once had raised between them had taken himself elsewhere and left them on peaceable terms.

Getzel never stopped by his sister's without a pocketful of candies. "All right, all you sweet-tooths," he would tell his nephews and nieces, "whoever guesses what Uncle Getzel has here gets twice as much." Though the children racked their brains, Uncle Getzel's sweets were not easily guessable, for Boruch Meir was always trying out new items in his store. Still, Getzel would be a sport and give all the sweet-tooths twice as much anyway. And while he did not have much of a sweet-tooth himself, having learned from Boruch Meir to control it, he could not teach his sister's children which sweets to chew and which to suck on without chewing and sucking on them too.

At such times Yona Toyber joined his sons and daughters and sat examining a candy between two fingers while his wife stood radiantly by. Yona, who had been no simpleton when he decided to marry the sister of a man who worked for a large firm, inspected each sweet he ate to make sure it contained no chocolate, which was something he was careful not to touch, having heard that it was suspected by the Rabbi of Barsan of being made with animal fat. A religious liberal in his attitude toward others, Toyber was quite strict with himself.

Yona Toyber was not a typical matchmaker. He was an abstemious eater and drinker and did not keep stacks of cards with the names of eligible young men and women written on them. Had he done so, he might have realized that it was high time his new brother-in-law was married too. Like any red-blooded youth his age, Getzel had not waited for a matchmaker to court the woman of his dreams. He was too shy, though, to confess that he needed one, not having the courage of Samson in the Bible, who, charmed by a Philistine wench, told his parents, "Now get ye her for me to wife."

In the end, his spirits low and his pockets empty, Getzel would leave his sister and her sweet-tooths to go home. He had played the candy man again in front of his brother-in-law and what did he have to show for it? Absolutely nothing. Perhaps he should have brought his two other sisters food and medicine instead. He was not exactly proud of the fact that Yossele, the carpenter's son who ran the buffet at the Society for Zion club, went hungry himself in order to feed Saltshi and Beiltshi.

The world, however, did not revolve around either Getzel or Yossele. Both of them existed to serve Hirshl, one in the store and one at the club. Not that Hirshl was necessarily the center of the universe either. But he came from a well-to-do home, had a home of his own, and was the only one of the three to be married. Moreover, his wife, Mina Ziemlich, had wealthy parents too. True, Hirshl had wanted Blume, but both God in heaven and Tsirl and Yona Toyber on earth had seen to it that he wound up with Mina.

Blume was still not married. Since the day she left his parents Hirshl had seen her only twice, once in the Mazals' front yard and once in the street with Knabenhut. For all anyone knew about her, she might have entered a nunnery. "Isn't it strange," Tsirl once remarked, "that we never see Blume anymore"—and indeed it did seem ungrateful of Blume not to have come to see her cousins even once. As is generally the case when all goes well with one, Hirshl saw nothing wrong with his behavior. If anyone had misbehaved it was Blume, who had not even paid a call on his new baby.

Hirshl was settling down. Even thinking of Blume no longer upset him. Could he be growing up at last? And yet, he reflected, if Mina were to die, perhaps Blume would marry him then. Not, God forbid, that he wished his wife dead. Should he ever be a widower, though, he would have to remarry someone, and who might that be if not Blume? If she did not agree to it out of love, she would surely agree to it out of pity. The thought of himself and his little orphan being left all alone in the world made his own heart well with pity for the two of them.

Hirshl grew fond of the word "orphan." Sometimes he even called his son by it. The first time that Mina heard him say "my little orphan" to Meshulam a chill ran down her spine. Eventually she grew used to it—or rather, to Hirshl's saying it, though not to the way it made her feel. Each time she heard her son called an orphan she shuddered. And yet she knew that Hirshl meant no harm. It was simply a word he liked and had grown used to.

Meshulam developed slowly. Every conceivable childhood illness afflicted him. A sickly infant to begin with, he was only made more so by the good intentions of those caring for him, who swaddled him so tightly and in so many clothes that he was always sweating and coming down with colds. The wet nurse was so eager to show her devotion that she gave him the breast whenever Mina, Tsirl, Bertha, or Sophia entered the room, even if it meant waking him from his sleep, while in the presence of Hirshl, Boruch Meir, or Gedalia she stood him on his feet to prove how strong he was, though his body was not ready for it, thus causing him to rupture his colon. Her own diet of coarse food and vodka did not do him any good either, nor did her habit of hanging soporific herbs above his head at night to keep him from crying and making her late for her trysts with her boyfriends.

Soon the doctors began to arrive. Each wrote out a prescription and gave Meshulam medicines. Some of these helped for a while but made him worse in the long run, others cured one complaint while creating several new ones. Bertha and Tsirl brought their women friends too, each an expert on childrearing, whose advice was so contradictory that, if worthless in itself, it at least had the merit of being impossible to carry out. The baby, however, showed no improvement.

Sometimes, seeing so many people fussing in vain over his son, Hirshl would think, If Blume were taking care of him, he would be all right by now. He pictured her on one side of the cradle and himself on the other, with the convalescing child between them. God in heaven knew that he was thinking only of Meshulam, since he was getting on well with Mina and was certainly no philanderer. Yet though, upon rousing himself from these fantasies, he guiltily would confess to having really thought only of himself, a moment later he would rail at his own conscience for being so sanctimonious. Then, frightened, he would bite his lip hard so as not to provoke the Fates.

In the end it was decided to bring the baby to Malikrowik. And while this was done less for Meshulam's sake than for Mina, who was too exhausted to take care of him any longer, the official reason given was that Meshulam needed fresh warm milk from the cow.

Bertha came for the child in the Ziemlichs' carriage. She

took her seat with him up front beside the wet nurse while Stach smiled at the horses and ran his hand along his whip. As the carriage started out, Mina, who was standing on the doorstep, began to cry. Though Hirshl wanted to embrace her, his concern for his son made his arms feel too weak to reach out.

36

THE HOUSE SEEMED empty once Meshulam was gone. Though Hirshl smoked one cigarette after another to calm himself, he still felt unsettled. Mina, tired from packing for the baby, went to bed early. Hirshl too lay down. But he could not find a comfortable position. Falling asleep, which had never been easy for him, was sure to be even less so on the first night without his son. After a while he got out of bed.

Mina awoke. "Are you up?" she asked.

"I thought I heard the baby crying," said Hirshl.

"But he's in the village," said Mina.

"I only said I thought it," Hirshl said.

"That's because you're used to it."

"Yes," Hirshl said. "We're creatures of habit."

Mina did not answer, and Hirshl tried to move softly so as not to keep her awake. She too breathed as quietly as she could while listening to his movements. He grew aware of her and stood still. His heart pounded hotly. He had never felt this way before, as if it were his first time alone in a room with a woman. Mina's breathing grew quicker. He too felt short of breath. "Are you awake?" he asked. Although his voice shook, he did not think she noticed it.

"Yes," said Mina from her bed.

Her eyes were wide open. She was thinking of her son, who had been taken away, and of her husband, who was standing over her. Hirshl was not thinking of his son or of anything. He was conscious only of the breathing woman before him.

The night was still. Not a sound came from the street. The slightest noise seemed much louder than it was. Mina's blanket moved. Hirshl's lips met hers. "It's you, Heinrich," she said when she could breath again. Hirshl clung to her with all his might and said nothing.

Now that Meshulam was in Malikrowik, Mina and Hirshl's life was changed. The wet nurse had gone with the baby, and, not having found a maid to replace her, Mina did the housework herself.

Mina was not an especially able housewife. Plenty of women were abler. But when all is well between a man and his wife, whatever she does is good enough for him.

Having work to do around the house put an end to Mina's boredom. Her pale complexion grew rosier, and a smile appeared on her mouth that had always been shaped like a yawn. Hirshl even liked the first wrinkles that had begun to show behind her ears; he called them her kiss lines and seemed as proud of them as if he had made them himself. Every morning he helped Mina prepare breakfast while interpreting her dreams for her. Dr. Freud in Vienna might have done it better, but not as far as Mina was concerned.

Hirshl enjoyed this time of the morning when he stood helping his wife in the kitchen. Not that Mina needed his help. He simply liked looking at her in her attractive house frock. Had not the milk and bread deliveries always arrived just when he most wanted to hug her, he might have been living in Paradise.

Half yielding to Hirshl's attentions and half fending them off, Mina would urge him to drink his coffee before it was cold. "You have some of it first," Hirshl would say. "But why should I drink from your cup," she would ask, "when I have a cup of my own?" "So that I can drink from your cup," Hirshl said. He talked like that at every meal.

Sometimes when they were together, Hirshl thought of

Blume. Not only did she never love me, he told himself, she never loved anyone at all. The reason she doesn't marry must be that it might give some man pleasure.

Mina's eyes shone with a blossom of light such as Hirshl had never seen. When she laid a hand on his shoulder, a pleasant warmth flowed into him from her. He saw that she was fuller. She felt him looking and blushed. He looked again. Could it be that he was right and she simply had not told him yet? Before he could ask, the glow of maternal contentment in her eyes told him everything. God in heaven had helped him to realize by himself.

Yet though Mina kept putting on weight, she had become nimbler. Her hands never rested for a moment. As soon as she was done with the housework, she took up the baby clothes she was knitting. They could not have been for Meshulam, who was already too big for them.

Hirshl, who hardly noticed Mina's clothes, was even less mindful of a baby's. The Christmas holidays were at hand and the store was busy. Already the gift packages were being prepared for the wives of the high officials. Not that Getzel and Feyvel could not be trusted with them, but a good merchant kept an eye on his staff.

Gedalia Ziemlich was in Szybusz one day and came to the store. Boruch Meir handed him a sheet of paper and Tsirl nodded toward some cartons. Hirshl was standing near his father-in-law; yet if he did not light up with satisfaction like Gedalia, neither did he look particularly annoyed. He had made, it would seem, his peace with the world, which could not be expected to change beeause of him. Not that some things did not change anyway. Though Hirshl's house, for example, had become a gathering place for his friends, it was abandoned by them for Gildenhorn's the minute Sophia's husband returned to Szybusz for the Christmas holidays.

Hirshl and Mina did not notice the change, or did not seem to mind it if they did. In any case, Mina was leaving for Malikrowik soon to be with her son. And since the government had begun to crack down on Jewish stores that kept open when the Christian ones were closed, Hirshl had time to go with her.

They traveled together. Meshulam was still behind for his age, but he had done better in the village than in town. Under his grandmother's care he was beginning to catch up.

Hirshl played with the child and made up all kinds of games for him. And though Hirshl bore not the slightest resemblance to his paternal uncle, after whom Meshulam was named, he did manage to write his son a poem, which he crooned for him thus:

> *The angels are bringing Meshulam my love*
> *A special present from above.*
> *And whether the gift is a girl or a boy*
> *It will give me and Meshulam great joy.*

Truer words were never spoken than Schiller's when he said that nowhere is there a man who has not written poems in his youth. And while Schiller may not have had a poem like Hirshl's in mind, it was certainly a sight better than calling one's own son an orphan.

Hirshl did not play with Meshulam all day. Sometimes, if Stach was in the barnyard attending to the horses or poking the dogs in the ribs, he went outside for a chat with him. The dogs did not mind old Knucklehead. They knew he had his problems and they patiently let him take these out on them—which was more than could be said for Meshulam's wet nurse, who slapped Stach's face when he got too familiar with her ribs. Though once she and Stach had been as thick as thieves, her stay in town had accustomed her to finer fare.

Mina spent most of her time with her mother. Bertha was a superb cook, and Mina was eager to learn from her. Now and then, however, she took a break from the kitchen and went for a walk with Hirshl.

Fresh snow fell on the gleaming white village, its smell fresh and gladdening too. Mina's little ears were a frosty pink. Yet after first feeling frozen they were now warm, and she soon saw that the cold was nothing to be afraid of.

The two of them crunched through the snow, which seemed to sing beneath their feet. Or was it really the snow that they heard? Sitting cross-legged in it and strumming as he sang was a blind musician—and though he could not have been one of Dr. Langsam's beggars, whom Hirshl had always pictured squatting in the hot summer sun of the doctor's hometown, his song that was boundlessly sad and sweet seemed to have no beginning and no end. Yet Hirshl and Mina stood perfectly still, as if waiting for him to finish it.

Suddenly Hirshl seized Mina's arm and said, "Let's go."

Had it not sent a shiver down her spine, she might have stopped to wonder at the harshness of his voice.

They had already taken several steps when Hirshl turned back and tossed the musician a coin. Had not the beggar been blind he would have been amazed by the sight of it, for it was bigger than any coin that anyone like him was ever given.

God in heaven knew what made Hirshl so restless. Though sometimes happy and sometimes sad, each mood of his seemed equally extreme.

Gradually he settled down again. One day it occurred to him that, though Mina had studied the piano, she had never asked for one on which to play for him. As anyone with as little interest in music as himself might have done, he felt grateful to her for having spared him.

37

TWICE A DAY the train stopped in Szybusz, and each time it brought with it new faces. Though there was not much difference among them apart from the state of their clothes, one

man's being clean and another's dirty, and their Yiddish pro-
nunciation, one man *tsva*-ing his *tsvay*s and another *tsvay*-ing
his *tsva*s, sometimes the train brought a passenger from
abroad who dressed and spoke completely differently.

Arnold Ziemlich was not exactly a new face in Szybusz,
having already been seen there at his cousin Mina's wedding.
In fact, his business in Szybusz was large and getting larger,
which should have come as a surprise to no one who had
bothered to count the number of chickens pecking in the
town's garbage. The chickens had no idea what made them
keep pecking and laying, but those who grew them and sold
them knew perfectly well that each single egg laid was for Herr
Arnold Ziemlich of Germany; while as for Herr Ziemlich,
though his customers were no wiser than the chickens, it being
entirely possible to eat an egg without knowing what tree it
grew on, he was only too aware of what made them keep
coming back for more. Besides, if a German were to eat eggs
from China his eyes might grow slantwise, while the eyes of
the good folk of Szybusz were big and blue.

Arnold Ziemlich had written Boruch Meir that he planned
to visit Gedalia in Malikrowik during the Christmas holidays
when his business was shut down, and true German that he
was, he kept his word.

Gedalia Ziemlich's house basked in jollity. Boruch Meir and
Tsirl came from Szybusz to greet the guest, and Bertha outdid
herself in the kitchen and set the table with her best china,
including the goose-shaped serving dish that pointed its angry
beak at Arnold Ziemlich. It was indeed a mystery how, when
Bertha was so pleased with every ladleful of gravy spooned
from it, the goose could look as sullen as it did.

Gedalia broke out a few bottles of homemade brandy from
his cabinet. In Germany one drank alcohol-flavored water that
did little more than wet the lips, but Gedalia's one-hundred-
and-eighty-proof goaded the tongue and greased the vocal
chords.

That was only the first glass of it, however. The second and the third had the curious effect of paralyzing the vocal chords completely while rendering one insensible to the fact that no one else was able to speak either.

Well, well, mused Boruch Meir, I've always thought my in-law Gedalia was the world's leading Ziemlich, and here the honor turns out to be Arnold Ziemlich's instead, since Gedalia's only daughter is now a Hurvitz, while Germany is full of little Ziemlichs. Someday there won't be a Ziemlich left in Malikrowik, even though they all came from here, but Germany will have lots of them. Maybe we should even plan a Ziemlich-Hurvitz wedding: my grandson Meshulam can marry one of Arnold Ziemlich's daughters, or else Mina will give birth to a daughter who can marry one of his sons.

Boruch Meir liked German Jews. In fact, ever since his first visit to the spa in Karlsbad, Boruch Meir had liked Germans in general.

Tsirl sat in silence, hardly eating. A great change had come over her, and she had ceased to be a passionate gourmand. It would have upset Bertha had she seen that Hirshl's mother was not touching her food, but her eyes were on her guest from Germany. Hirshl too, though looking smart in his dress clothes, seemed far from joyful. Yet great joy awaited him. God in heaven was preparing it Himself. It was plain for all to see that Mina was about to give her family another son or daughter.

Tsirl's eyes narrowed. Not that she had anything against foreigners. But why all the fuss over this one? When it came right down to it, he was the son of a man who was buried in an unknown grave.

It could not be denied, however, that Arnold Ziemlich's visit had the merit of reuniting Hirshl, Mina, Boruch Meir, Tsirl, Gedalia, and Bertha in Malikrowik. Only Yona Toyber was missing—and when it came right down to it, he would have been superfluous, for Hirshl and Mina were married already and had no further need of a matchmaker until

Meshulam grew up. And to keep him from growing up all alone, they were giving him a new brother or sister.

Meshulam's brother was born with a smile on his face. He was a perfectly formed child. Mina soon got over her confinement and made an ideal mother. She and Hirshl found a thousand different things to love in the baby and called him by a thousand different names. A day did not pass without a new one being given him. Some of these names made sense and some did not. He had so many of them that the one he was born with was forgotten.

A thousand times a day Hirshl and Mina came to the baby's cradle to admire him. "Look, he just smiled!" "Did you hear him sneeze?" "What a darling nose he has." "He blew a kiss, look." "I swear, he understands everything!" "The pillow is crushing his ear."

The baby lay in the cradle, showing off for them, while his older brother grew up an hour's walk away. Gedalia and Bertha did everything for Meshulam as though he were their own child. Still, he was not indulged like his brother, for Mina's parents were no longer young and had forgotten how to talk to a small boy. Not that Meshulam was badly off. His little brother had it better, though.

"Mina," Hirshl asked her as they were standing by the baby's cradle, "what are you thinking about?"

"About his brother," said Mina.

"It's good that he's with your parents."

"Yes," Mina said. "I think so too."

"But for a different reason than I do," said Hirshl.

"Why, what reason is that?"

"That love can't be divided."

"I thought," said Mina, "that it's the nature of love to always have room for one more."

Hirshl looked down and said, "No, that's not so. Love comes to us only when no one stands between it and us."

God in heaven knew that he was thinking only of the baby.

229

Hirshl and Mina's story is over, but Blume's is not. Everything that happened to Blume Nacht would fill another book. And were we to write about Getzel Stein too, who was mentioned here only in passing, and about all the other characters in our simple story, much ink would be spilled and many quills broken before we were done.

God in heaven knows when that will be.

Afterword by Hillel Halkin

How simple is *A Simple Story?* Or, to ask the same thing differently: How ironic is its title? How we read it depends on our answer to this question.

For on the face of it, the story *is* a simple one—or rather, a simple one with a twist, since it differs in one important respect from other simple stories that it resembles. That is, in its opening chapters Agnon's novel appears to have all the makings of a conventional romance: boy meets girl, boy and girl fall in love, boy and girl's love meets an obstacle. As experienced readers, we know that the story can now go one of two ways. In the first of these, which might be called the "Rapunzel variation," the lovers are cruelly separated, yet after many trials demanding great steadfastness on their part they are happily reunited. Such is the stuff of fairy tales, stage comedies, Hollywood movies, fictional potboilers, women's comic books, and not a few serious novels from *Pamela* to *Lady Chatterley's Lover*. The second variation might be named after Tristram and Isolde and ends as shatteringly as the first ends triumphantly: here the separation of the lovers proves insuperable and concludes with final heartbreak and often death. We encounter it in mythology (as in the story of Orpheus), in dramatic tragedy (*Romeo and Juliet*), and once again, starting with *The Sorrows of Young Werther*, in more than one modern novel.

Now, until we are fairly near the end of *A Simple Story* Agnon does nothing to disabuse us of our illusion that it will

231

turn out to be yet another tale of victorious or tragic romantic love. In fact, stringing us along, he does everything to encourage this belief. At first we are inclined to think the novel will follow the Rapunzel variation: most likely Hirshl will elope with Blume before his planned wedding with Mina, and the rest of the story will relate the lovers' struggle to overcome the hardship and opprobrium to which this exposes them. By the middle of the book, once Hirshl and Mina are unhappily married, we have begun to suspect that the Tristram and Isolde variation is being brought into play: either Hirshl will leave Mina and run away with Blume, in which case the disgrace may prove so great that it drags them both down with it, or else—a possibility that looms larger as Blume rejects Hirshl's advances and Hirshl teeters on the edge of madness and plunges into it—he will lose his sanity forever, or even his life, because he cannot take such a step. The one thing that we are not prepared for—the one thing indeed that must not happen in a romance, because it violates every canon of romantic love—is that Hirshl, the pining lover, will be restored to full health, forget about Blume, his true love, and live happily ever after with Mina, the woman forced on him by his parents. Though Agnon makes us laugh often in *A Simple Story*, which has some marvelously funny passages, the last laugh, it must be conceded, is his—and it comes at our expense.

In a word, much to our surprise, *A Simple Story* turns out to be an anti-romance. A careful rereading of it makes one wonder whether, in writing it, Agnon was not surprised by this too. Though we have no way of knowing how it was originally conceived, not only is there a curious shrinking of Blume's role in the course of the book, prompting its author to bid us adieu with the implied promise—one that he never kept—to write a sequel about her, there is also, coinciding with her vanishing, a perceptible shift from the romantic, almost sentimental tone of the novel's beginning to the comic (though by no means untender) one of its middle and end. Each of these registers had been used before by Agnon in a novel set in Szybusz, the town that serves as the locale for

232

several of his books: the romantic-sentimental in *In the Flower of Her Youth* (1921), which tells the story of Akavia and Tirza Mazal, who appear again as minor characters in *A Simple Story*, and the comic-burlesque in the social satire *Young and Old Together* (1923). In *A Simple Story*, published in 1935, when he was at the height of his creative powers, Agnon begins on the former note and then veers increasingly toward the latter, though it is one of the strengths of the novel that the two are played off against each other until the very end. Certainly, though, the more the story progresses, the more broadly humorous it becomes.

Indeed, whether *A Simple Story* changes course because Blume fades into the background or whether she fades into the background because Agnon wished to change course, it is evidently her disappearance that released his great comic talents, for she is one of two characters in this many-charactered book who is not at least a partly comic figure. The other is Dr. Langsam, the old neurologist who cures Hirshl of his madness, and he and Blume represent the two poles between which Szybusz exists. Blume is all Innocence; though far from naive (she is much less so in fact than Hirshl, having received her share of hard blows in her life and having learned the lesson of each), she mysteriously retains a charmed virginity, as though she really were the princess in the fairy tale to whom she is more than once compared. Langsam, on the other hand, is the embodiment of Experience; he cannot be treated ironically because he is a master ironist himself, although a most compassionate one. But the people of Szybusz are neither innocent nor experienced. They are too worldly-wise to be the first and too narrow-minded to be the second, and, well aware of the hypocrisies of others but largely unconscious of their own, they are easily poked fun at. *A Simple Story* makes the most of the opportunity.

Yet is the world of Szybusz merely a comic one? Once again we have reached a crossroads in our reading of the novel. For if the life of the town has nothing serious to recommend it, then Hirshl's reconciliation with it as expressed by his final

233

accommodation to his arranged marriage is a pitiful surrender, a sacrifice of his manhood on the altar of a ludicrous social respectability. This would be one kind of anti-romance, in which the fault lies not with romantic love but with the cowardly failure to assert it. Suppose, however, that the values of Szybuszian society are ultimately meant to be taken by us as positive, and that the comedy of *A Simple Story*, while aimed at its characters' foibles, comes to point out to us their real virtues as well? We would then have a different story, one whose moral might be that the rejection of romantic love in favor of social convention, though exacting a heavy price, is part of putting one's adolescence behind one and becoming, rather than failing to become, a man. One way or another, before we can make up our minds about Hirshl we must make up our minds about Szybusz.

The town of Buczacz, in which Agnon was born in 1888 (in his fiction he playfully changed its name to Szybusz, the word *shibush* in Hebrew meaning "error" or "muddle"), was situated at the extreme eastern end of the Austro-Hungarian Empire, about one hundred miles east of Stanislaw (Stanislawow) and two hundred southeast of the provincial capital of Lemberg, today the Ukrainian city of Lvov. The region of Galicia to which it belonged had been annexed by Austria-Hungary in the first partition of Poland in 1772 and was inhabited by peoples speaking four different languages—German, Polish, Ukrainian, and Yiddish. In eastern Galicia the Germans were the least numerous of these elements and consisted mainly of the imperial bureaucrats entrusted with administering the area. The Poles and the Ukrainians, who had a long history of national enmity between them, were the two largest groups, the Ukrainians comprising the peasantry, whereas the Poles were concentrated in the towns and cities, like the Jews. Indeed, although the Jews constituted perhaps a tenth of the population of Galicia as a whole, they were a far higher percentage—in some places even a majority—of its urban inhabitants. Small shopkeepers, artisans, and petty traders, their economic situation was none too good, especially in the far east of the province, which was among the empire's most remote and backward corners.

Yet if they were often poor and commonly despised by their Polish and Ukrainian neighbors, the Jews of Galicia were considerably better off than their millions of brethren in Czarist Russia and Poland, whose Eastern-European Jewish culture they shared. Indeed, in the same years of the late nineteenth and early twentieth centuries that saw the Jews of the Russian Empire subjected to ever worsening pogroms, residential restrictions, and a host of other anti-Semitic acts and policies, Galician Jewry was enjoying an unprecedented epoch of security and equality under the lengthy and benevolent reign of the Kaiser Franz Josef. Such had not always been the case. Although as far back as 1782 the emperor Josef II had issued a Toleration Act removing a number of disabilities imposed on them, the Jews of Galicia were still the frequent victims of government discrimination in the first half of the nineteenth century. Beginning with the accession of Franz Josef in 1848, however, conditions improved steadily, especially after 1868, when the last anti-Jewish legislation was repealed and a series of sweeping constitutional reforms was instituted in the empire as a whole. From now on Jews paid no special taxes, could live and travel where they pleased, were free to engage in any business or profession, had the right to educate their children in their own schools, and could even vote and stand for office in local and municipal elections. Above all, they could live without the fear of violence or persecution, feeling safe in the confidence that they were protected from hostile or arbitrary forces by a powerful, enlightened, and law-abiding regime.

It was perhaps this fundamental sense of security, so at variance with the Eastern-European Jewish experience elsewhere, that provoked the Jews of Russia and Poland into their use of the term *a galitsianer yid*, "a Galician Jew," to denote a person rather smugly self-satisfied with himself and his condition. The expression suggests more than just that, though, for a genuine *galitsianer* must have other qualities too: a highly practical turn of mind, commercial craftiness, a gift for haggling and outsmarting, native intelligence coupled with a profound lack of intellectual curiosity, religiosity without deep religious feelings, and, not least of all, a sly sense of humor that is not averse to taking pleasure in the misfortunes of others. Like all ethnic stereotypes—and there was not a region of Eastern Europe whose Jews did not have their sobriquets, not always complimentary, for other Jews—that of the *galitsianer* contained much exaggeration; like all such stereotypes too, however, it contained a measure of truth. Thus, while sharing the deep respect for religious learning that was universal among Eastern-European Jewry, the Jews of Galicia were far removed from the great centers of Talmudic study in Lithuania and from the highly intellectual approach to religion and its texts that prevailed there; swept in the late eighteenth and early nineteenth centuries by the Hasidic revival (indeed the Baal Shem Tov, the founder of Hasidism, began his career in Galicia), their long-entrenched Hasidic dynasties inculcated a conservative pietism less theologically daring and emotionally soulful than that practiced in parts of Poland or Russia; scarcely touched by the cultural influence of such Jewishly sophisticated large cities as Warsaw or Vilna to the north, or Odessa to the east, their highly mercantilized life also lacked the almost peasantlike rusticity that could be found among the Jews of the even more remote Carpathian Mountains to the south; while at the same time, though they inhabited a provincial backwater, their Austrian citizenship and the liberal monarchy of Franz Josef gave them a superior sense of being more Western and advanced than their co-religionists living under Czarist rule. In a word, though ultimately not very different from the other Jews of Eastern Europe, they formed a distinct subculture of their own.

This subculture is that of Szybusz, and not a few of the characters in *A Simple Story,* above all Hirshl's parents, Boruch Meir and Tsirl, are *galitsianers* to the core. Shrewd but simple, careful to render to both God and Caesar, liking a good laugh yet laughable themselves, they are pillars of their community and its ideal types. Indeed, honest, hard-working, and financially successful on the one hand, yet tolerant, sociable, and mindful of their public obligations on the other, they came close to realizing the ideal of European bourgeois society, of which the Jewish community of Szy-busz—admixed in whose indigenous value system is not a little of the Austrian *Gemütlichkeit*—is a poor but undeniable cousin. Despite the pervasive small-town Jewishness of Hirshl's environment, therefore, the collision between him and the world of his parents is more than just a parochial one pitting a quaint religious tradition with its anachronistic custom of matchmaking against a young man who has fallen in love with the wrong person. On the contrary: it is part of the same conflict between bourgeois civilization and Eros that plays such a prominent role in the novels of Mann, Proust, and other modern European writers, and—with a suitable change of scenery—it would be as credible in the Vienna or Paris of the early 1900s as it is in the Szybusz of those years. (Although no dates are mentioned in *A Simple Story,* several historical references in the novel, especially one to the Russo-Japanese War, establish that the story takes place in the first decade of the twentieth century.)

Nor should we be too quick to assume, as some of Agnon's critics have been, that Agnon's sympathies in this conflict are essentially on the side of Eros. Granted, the world that Hirshl makes his peace with has little room in it for strong passion; true too, it is often shallow, petty, grasping, and two-faced; yet to say of it, as does the critic Boruch Hochman,* that it is "a milieu which has been shown to be inimical to every value of youth, life, love, or for that matter, authentic tradition," so that, in settling for an existence like his parents', Hirshl is in for a "dreadful" future, involves, I believe, a misreading of *A Simple Story* that comes from projecting our own modernist—that is to say, anti-bourgeois—biases onto it. Indeed, the fact of the matter is that, if we set our cultural prejudices aside and

*Hochman's excellent *The Fiction of S. Y. Agnon* is the best study of Agnon available in English and is recommended to anyone wishing to know more about his work.

read the book as it is written, not only does Agnon clearly *like* the characters he has created, he writes about them with a buoyancy and affection that compel us to like them too. They may not be *our* ideals; however great their limitations, though, we can hardly deny them their attractive qualities. They are generally quick-witted and good-natured; they are, though often insensitive, rarely deliberately unkind; they have an admirable sense of social and family solidarity; and, far from being "inimical to life," they enjoy its simple pleasures with great gusto. Even the most potentially disagreeable of them are by no means negatively portrayed. Thus, for example, Mina, after striking us at first as an empty-headed shtetl debutante, turns out to be a young woman of considerable mettle and resourcefulness, while Tsirl, who—clever, enterprising, amiable, lively, selfish, complacent, controlling, and sometimes cruel—embodies all the good and bad that can be found in Szybuszian society, probably has as much of Agnon himself in her as any other character in the novel.

(If this seems a questionable assertion, I might back it up with a story told me by the Israeli author Amos Oz. Once, when he was a young university student in Jerusalem, Oz went to pay an admirer's call on Agnon, who was then a venerable figure in his seventies. Agnon received him graciously and chatted about his work for a while, after which he inquired—unfortunately I cannot reproduce here how Oz, an excellent mimic, imitated the antiquated East-European Hebrew that Agnon insisted on talking to the end of his life—what other Hebrew authors his visitor liked. Oz mentioned Hayyim Hazzaz, Agnon's contemporary and chief rival for the doyenship of Hebrew literature, and was astonished to be answered, "Hazzaz? Who is that? I never heard of him." Thinking he had not been heard properly, Oz repeated the name—only for Agnon to reiterate that it was unfamiliar, rise from his chair, go over to a bookcase, take down a heavy directory of Hebrew writers, leaf through it to the letter "H," and show the bewildered student of literature that there was no Hazzaz in it. The conversation passed on to other things until, when Agnon left the room for a minute, Oz went to have a

238

look at the book in question—and discovered that it was a nineteenth-century volume published before either Agnon or Hazzaz was born! Is not this episode an almost exact replica of the scene in *A Simple Story* in which Tsirl expresses her opinion of Kurtz and his unwanted appearance by pretending not to realize that he is there?)

I relate this story to point out not only that Agnon, the Nobel Prize laureate translated into dozens of languages, was a *galitsianer* himself with a penchant for pulling legs, but also that often in *A Simple Story*, when he appears to be laughing with us at his characters, he is at the same time laughing with his characters at us. You, my readers, he is saying, may find the people that I write about comic, and perhaps they are; but can you be sure that in finding them so you have not become comic yourselves, since your judgments of them reveal your own twentieth-century standards, which may be as ludicrous as, or even more so than, theirs? Indeed, though Agnon is a great leg puller, it is not always apparent in his work whose leg is being pulled. Take the case of the narrator of *A Simple Story*, with his pious homilies and ritually obeisant "God in heaven." Are the latter really so emptily sentimental, as Hochman claims, that they "can only undercut any faith in [God's] relevance to the ongoing business of life," with the result that "Agnon's irony is directed as much against the narrator as against the burgher world of the novel"? Or is it possible that it is we who are having our noses tweaked for reacting this way—that is, for no longer casually being able to see divine providence everywhere, as did our less sophisticated ancestors, so that we must impatiently dismiss any reference to it as hollow twaddle? If *épater les bourgeois*, shocking the conventional-minded, was one of the slogans of modernism in the arts, it is a favorite game of Agnon's to invert the injunction and scandalize the modernist in his reader. His folksy narrators, who remind one of the stock figure of the country bumpkin in the jokes who outslicks the city slicker in the end, often do just that.

A mock naive antimodernism is in fact Agnon's preferred

fictional stance, so much so that he sometimes doubles it backward in time, first twitting our own age with an earlier one and
then teasing that with an even more distant past. (Thus, in *A
Simple Story*, while satirizing modern medicine, the Knaben-
huts and Getzel Steins who wish to change the world, or the
Gildenhorns and Schleiens who actually are changing it, the
narrator often implies that this world itself has deteriorated
sadly from that of its forebears, who were in all respects more
stalwart and serious men.) "Older is better" could be his
motto, and though Agnon writes about the world of his Galician youth and childhood with a nostalgia that is unusual in
modern East-European Hebrew literature, where this period
of life is more often remembered with the threatening shadow
of a hostile environment lying heavily over it, his work repeat-
edly harks back to a vaguely situated Golden Age whose loss it
thematically laments. Whether this is a mere literary posture
or an accurate representation of his historical beliefs is difficult
to say; there can be little doubt, however, that he himself, an
observant Jew all his life except for a brief period in early
adulthood, was of a deeply conservative turn of mind. Politics
as such never seem to have interested him much; he rarely
wrote about them directly, and his sense of them could probably be summed up in the words of the first-century rabbi
Hanina S'gan ha-Kohanim, who is quoted in *The Ethics of the
Fathers* as saying, "Pray for the welfare of the State, because
the fear of it alone keeps each man from swallowing his neighbor alive." Agnon's own profound fear of anarchy was above
all moral and cultural, and it is the implicit message of nearly
all his work that without both the social system and the indi-
vidual discipline that enable men to keep a tight rein on themselves—a system and discipline that are admirably provided
by the commandments of Judaism—the human self and its
relationships with the world are in perpetual danger of revert-
ing to chaos. Indeed, modern life is for Agnon practically
synonymous with chaos, and, in one form or another, his
fiction is a persistent rejection of it. (Although this aspect of
his writing is all but untranslatable, Agnon's repudiation of

modernity is even reflected in his Hebrew prose style, which, based on his own inventive and immensely erudite adaptation of classical rabbinic diction, stubbornly—one might almost say defiantly—refused to make any concessions to the enormous changes that took place in the Hebrew language in the course of its twentieth-century revival.)

And because romantic love too, with its strong irrational component, is a potentially chaotic and lawless force, a premodern Szybusz must strive to neutralize or contain it in self-defense. (The fact that we and Agnon know what the Hurvitzes and the Ziemlichs do not, though they too have an inkling of it, namely, that Szybusz and all that it stands for are a historically doomed cause, may add another ironical dimension to the novel, but it is hardly the central issue in it.) It should be noted, though, that the enemy in Szybusz is by no means sexuality itself. Szybuszian society is not particularly puritanical, and neither, despite the rather Victorian themes of the novel, is Agnon in writing about it. On the contrary, just as the narrator of *A Simple Story* is not embarrassed to attribute the survival of Hirshl and Mina's marriage in its early stages to the attractions of sex alone, so the love they finally come to feel for each other is born in a supremely sexual moment that is described with both great power and delicacy. The enemy is social disorder. The world of Szybusz would not come to an end if Hirshl married Blume, but it is a world that rests on parental authority, family alliances, and the transmission of accepted tradition, all of which would be challenged if he did. Marriage is its most sacred institution because it stands at the intersection of these factors, and the moment it ceases to be such, social stability commences to vanish. Besides which, as Boruch Meir and Tsirl know from their own experience, even if one does not marry because of love, one may still end by loving because of marriage.

Is *A Simple Story* then an antiromantic comedy in which the adolescent folly of a young man's love is nipped in the nick of time and the social order happily preserved? Not necessarily.

There is nothing foolish about Hirshl's love for Blume, nor is it described as anything but genuine, heartfelt, and pure. In fact, Hirshl *can* marry Blume without ultimate ruination if he insists on it— everything we know about his parents tells us that, if he were to fight for his love for her, they would acquiesce, however unhappily, in the end. Why does he not? The narrator of *A Simple Story* offers us no less than four different explanations, which can be taken singly or together. One is that Hirshl stumbles into his engagment to Mina through an inadvertent comedy of errors from which he is simply unable to extricate himself. Another is weakness of character: if he were not such a mother's boy he would break off the engagement—or, what is more likely, would never allow it to take place. A third reason is the deep unconscious identification that he feels with his father: just as Boruch Meir jilted *his* cousin, Blume's mother, Mirl, in order to marry Tsirl, so Hirshl, in the mysterious way that children often have of recapitulating their parents' lives even as they are rebelling against them, does the same thing. And finally, we are offered the explanation of fate—or, if one wills, of Providence: Hirshl marries Mina because it has been decided in Heaven that he must, and the rest is simply the working out of the divine plan for him. Though falling in love with Blume may jeopardize that plan, it is hardly blameworthy in itself.

Similarly, we are given our choice of reasons for Hirshl's mental breakdown. It may be the result of a hereditary illness that has afflicted his uncle, his grandfather, and his great-great-grandfather before him. It may be brought on by a combination of emotional tension, worry, lack of sleep, physical exhaustion, and too many barbiturates. It may be the only way out of the insoluble conflict in his life between his unappeasable desire for Blume and the social and marital roles he is forced to play. And it may be the expression of a severe oedipal complex with its attendant castration fears, as a result of which Hirshl both identifies with his own masculinity, as symbolized by the rooster or cock (several times archaically referred to in the Hebrew as *gever*, a word whose common meaning is "man"), and is convinced that he must sacrifice or "slaughter" it. Such overdetermination is psychologically true to life; it is also one of Agnon's typical ways of baiting his readers and forcing them to reveal their own proclivities by choosing the level of meaning that they feel most comfortable with.

Deep within himself Hirshl is perhaps even afraid of Blume and of the desire she arouses in him, for she is not only beauty incarnate in his eyes but mystery incarnate too. Her very name, as has been pointed out, underlines this duality, Blume in Yiddish meaning "flower" and Nacht meaning "night." She is indeed a "night flower" for Hirshl, the plucking of which depends on his venturing into unknown realms, sexual, emotional, and social, of life and self—and by the time he feels brave or desperate enough to do this on his nocturnal walks to the Mazals' house, Blume feels compelled to reject him. Although we are left to speculate about what might have happened if she did not, or if Hirshl had proposed to her in time, there are two sets of minor characters in *A Simple Story* who serve as markers here. One is Akavia and Tirza Mazal, about whose marriage we know—although their history is only hinted at in the novel—that it is a happy consummation of a premarital romance.* (It also, however—either because they are so engrossed in each other or because they no longer fit into any accepted social mold—has removed them from the life of the town, on whose secluded outskirts they live by themselves.) The other pair is Mottshi Shaynbart and Dr. Langsam's wife, who has killed herself, we are told, after an unhappy love affair with him. In a word, we are given a glimpse of the two romantic variations that the plot of *A Simple Story* turns its back on—and whether Agnon is saying that the innocent romance may end happily like Rapunzel's

*Tirza and Akavia's story is told fully in *In the Flower of Her Youth*, which relates how Akavia, a middle-aged bachelor who was in love with Tirza's dead mother, is fallen in love with by Tirza, whose father he is old enough to be. Though the match is highly unconventional, and is opposed at first not only by Tirza's father but by Akavia too, Tirza's love wins out in the end and she and Akavia are wed.

but the adulterous one must end tragically like Isolde's, or whether he is simply reminding us that both possibilities exist, we are being told in either case that romantic love can be a gamble with one's position in society, and even with one's life, that Hirshl at one point, and Blume at another, are not willing to take. Does *A Simple Story* suggest that they should be? Or that, on the contrary, they are wise not to be? It does neither. This too is a question whose answer is left entirely up to us.

Dr. Langsam, the only character in *A Simple Story* who is not only clever but wise, does not even bother to ask it. Perhaps Hirshl would have been a happier and more fully alive person with Blume than he can ever be with Mina; perhaps a romance between the cousins would have had a disastrous end, like that of the doctor's own wife. Since as a physician he must work with what it is and not with what might have been, none of this matters very much. And what *is* is that, willingly or not, Hirshl has thrown in his lot with Szybusz rather than with Blume and must be helped to make his peace with the fact. To accomplish this the old doctor assumes a cunningly indirect strategy. On the one hand, by means of his seemingly aimless stories, he builds up in his patient a positive image of small-town Jewish life, thus getting him to accept that the conventional society of the Galician shtetl in which he is condemned to live has a dignity and a value of its own and that there is no need to feel shame or anger at belonging to it. On the other hand, by recreating a semblance of the maternal warmth and care that Hirshl never received as a child, he encourages a transference that frees Hirshl of the unconscious rage felt toward his parents and especially toward his mother. Like Agnon the novelist, Langsam the psychologist, with his dislike of modern ways, is not as simple as he at first appears to be; there is a great deal of sophistication in his outwardly artless methods, which succeed precisely because Hirshl fails to see them for what they are.

The result of Dr. Langsam's treatment, with all the painful renunciation and acceptance that it involves, is strikingly borne out in the little scene of the blind musician that occurs in the novel's last pages. At first Hirshl is entranced by the lyric sweetness of the beggar's music; yet quickly it becomes unbearable for him, because, although he may not be consciously aware of it, its haunting beauty reminds him of his love for Blume that is forever lost. The harshness of his voice as he urges Mina away from the scene has both rejection and grief in it, for he is saying goodbye for the last time to a part of himself that he knows will never be realized. (Indeed, a few lines further on we are told that even the piano music rotely played by Mina would be more than he could stand.) A moment later, however, he turns around and throws the beggar a large coin. This is not just a perfunctory act; it is, the narrative informs us, a generous gift and no doubt a precedent for the future. Though Hirshl will never be all that he might have been, he will be like his father an active and responsible member of a humane if often trivial society, one of whose major precepts is the giving of charity and the caring for the less fortunate. As in Dr. Langsam's musings about "passing on" good in the world, Hirshl, having been helped by the doctor whom he has proceeded to forget, now helps someone else himself. It may not seem like much in the ultimate scale of things, but it is not such a trifle either.

Comedy, which labors to convince us during its brief hour on stage that despite life's many pratfalls all things turn out for the best, often concludes by gaily pairing off its characters so that everyone has someone in the end. *A Simple Story* is no exception to this rule. As the novel draws to its close Hirshl and Mina have each other and their new baby; the Ziemlichs have Meshulam; Yona Toyber has Getzel Stein's hunchbacked sister; Kurtz has the Hurvitzes' ex-maid; Dr. Knabenhut has a rich wife to support him; Arnold Ziemlich has his long-lost family in Malikrowik; and Boruch Meir is already dreaming of a Ziemlich-Hurvitz wedding, that is, of the royal marriage of cousins that has eluded him and his son. Only Getzel Stein and Blume are left out in the cold. About Getzel we hardly need worry: he is a practical and assiduous young man who undoubtedly will get over his disappointment in love and find himself a suitable partner. Blume is another story, though. A charmed mystery to us as she is to Hirshl—indeed, we hardly know her any better at the end of *A Simple Story* than we do at the outset—we leave her feeling uncertain what the future holds in store for her. Perhaps, having refused to surrender that bright kernel of herself that Hirshl has relinquished, she will continue to grow and will someday meet her equal, which Hirshl has proven not to be. Perhaps she will withdraw even more deeply into the protective armor of pride and self-reliance that already surrounds her. In either case, it is easy to imagine her seeking her destiny elsewhere, for, homeless as she is, the world must be her home as Szybusz is the Szybuszian's. The novel ends with her as it began with her, and so reminds us that there is more suffering, loneliness, and possibility in life than the comic stage can accommodate. It is a tribute to the evocative powers of this not so simple story that, thinking of Blume, though we know that she exists only in its pages, we cannot help wishing her well.

DATE DUE